VITAL: THE FUTURE OF HEALTHCARE

Vital: The Future of Healthcare

ISBN: 978-1-955969-02-4 (paperback)
ISBN: 978-1-955969-05-5 (ebook)
Library of Congress Control Number: 2021948333
All rights reserved.

Book layout & design: Mark Givens
Editor: RM Ambrose

Printed and bound in the United States
Distributed by Ingram

Published by Inlandia Institute
Riverside, California
www.InlandiaInstitute.org
First Edition

VITAL: THE FUTURE OF HEALTHCARE

Edited By
RM Ambrose

Inlandia Books
Riverside, California

For the healthcare workers
The essential workers
The laid-off workers
The survivors
And the ones taken by Covid

Contents

Introduction

There is no Science Fiction without Medical Science Fiction. It is not a subgenre; it is the very foundation. Intrinsic. Endemic.

This genre was born like Athena from the head of Mary Shelley. Victor Frankenstein's Promethean act of creation, and then neglect, of an intelligent and sensitive person is a narrative examination of ethics in science, still relevant two hundred years (and two pandemics?) later.

Perversely, Science Fiction itself has been diagnosed as a pathology. As Gavin Miller points out in "Fan of sci-fi: Psychologists have you in their sights," the broader SF/F genre continues to be misunderstood and dismissed. However, as Esther Jones observes in "Science fiction builds mental resiliency in young readers" mounting research shows that fiction reading, and particularly science fiction, can build empathy and critical thinking.

Useful skills for the people designing, deliberately or accidentally, patient experience today. Imagine artists weaving stories that create a shared language of ideas. A language designers, developers, administrators, and Healthcare providers can use to improve patient experience. Well-written stories help the reader, the designer, to develop empathy and see through the patient's eyes.

Furthermore, reading Science Fiction can help cure specific problems of the Healthcare industry. Following a handful of jurisdictions in 2019, hundreds of US cities, counties, and state governments have declared racism a public health crisis. As Ashley Abramson writes in "How Sci-Fi Creates Better Doctors," Science Fiction teaches providers to combat racial bias in Healthcare.

Science Fiction also helps us come to grips with the issues of our fast-changing world. Technology advances so fast society cannot keep up. Politics and society have been changing at a tremendous rate as well, accelerated by technology. Stories of the future help us conceptualize these problems, and maybe some solutions as well.

Although, the pace of change is a challenge for writers and editors, too. Almost a decade ago, novelist Charles Stross blogged that he couldn't write a third novel in his near-future Scottish detective series because, among other things, there was a Scottish Independence Referendum scheduled in 2014, shortly before the book would be published, and he didn't know if Scotland would still be in the UK by then. Since then, the UK left the EU (being in the EU was one of the reasons many Scotts voted against independence), and Brexit might trigger another Scottish referendum.

To some degree, I experienced the same problem with this book. Covid was *not* on my mind when I conceived of this project so many years ago. I did have a list of story themes that included "Epidemic/ Pandemic." And I even thought about the Ebola outbreak in West Africa, and later the narratives of distrust, conspiracy theories that the virus wasn't real, which complicated efforts to control that outbreak.

As I revised this introduction, a beloved family member who worked as a nurse but believed Covid conspiracy theories and refused to get vaccinated, died of Covid. The state mandated vaccination of Healthcare workers just went into effect, and could have saved their life in spite of their beliefs, but was a couple months too late.

Many of the stories I selected took on new meaning due to Covid. In fact they, continue to take on new meaning for me as the pandemic progresses. I'm sure their meaning will continue to evolve after this book is published.

I also changed the beneficiary of the book - although I'd always intended this to be a charity anthology. When the World Health Organization's funding came under threat due to the US potentially pulling out - in the middle of a one-hundred-year pandemic, no less - the WHO's Covid-19 Solidarity Response Fund became the obvious choice. And even though President Biden has reversed his predecessor's course on the WHO, the worldwide vaccine roll out still desperately needs our help.

The US Healthcare system's problems are unique and numerous, and it would be easy to make this book all about America. But health is a universal human need, and Viruses don't heed borders. So, I have included some story translations or stories from non-Anglophone countries, including Spain, China, and the Czech Republic. I wish I could have included many more.

The pandemic shook the planet, but through an unprecedented monetary investment from govern-ments, and building on dedicated ongoing research, we have witnessed amazing breakthroughs in science.

Messenger RNA (MRNA) vaccines, like Pfizer's and Moderna's, were Science Fiction just a few years ago, and now they're changing the course of the disease. One day, maybe MRNA therapeutics will be used to fight Cancer.

As I started writing this introduction, the Biden administration announced plans to invest $3.2 Billion in the development of antiviral drugs - rather than vaccines to prevent illness, actual treatments to cure viral infections. Viruses, like parasitic little zombies, are notoriously hard to treat because they're not really alive and only reproduce by hijacking our cells.

The deadliest viruses are too deadly and tend to "burn out" before they infect too many people. Perhaps it's because viruses are seen as a remote threat (e.g., Ebola) or a low threat (the common cold), but it's tragic that it took the Covid death toll to justify this invest-ment. Will support for this research burn out before a breakthrough?

The pandemic may have changed this project, and changed how you will read these stories, but it is not just about the pandemic. In fact, most stories were written before the pandemic. Of those written during Covid, only one addresses it directly. I chose this theme because medicine touches nearly every important aspect of our lives, from the problem of conspiracy theories on social media to gun violence.

In this volume you'll find stories dealing with climate change, systemic racism, human sexuality, machine learning, and privacy. And of course these stories tackle core Healthcare themes like bioethics, greed in the pharmaceutical industry, the perils of implanted human-computer interfaces, the elder care crisis, and access to Healthcare.

Rather than highlighting specific stories and their themes here, for each story I provide a brief introduction or forward. And when you encounter a great story by an author you're not familiar with, I encourage you to flip to their bio at the end of the book.

The ideas driving these stories come from writers who are also professional scientists, one a medical doctor, another a philosopher, and many are educators. Some are New York Times bestsellers and Hugo, Nebula, Locus, and Sturgeon award winners, among other accolades. I've packed an illustrious group into this little volume.

Taking on issues like systemic racism and climate change, and my choice to donate to the WHO Covid fund in response to President Trump's attempt to pull their funding? You might think this is a political book. Sadly, I don't think it is possible to be apolitical anymore, especially in a book that deals with science. But I know that Republicans and conservatives in general hold a variety of opinions on these issues, so this is not just a liberal book. And there's a big difference between discussing policy compared to shouting down and denigrating those who disagree with you.

Regardless of your political bent, I hope you will find this book thought-provoking and engaging. As I've pointed out already, just reading science fiction helps us build empathy. This is because a powerful story isn't just a polemic on an issue that's also entertaining, it humanizes an issue with characters and engages you on an emotional as well as an intellectual level, whether or not you agree with it. I think that is good art. And empathy is how we build social connections. In a time of such division, I think empathy is extremely important.

If reading Science Fiction builds empathy, it is not a disease, it is a cure. And this book aims to contribute to the future of Healthcare, not just through ideas and the intrinsic benefits of reading Science Fiction, but through actual monetary donations to fight the pandemic worldwide. Read on, and make a difference!

—RM Ambrose

The Public Health Officer Who Cried Wolf

The problem with public health officials is that they're always talking about doom and gloom. People don't like to hear that. The problem with public health officials is that they were right.

In fact, it's kind of a problem with Healthcare as a whole. It's hard to market Healthcare. People don't enjoy thinking about getting sick or injured.

For decades before the pandemic, public health departments across the US went through budget cuts. Trying to ramp up for a pandemic when they had been so underfunded proved an impossible task. Not unlike the program in Annalee Newitz's 2019 Sturgeon Award-winning story.

When Robot and Crow Saved East St. Louis

by Annalee Newitz

It was time to start the weekly circuit. Robot leapt vertically into the air from its perch atop the History Museum in Forest Park, rotors humming and limbs withdrawn into the smooth oval of its chassis. From a distance, it was a pale blue flying egg, slightly scuffed, with a propeller beanie on top. Two animated eyes glowed from the front end of its smooth carapace like emotive headlights. When it landed, all four legs and head extended from portals in its protective shell, the drone was more like a strangely symmetrical poodle or a cartoon turtle. Mounted on an actuator, its full face was revealed, headlight eyes situated above a short, soft snout whose purple mouth was built for smiling, grimacing, and a range of other, more subtle expressions.

The Centers for Disease Control team back in Atlanta designed Robot to be cute, to earn people's trust immediately. To catch epidemics before they started, Robot flew from building to building, talking to people about how they felt. Nobody wanted to chat with an ugly box. Robot behaved like a cheery little buddy, checking for sick people. That's how Robot's admin Bey taught Robot to say it: "Checking for sick people." Bey's job was to program Robot with the social skills necessary to avoid calling it health surveillance.

Robot liked to start with the Loop. Maybe "like" was

the wrong word. It was an urge that came from Robot's mapping system, which webbed the St. Louis metropolitan area in a grid where 0,0 was at Center and Washington. The intersection was nested at the center of the U-shaped streets that local humans called the Loop. A gated community next to Washington University, the Loop was full of smart mansions and autonomous cars that pinged Robot listlessly. Though it was late summer, Robot was on high alert for infectious disease outbreaks. Flu season got longer every year, especially in high-density sprawls like St. Louis, where so many people spread their tiny airborne globs of viruses.

Flying in low, Robot followed the curving streets, glancing into windows to track how many humans were eating dinner and whether that number matched previous scans. Wild rabbits dashed across lawns and fireflies signaled to their mates using pheromones and photons. Robot chose a doorway at random, initiating a face-to-face check with humans. In this neighborhood, they were used to it.

A human opened the service window. The subject had long, straight hair and skin the color of a peeled peanut.

"Hello. I am your friendly neighborhood flu fighter! Please cough into this tissue and hold it up to the scanner please!" Robot hovered at eye-level, reached into its ventral service trunk, and withdrew a sterile sheet with a gripper. This action earned a smile. Robot smiled back, stretching its dog-turtle mouth and plumping its cheeks. Humans valued nonverbal emotional communication, and it was programmed with an entire repertoire of simple exchanges:

If human is angry, then Robot is sad.

If human is rude, then Robot is embarrassed.

If human is happy, then Robot is happy.

The human coughed and Robot did a quick metagenomic scan, flagging key viral and bacterial DNA before uploading sequence data to the cloud. Other bots would run the results against a library of known infectious diseases and alert the CDC if any were on the year's rolling list.

Six days later, Robot headed across the Mississippi River to East St. Louis. Here, heat and rain had eroded the pavement until its surface was as pocked and fissured as human skin. The first time Robot performed health surveillance in this area, nothing fit its generic social programming. Buildings marked as unoccupied were clearly full of humans. Occupant records did not match the names and faces of occupants. People spoke with languages and words that did not match known databases. As a result, Robot could not gather adequate data. When Robot requested help with this problem, Bey was the only CDC admin who responded. She communicated with Robot from Atlanta via cellular network, using audio.

"Not all humans behave or speak the same way," she told Robot. "But you can learn to talk to anyone. Gather data. Extrapolate from context. Use this." And she sent Robot a blob of code for natural language acquisition and translation. Very quickly, Robot learned that humans used slang, dialects, sociolects, and undocumented lexicons. Bey also sent several data sets taken from an urban studies lab, which supplemented

Robot's map data. It turned out that not all humans lived in the same domicile for two years on average; not all residences had cars and rabbits outside. Some humans lived in places that were not tagged as domestic spaces. Some humans did not use government-assigned identifiers. But all of them could get sick.

There was a small neighborhood of soft textile homes underneath the freeway. It did not exist on official maps. Robot knew it because of Bey's algorithms.

"Hello!" Robot said, landing on the porch of a blue fabric house. It spoke a dialect that was popular here. "I am checking to make sure you are healthy! Please say hello!"

A human rustled inside, then unzipped the door.

"Hi Robot." The human had brown eyes and facial symmetry that matched previous records. It was the same human as last month.

"Please cough into this tissue and allow me to scan."

The human smiled, and Robot knew why. The word for cough in this dialect was a pun for something the humans found endlessly amusing. There was a more formal word for cough, but compliance was higher if Robot used the pun. Higher compliance rates meant better data.

"Robot, I think my friend Shareeka is sick. Can you please check on her?" The human was worried, and Robot responded with a sad/concerned expression.

"Where is Shareeka?"

"She's in the new building on State near 14th? On

the upper floors that aren't finished. I bet you could fly right in."

"Thank you for your help."

The human petted Robot's head. It was the most common form of physical affection that Robot had documented in its four years and eight months in the St. Louis metropolitan area.

Protocol held that Robot should follow up on disease reports immediately, so it flew to the new building on State. Like the textile neighborhood, this building was not a designated residential area. It was a gray box on Robot's official map. But visual sensors showed a reflective spire, with 20 floors wrapped in steel and glass. Five floors rose like a skeletal crown on top, exposing its steel beams, pipes, and drywall. Coming from inside were the sounds of human life: music, conversations in six languages, babies crying, food sizzling on hot plates. Robot could see electricity cascading down wires from solar panels bolted to the outside of windows. Residents tuned the data network with satellite dishes made from woks and metal cans. From Robot's perspective, it was exactly like other residential buildings with a few cosmetic differences.

Extending its feet and head, Robot landed on the lowest open floor, then walked to the interior, asking for Shareeka. A juvenile human opened a green door and said hello. The human had short hair, woven into pink extensions, and a well-worn text reader in one hand.

"Hello! I am Robot, and I want to make sure you are healthy. A nice person told me that Shareeka might be sick. Can I meet Shareeka?" Robot used the same dialect it had in the fabric neighborhood, adding enhancement words that signaled benevolence.

The human made a neck motion that meant "no."

"I am a friend who only cares about whether you are well. I am worried about Shareeka." Robot made a sad face.

The human made a sad face too. "Shareeka left a couple of days ago. I don't know where she is."

"How do you feel today?"

"I'm kind of stressed out about school," the human said. "How are you feeling?"

It was very rare for a human to ask Robot how it felt, and there was no stock answer or expression available. So Robot answered as literally as possible. "I am not sick because I am a machine. But I am worried that you are sick. Would you cough into this tissue and allow me to scan it?"

"Are you going to sequence the DNA right now?" The human was intrigued.

"Yes! But I will work with bots on the data network to figure out if anything dangerous is in there."

"I know. You have a list of known infectious diseases and you'll search for a match. We learned about it in biology class." The human smiled, and Robot smiled back.

"Yes! That is what I will do." It held out the tissue.

The human coughed on it and studied Robot very carefully as it conducted the scan.

"How do you make sure that you don't mistake somebody else's microbiome for mine? Do you sterilize your hand every time?"

"Yes I do." Robot uploaded its data and talked at the same time. "What is your name?"

"Everybody calls me Jalebi."

"You are named after a fried, spiral-shaped sweet soaked in sugar water." Humans enjoyed it when Robot recognized the meaning behind their names.

Jalebi nodded. "When I was a kid, I ate so many that I passed out. Too much sugar. So my brother started calling me Jalebi."

Robot was having difficulty making a connection to the cloud. "I am going to go back outside to talk to the network. It was nice to meet you Jalebi."

"Wait—what's your name?"

"Robot."

"That's your name? I thought that was your ... race." Jalebi used an ambiguous word that could also mean "species."

"It's my name," Robot replied.

Robot stood in the darkness beneath the moon, above the neighborhood lights, in the unfinished hallway open to the air, and called for the cloud. There was nothing. It called for Bey. There was no answer. It sent an emergency email to the CDC surveillance team list and got an error message. It called and called, charging up every morning in the sunlight and powering down at midnight. After seven days, it got a text message from an unknown private number:

Hi Robot. It's Bey. I can't be your admin anymore. I'm really sorry because it was nice to know you. Unfortunately the CDC lost its funding. I work at Amazon Health now, but we aren't allowed to network with open drones like you. I don't think anyone is going to shut you down or collect you, so I guess you can do whatever you want. If anything really bad happens, text me here on my private number. I hope the language acquisition algorithm is still helping!

For the first time, Robot made a sad face that nobody could see. It wasn't sure what "really bad" meant, but its models of human communication suggested that Bey referred to an outbreak. The problem was that Robot had no way to conduct a typical surveillance circuit without somewhere to upload its data for analysis. Plus, it was going to run out of sterile tissues. That's what happened last year when the government shut down and Walgreens froze its CDC account. Robot used the government shutdown scenario to model its current situation, and predicted that it meant the Walgreens account would be frozen for an indeterminate length of time. The 5,346 sterile tissues remaining in its chassis were the last it would ever have. The sterilizing gel for its gripper was already running low.

Bey said Robot could do whatever it wanted, which was the kind of thing humans said when they expected it to predict which data-gathering task should be prioritized. Based on current supply levels and its onboard analysis capabilities, Robot determined it should focus on learning local languages and human social habitation practices. It would attempt to reach the cloud every morning, and would reprioritize if disease analysis systems became available again. Robot thrust its head out of the pocked oval of its body, a determined smile on its face. In the absence of a human, the expression was intended only for a theoretical model of a person who always cared what Robot thought and did.

A crow stood next to Robot on the building's edge, looping its leg over one wing to scratch its head. It regarded Robot for a second, then said something before flying away. The phonemes were part of an unknown language, and Robot added them to a sparse data set it had gathered from other crows in the area. Now that it could do what it wanted, Robot reasoned, it was time to make that data set robust. Many crows flew up here and perched, often in groups of three or four, and their sounds followed the same general patterns as any natural language. It could learn a lot by staying right here, down the hall from Jalebi's habitat. The days grew shorter and new constellations rose in the sky.

Robot started to pick up a few phrases from context. In the mornings and evenings, the crows discussed the sun's position and its relationship to likely sources of food. Soon, Robot could piece together bits of syntax, using brackets to designate uncertain or unknown meanings: "[Food type] four [measurement units] north of the morning sun." There were also location calls, which it roughly translated to "Food here!" and "I'm [name] here!" and "Get over here [you]!" Its first translation breakthrough came one morning when a statistically unusual number of crows gathered near its perch. Robot counted 23 birds at one point, many of whom were quite large. Maybe they were from different subspecies? Or elder crows? From what Robot had learned by querying the internet, zoologists drew the line between crow species arbitrarily based on calls and cultural differences.

This seemed like an important meeting, so perhaps multiple crow groups were invited in a show of corvid solidarity. Robot recorded hundreds of new words. It learned a few of the birds' names as well. Suddenly, one of the ravens gave a location call: "There! North five [measurement units]! Group!" They took off at once, and Robot followed them. It was time to test out its ability to communicate, by using a location call. "I'm here! Joining group!"

A crow flew alongside Robot and answered. "I'm here! 3cry!" 3cry was Robot's approximation of the bird's name, which it recorded as a series of three high-pitched phonemes issued in rapid succession.

Other birds answered with their own names. "I'm here! 2chop1caw! I'm here! 4cry! I'm here! 2chop!" Robot now had a running list of phonemes used in crow names, and tried to record them faithfully.

They flew as a loose pack, not forming a V the way other birds did. Crows usually preferred smaller social groups and didn't care about staying in a tidy line. They only came together in large numbers to deal with issues serious enough that even an egg-shaped drone was permitted to come along.

"Enemy! Enemy!" One of the ravens barked out the word, its accent slightly different from the crows. Far ahead, a hawk coasted on the updrafts from the city in a large, lazy circle.

"Egg killer!"

"Trespasser!"

"Attack from above!"

The birds called names and orders to each other,

soaring over the hawk's head and dive-bombing it. Though hawks have excellent vision from the front of their faces, they also have two major blind spots above and behind. This particular hawk was immediately thrown off its trajectory by a mob of angry crows clipping it from out of nowhere.

3cry called to Robot. "Come here! Above to below!"

Robot modeled several scenarios, and settled on one that would knock the hawk out of the updraft without causing any health risks to the bird. Communicating with the crows was important, but the health of living beings was paramount. Coming down gently on the hawk's back, Robot pushed lightly, keeping up with the bird's speed while also altering its course. The hawk let out an incomprehensible scream and dove, escaping the crows by heading across the Mississippi.

"Out of here!"

"Go!"

"End group!"

Four crows followed after the hawk, but the rest of the corvids scattered. Robot flew back toward Jalebi's building, modeling possible new words by correlating matching sounds from different birds. 3cry followed close behind.

"I'm here! 3cry! Female! You are here!"

Robot predicted that 3cry was asking for its name and gender. It replied using crow words, then switched to a human word for Robot. It did not yet know the word for "nongendered" in crow language, so it did not offer a designation. 3cry flew silently for a while. They landed on the building and looked at the horizon.

Robot offered a friendly greeting in crow language. "Afternoon time."

"Enemy gone. Robot is here." 3cry pronounced its name perfectly. "Human sound."

Robot searched for the right words from its limited vocabulary. "Humans are here. With my group."

3cry cleaned her right wing, chewed on a mite, and cocked her head at Robot. "Humans are not a group. They can't speak. They reject food."

"They speak with other sounds." Robot's vocabulary was growing bigger the more they talked. "They eat other food."

3cry made a soft clucking noise that meant the same thing as human laughter. "You are a fool."

Robot predicted that assent was the best response. "Yes I am."

"Yes you are." 3cry leaned over and gently poked a bit of dirt from the edge of Robot's mouth.

Robot plucked a broken feather off 3cry's back.

When they cleaned each other, it was like when a human smiled at Robot and Robot smiled back.

3cry and Robot became what the crows called a group, which meant that they flew together during the day. They met in the mornings, on the ledge, after Robot's daily attempt to reach the CDC. Robot didn't need food, but it was good at identifying potential sources of sustenance for 3cry. "Food here!" it would say, hovering over a fragrant bin. After scavenging with 3cry through city waste, it was easy to understand why she thought humans rejected food and were therefore basically non-sentient.

Over weeks, their conversations became more complex, but many concepts defied translation. Robot still didn't understand the crows' unit of measurement for distances. And 3cry didn't understand Robot's interest in health. From what Robot could discover, crows understood the concepts of death and near-death, but didn't talk about disease specifically. Disease was one of many ideas that could be described with the word "near-death," which also happened to be a pun on the word for unripe food. Many crow words were puns, which made translation even more difficult.

For conversations about health, Robot relied more and more on Jalebi. She had figured out that it was roosting with 3cry on the ledge near her habitat, and came to visit for what she called "study sessions." Using text devices, she gathered data very slowly, then synthesized it even more slowly. Robot spent hours quizzing Jalebi about molecular structures and chemical interactions, marveling at the concept of a mind that came online without this information. Still, Robot liked to have a human face to mirror its own expressions. It felt unquantifiably more satisfying to smile at a human than it did to smile at its own internal representation of a human. After so long in the company of 3cry and Jalebi, Robot began to question what, exactly, that internal representation might really be. Maybe it wasn't a human at all. Maybe it was a self-representation, and Robot had been smiling at itself all along.

Usually when Jalebi came to the ledge with her textbooks, 3cry left with a string of curses. These weren't necessarily hostile—crows liked to insult each other, and often did it with great affection. Mostly they thought it was hilarious that humans couldn't understand words. So crows rained their most creative snark on human heads, marveling at how oblivious they were to the humiliations they suffered from the beaks of people flying overhead. But one afternoon, 3cry arrived during their study session and did not fly away.

Jalebi was musing about something she'd learned in a recent lesson about atomic structure. "What if it turns out we really are spreading cancer to each other on a quantum level?" she asked.

"Human squawking!" 3cry yelled. "Shit and plastic! Featherless fool!"

Robot decided to ignore the insults. "Afternoon time," it said pleasantly. "Human here! Jalebi! Part of the group."

"Group does not include living sandwiches." 3cry laughed.

Jalebi watched, wide-eyed. "Can you speak crow language?"

"A little," Robot said. "My vocabulary is small, but I can say a few things. This is 3cry. She's ... my friend." As it said the word, Robot realized it was true. Thanks to Bey's social programming, it knew that groups were statistically likely to be made up of friends or kin. Since Robots have no kin, that meant Jalebi was a friend too.

Jalebi tried to make the sound of 3cry's name and the bird ignored it.

"I found something you like, Robot. Near-death. All

over a human tree."

"She said your name perfectly! I read that crows can imitate words, but I'd never heard it before!"

3cry glanced at Jalebi, then at Robot. "Annoying Jalebi."

"She said my name too! That's so cool!"

But Robot wasn't paying attention to the interesting language data points. It predicted 3cry had found a disease outbreak, and that took precedence over all other inputs.

"I have to go," it said to Jalebi. To 3cry, it added, "Take me there."

Robot followed 3cry in a southeasterly direction, eventually alighting at the top of a building on Missouri Street. Like Jalebi's home, this building was partly open to the air. Its layout suggested that it might have been a public building like the CDC; there were long hallways lined with small rooms like offices. Water sources were isolated in a few areas, unlike in a typical habitat, where water welled up in multiple rooms. But it was definitely a human habitat now, with soft bedding and buckets for water and data access points made from cans. As they flew down a stairwell, Robot tried to estimate the population of the building based on noise, heat, and live wires. It settled on a 75 percent probability of 50 humans on each upper floor, with populations growing as they descended.

"Here!" 3cry landed on a railing in front of a door marked 2, for second floor. "Near-death!"

"Thank you."

"End group," 3cry said, taking to the air. The phrase

was one way crows said goodbye.

"Until morning," Robot replied, already using a gripper to tug the door open.

The corridor was full of light from scratched windows along the left-hand side, illuminating dozens of doors to habitats that were once something else. Classrooms? Offices? Consulting rooms? Robot flew slowly past them, modeling possibilities and looking for humans. The fourth door was propped open, and several humans were inside. Their breathing was labored, and one was crying. Something had knocked out the walls between rooms, creating a wide-open space full of cloth dwellings, plush bedding, and piles of bright plastic containers.

It was time to land. Humans didn't like it when Robot flew overhead, and besides, the face and legs were part of what made it seem so friendly. Walking over to one of the humans wrapped in blankets, Robot smiled and waved a tiny gripper in greeting.

Patchy black hair covered the human's head, and cracks had formed in the lips that didn't smile. With no baseline language established, Robot estimated that it should try the dialect spoken in Jalebi's building. "I'm a friend who is worried about your health! Can you cough into a tissue for me?" The human stared at Robot's face and blinked, before succumbing to a coughing fit. For Robot, it didn't matter whether the coughs were intentional or not. It took a sample and moved on to the next human.

"Hello!" Robot said to the juvenile, who was using a mobile device to access the internet.

"Are you a cop?" The juvenile used a sociolect of

English that was common in East St. Louis.

"I'm a friend who checks to make sure you are healthy! I share information with doctors, not police." The human frowned and Robot made a sad face. "A lot of people here are sick. I would like to help."

"Nobody is going to help, stupid drone. Hospital for citizens only, yeah?"

"Please cough into the tissue, so I can figure out why you are sick."

Another human spoke up, head emerging from a cloth shelter. "What are you going to do about it?"

Robot stood still for several microseconds, modeling possibilities and considering what language would be the most soothing. "I am going to find out what is causing your illness. This is an emergency. I will find help. I promise. Please cough into the tissue."

One by one, the humans complied. Robot flew from room to room, checking for disease. After sequencing several samples, it found the same virus strain in multiple humans. This met the definition of an outbreak. It was time to call Bey.

"Is that you, Robot? I can't believe you're still running! It's been ... what? Over a year?"

"Something really bad is happening in East St. Louis," Robot said, deploying the exact words Bey had used to delineate when it would be appropriate to call her. "There is an outbreak. I need to send you data."

"Do you have sequence? Maybe I can ... " Robot heard background noise, as if Bey were moving something on her desk. "Can you send it as an anonymous dump to this address?" She sent the directions to a temporary storage cloud, and Robot deposited data from 127 samples it had taken from humans in the building.

"We have a system for anonymous reporting, part of this new Amazon Health philanthropy project." Bey paused. "Got it! Let me analyze this really fast and see if it's more than just a garden-variety ... oh shit."

Robot predicted that she was not saying shit for the same reason 3cry did. "What is it?" Robot asked, putting on a fearful expression for itself.

"This is really bad, like you said. We need to get someone in there. Unfortunately, Illinois doesn't have a state health department. Maybe there's a local group or ... " Bey was typing. "OK, Robot, I found something. There's a nonprofit health collective in East St. Louis called Community Immunity. They could probably manufacture vaccines and a therapy. It's a known pathogen, but hasn't ever been spotted in the Midwest before. So all they need is this file." Bey sent a small amount of data. "Do you have anyone who can help you? You might need a human. Sometimes people are hostile to drones, even cute ones."

Two hours later, Robot was describing the situation to Jalebi. It was evening, and 3cry was likely sleeping with other members of her group. But Jalebi was wide awake and extremely agitated. "You're talking about that health collective on MLK Drive! I've seen it!"

Robot nodded, smiling. "Can we go there now?"

Jalebi glanced toward the door to her habitat. "Yeah. My mom won't be home until morning anyway."

Community Immunity was located in the husk of an old strip mall, its gleaming counters and wet lab hidden behind windows duct taped with tinfoil and cardboard. Bey was right that Robot needed a human. Jalebi had to pretend that Robot was her school project, and Robot had to pretend that Jalebi had programmed it to look for outbreaks. Once the humans at Community Immunity had the data, they made unhappy faces and said "oh shit" in the same way Bey had.

A human with purple hair and a prosthetic arm offered Jalebi a seat and some hot tea. The human spoke the same sociolect of English that Bey used. "It's very good that you brought this to us. You are a good citizen." Then the human looked at Robot. "Thank you, Robot, for giving us the file with an open therapy and vax recipe."

"I am happy to help. I don't like it when people are sick."

This human, unlike the others, seemed to know that Robot was the person who found the outbreak. "I'm Janelle, by the way. She/her pronouns. Do you know if there are other places where H18N2 is infecting people?" Robot liked the way Janelle identified herself by name and gender, the way crows did.

"A friend told me about this outbreak. I don't know if there are others." Robot deliberately chose vague language. After Bey's warning, it did not want to reveal its data-gathering techniques.

Janelle took it in stride. "Can your ... uh ... friend help find more? We can manufacture a therapy and a vax tonight, but we need to get it out there fast before this sucker mutates."

Robot nodded. "Tomorrow. I will try to find more."

When 3cry arrived in the morning, Robot had to strain

against the boundaries of its vocabulary to make itself understood. "Need group. Find near-death enemy."

"Enemy?" 3cry scratched her head.

"Enemy for humans," Robot admitted. But then it had an idea. "Enemy causes human death. Dead humans mean less food."

Despite butchering the crow syntax, Robot thought it had made 3cry understand. Plus, sometimes crows just liked an excuse to get the mob together. "Begin group!" 3cry yelled, taking off. Robot leapt into the air behind her. They flew over East St. Louis, calling for the big group that had taken out the hawk. "Begin group! Begin group!" More birds joined them. "Here! I'm here!" They called their names and swirled to roost in a tree at the edge of the Mississippi River, where freeway met water.

"Find near-death!" 3cry said, then issued some directions and specification words that Robot did not understand.

"Near-death! There! [Measurement unit] north!" The words came from a big crow named 2chop1caw, jumping into flight. Most of the group followed, possibly to assess what exactly 3cry meant by "near-death." 2chop1caw led them to a fabric habitat nearby, where Robot quickly identified three sick people. The virus matched the H18N2 signature identified at Community Immunity.

"More near-death! Where else? Begin group!" Robot called the birds to the air again, and they fanned out over the city, making a racket and hurling their best insults. Each time they uncovered a new outbreak, they gave their loudest calls, sometimes passing those calls to the next bird, until Robot could follow their cries back to the source. By the end of the day, they had discovered five small outbreaks.

"End group!" 3cry yelled, following Robot back toward MLK. The crows called farewells and locations to each other. "End group!" "Evening time!" "I'm here!" "You there!" "Food!" "Death!" This was followed by laughter, because food and death diverged into many puns far beyond Robot's comprehension.

3cry appeared to have decided that she was roosting with Robot for the evening. When they landed, she hooked her claws around its rotor pole, and clung there as Robot signaled arrival to the door of Community Immunity. Robot didn't mind. Humans found small animals disarming, and that always led to greater compliance.

Jalebi was there with Janelle, looking at something on a monitor. "Hi Robot!"

"We have data on the location of more outbreaks."

Janelle laughed. "Really? Did your little feathered friend help?"

"Her name is 3cry!" Jalebi failed to pronounce 3cry's name again. And, once again, 3cry ignored it, jumping off Robot and using her beak to straighten the feathers under her right wing. Robot reached over and plucked one out that was bothering her.

"Where can I put this data?" Robot aimed a concerned expression at Jalebi and Janelle.

"Put it here for now." Janelle waved a mobile device near Robot, setting it to accept uploads. "Jalebi, do you want to help us synthesize those doses of nasal spray? Looks like we'll need at least 500. And then we'll start making vax doses for injection."

"Yes! Absolutely!" Jalebi acted like a crow about to charge into the air. But she was only racing across the room to boot up a mixer.

Janelle had a thoughtful expression on her face. "Did this crow really help you find the outbreaks?"

"Yes. The crows think humans are idiots, but they appreciate your garbage."

Janelle laughed for a long time, and Robot was not entirely sure why.

When Jalebi returned, she sat down alongside Robot and 3cry and smiled. "This place is really cool. I like it here."

"Maybe this is your group," Robot guessed.

"Maybe." Jalebi cocked her head like 3cry. Then she scooped up a tiny tube full of wound adhesive. "Here, hand me that beautiful feather." Robot dropped 3cry's feather into her hand. Dabbing a bit of adhesive on Robot's back, she stuck the feather to its shell next to the place where its rotor pole emerged.

3cry was startled. "I like it," she said. "That human is a fool."

"Yes she is," Robot agreed. "You are also a fool."

"Yes I am."

The three people roosted contentedly next to each other on the floor, watching Janelle and the humans preparing antivirals for other humans. It was a scenario that Robot would not have predicted. But now it could. Robot smiled to itself, organized the data, and retrained its model for friendship.

It Could Have Been Worse

If only we'd had benevolent little robots and cooperative corvids to help us nip Covid-19 in the pandemic bud.

I love a happy ending, but outbreaks often don't end so happily, as we're all too familiar.

Epidemics and pandemics loom large in Science Fiction, using plagues as a mechanism for the collapse or transmutation of society. Honestly, it's hard to assemble a medical-themed anthology without including some.

I lined up most of the stories you are reading long before the news of a novel coronavirus. But there's one pandemic-themed story I acquired during Covid.

Tananarive Due's Nayima trilogy culminates with "Carriers." But I'd argue that you can read the first two stories as prequels. So, start here and pick up "Removal Order" and "Herd Immunity" later.

Carriers

by Tananarive Due

Republic of Sacramento
Carrier Territories

Nayima's sleep had turned restless as she aged, so the rattling from the chicken coop outside woke her before her hens raised the alarm. The intruder was likely either feline or human, and she hoped it was the former. A cat, no matter how big, wasn't as dangerous as a person.

Nayima ignored the sharp throb in her knee when she jumped from her bed and ran outside with her sawed-off in time to see a hound-sized tabby scurrying away with a young hen pinned in its teeth, a snow globe of downy white feathers trailing behind. The army of night cats scattered in swishing bushes and brittle leaves. The giant thief paused to look back at her, his eyes glowing gold with threat. The cats were getting bigger.

Nayima had been saving that hen for Sunday dinner, but she was too winded to chase the thief. Now both knees throbbed. And her lower back, right on schedule. She fired once into the dark and hoped she'd hit him.

Fucking cats.

The dark was thick to the forsaken east, but to the west she saw the gentle orange glow from the colony in Sacramento, the fortress she would never enter. The town folk had electricity to spare, since their lights never went fully dark anymore. They were building a real-life Emerald City from the ruins, with bright lights and fresh water flowing in the streets—literally, after the levees flooded back in the '20s.

By contrast, her tract, Nayimaland, was two-hundred acres of dead farmland she shared with feral cats made bold because food was scarce—taken by drought, not the Plague. The late State of California had yet more dying to do.

Nayima felt thirsty, but she didn't stop at her sealed barrel to take a scoop. She couldn't guess how long her standing water would have to last. Sacramento owed her water credits, but she would be a fool to trust their promises.

At the rear of the chicken coop, Nayima found the hole the cat had torn in the mesh and lashed loose wires to close it. The hens were unsettled, so she could expect broken eggs. And she couldn't afford to cook one of her reliable laying hens, so she'd have to wait for meat at least another week, until trading day.

By the time Nayima came back to her porch, her two house cats, Tango and Buster, had gathered enough courage to poke their heads up in the window. For an instant, her pets looked like the thief cat, no better.

"It's okay, babies," she said. "One of 'em got a chicken."

Buster, still aloof, raised his tail good night and went to his sofa. But Tango followed her to her bedroom and jumped beside her to sleep. Nayima preferred a bare mattress to the full bed that had been in this room—fewer places for intruders to hide and surprise her. She slept beneath the window, where she could always open her eyes and see the sky. Tango rested his weight against her; precious warmth and a thrumming heartbeat to calm her nerves.

"I can't feed you all," she told Tango. "I'm crazy for taking in just you two."

Tango slowly blinked his endless green eyes at her, his cat language for love. Nayima returned Tango's long, slow blink.

*　　*　　*

Nayima thought the jangling bells outside soon after dawn meant that a cat had been caught in a cage, but when she went to investigate, she found Raul's mud-painted red pickup slewed across the dirt path to her ranch house. He was cursing in Spanish. His front tire had caught a camouflaged cage, and he was stooping to check the damage. At least a dozen sets of cats' eyes floated like marbles in the dry shrubbery.

"Don't shoot!" Raul called to her. He knew she had her little sawed-off without looking back. "You'll blow off your own culo with that rusty thing one day. ¿Es todo, Nayima?"

Despite the disturbance and his complaining, Nayima was glad to see Raul. He looked grand in morning sunshine. Raul's eyes drooped slightly, giving the impression of drowsiness, but he was handsome, with a fine jaw and silvering hair he wore in two long braids like his Apache forebears. Since reconciliation and the allotment of the Carrier Territories eight years ago, Raul looked younger every time she saw him.

Nayima had turned sixty-one or sixty-two in December—she barely tracked her age anymore—and she and Raul were among the youngest left, so most carriers had died before the territories were allotted. In their human cages.

Captivity had been their repayment for the treatment and vaccine from the antibodies in their blood. They were outcasts, despite zero human transmissions of the virus after Year One. The single new case twenty-five years ago had been a lab accident, and the serum had knocked it out quick.

The Ward B carriers Nayima had barely known still lived communally, or close enough to walk to each other's ranches. But Nayima had chosen seclusion on an airy expanse of unruly farmland that stretched as far as she could see. In containment, she'd never had the luxury of community, except Raul. She had enough human contact on her market trips, where she made transactions through a wall. Or her hour-long ride on her ATV to see Raul, if she wanted conversation. Other people wearied her.

"Sorry—cat problem," she told Raul. "Did it rip?" She had a few worn tires in her shed from the previous owner, but they were at least forty years old.

Raul exhaled, relieved. "No, creo que está bien."

She squatted beside him, close enough to smell the sun on his clothes. She had not seen Raul in at least thirty days. He had begged her to share his house, but she had refused. She needed to talk to him from time to time, but she remembered why she did not want to live with him, and why she had slept with him only once: Raul's persistent recollections about his old neighborhood in Rancho Cucamonga and his grand-parents' house in Nogales were unbearable. He always wanted to talk about the days before the Plague.

But after forty years, he was family. He'd been a gangly fifteen-year-old when the lab-coats captured him. Shivering and crying, he had webbed his fingers to reach toward her hand against the sheet of glass.

Nayima missed skin. She felt sorry for the new children, being raised not to touch. She absently ran her fingertips along the dirt-packed ridges in the tire's warm rubber.

"Do you have meat?" she said.

"Five pounds of dried beef," he said. Nayima didn't care much for beef, but meat was meat. "In the back of the truck. And a couple of water barrels."

Water barrels? A gift that large probably wasn't from Raul alone, and she didn't like owing anyone.

"From Sacramento?"

"You're doing a school talk today, I heard. Liaison's office asked me to come out."

Nayima's temper flared. She could swear she'd felt a ping at her right temple an hour before, waking her from fractured sleep. The lab-coats denied that they abused her tracking chip, but was it a coincidence she had a school obligation that day? And how dare they send so little water!

Nayima was so angry that her first words came in Spanish, because she wanted Raul's full attention. He had taught her Spanish, just as she had taught him so much else, patient lessons through locked doors. "Que me deben créditos, Raul. They owe a lot more than two barrels."

"You'll get your créditos. This is just..." He waved his

hand, summoning the right word. Then he gave up. "Por favor, Nayima. Take them. You earned them." He tested the air pressure in his tire with a pound of his fist. "Gracias a Díos this is okay."

Nayima's shaky faith had been shattered during the Plague, but Raul still held fast to his God. He told us the Apocalypse was coming in Revelation, he always said, as if that excused it all. Nayima still believed Sunday dinner should be special, but only to honor the memory of her grandmother's weekly feasts.

Two new orange water barrels stood in the bed of Raul's truck. Large ones. She needed more credits to get her faucets running, but the barrels would last a while. Nayima climbed up, grabbing the bed's door to swing her leg over. She winced at the pain in her knees as she landed. She treasured the freedom to move her body, but movement came with a cost.

"¿Estás bien, querida?" Raul said.

"Just my knees. Stop fussing."

Nayima fumbled with an unmarked plastic crate tied beside the closest barrel.

"Don't open that yet," Raul said.

But she already had. Inside, she found the beef, wrapped in paper and twine. Still not quite dry, judging by the grease spots.

But she forgot the jerky when she saw two dolls, both long-haired girls, one with brown skin, one white. The dolls' hands were painted with blue plastic gloves, but nothing else. They had lost their clothes, lying atop a folded, obscenely pink blanket.

"What the hell's this?" Nayima said.

Raul walked closer as if he carried a heavy sack across his shoulders. "I wanted to talk to you," he said, voice low. He reached toward her. "Come down. Walk with me."

"Bullshit," she said. "Why is Sacramento sending me dolls?"

"Bajar de la truck," Raul insisted. "Por favor. Let's walk. I have to tell you something."

Nayima was certain Raul had sold her out in some way, she just couldn't guess how. Raul had always been more willing to play political games; he'd been so much younger when he'd been found, raised without knowing any better. So Raul's house had expensive solar panels that kept his water piping hot and other niceties she did not bother to covet. His old pickup truck, which ran on precious ethanol and gasoline, was another of his luxuries for the extra time and blood he was always willing to give the lab-coats.

Nayima climbed out of the truck more carefully than she'd climbed in, refusing Raul's aid. Living in small spaces for most of her life had left her joints irritable and stiff, even with daily exercises to loosen them. If she'd had the energy or balance, she would have shoved Raul down on his ass.

"Start talking," she said. "What have you done?"

"Put the gun down first."

Nayima hadn't realized she was pointing the shotgun at him. She lowered it. "Tell me ahora, Raul. No hay más secretos." Raul's secrets stung more than anyone else's.

"I won a ruling," Raul said.

"About what? Free toys?"

Raul stared out toward the thirsty grasslands. "I have a library portal at my house..." he began.

Of course he did. Toys and gadgets. That was Raul.

Raul went on. "I did some research on... the embryos."

Nayima's cheek flared as if he'd struck her. During Reconciliation, she and Raul had learned that dozens of embryos had been created from her eggs and his sperm, more than they'd known. They had been the cocktail du jour: something about their blood types. Her heart gave a sudden sick tumbling in her chest, as if to drown him out.

"There's a bebé, Nayima," he said, whispering like wind. "One survived."

The world went white. Her eyesight, her thoughts, lost.

"What? When?"

"She just turned four," he said. "She's still in the research compound."

There was a she somewhere?

"How long have you known?"

"Six months," he said. "When I got the portal. I saw rumors of the surviving infant, did the research. She's one of ours. They never told us."

Now Nayima's sacrifices seemed fresh: the involuntary harvesting of her eggs, three first-trimester miscarriages after forced insemination, a succession of unviable embryos created in labs, and two premature live births of infants from artificial wombs who had never survived beyond a day. Pieces of her chopped away.

"We can't reproduce," she said.

"But one lived," Raul said. "They don't know why."

"You've known all this time? And you never told me?"

He sighed. "Lo siento, Nayima. I hated hiding it. But I knew it would upset you. Or you might work against me. I didn't want to say anything until I got a ruling. As the biological father, I have rights."

"Carriers don't have rights."

"Parental rights," Raul said. "For the first time—yes, we do."

Nayima despised herself for her volcanic emotions. How could Raul be naïve enough to believe Sacramento's lies? If there was a surviving child—which she did not believe—they would not release their precious property to carriers.

"It's a trick," she said. "To get us to go back there."

Raul shook his head slowly. Impossibly, he smiled. "No, Nayima," he said. "They're sending her to us. To you. She's free under Reconciliation to be with her parents. All you have to do is sign the consent when they come."

Nayima needed to sit, so she ignored her sore joints and sat where she'd been standing, on the caked dirt of her road. The air felt thick and heavy in her lungs.

"No," Nayima said. Saying the word gave her strength. "No no no. We can't. It's a trap. Even if there's a girl..." It was so improbable, Nayima could barely say the words. "And there isn't... But even if there is, why would they offer her except as a weapon against us? To threaten us? To control us? Why do they keep trying so hard to make children from us? She's not from my womb, so she doesn't have the antibodies. Think about it! We're just...reserves for them. A blood supply, if they ever need it. That's the only reason we're still alive."

Raul's eyes dropped. He couldn't deny it.

"She's our child," Raul said. "Ella es nuestra bebé. We can't leave her there."

"You can't—but I can," she said. "Watch me."

Raul's voice cracked. "The ruling says both living parents must consent. I need you with me on this, Nayima."

"I'm an old woman now!" Nayima said. Her throat burned hot.

"And I'm fifty-six," Raul said. "But we had una hija together. The marshals are bringing her here tomorrow."

"You're sending marshals to me?" The last time marshals came to see her in the territories after only nine months, a pack of them had removed her from the house she had chosen and stolen half of her chickens, shooting a dozen dead just for fun. Her earliest taste of freedom had been a false start, victim to a government property dispute.

"Marshals aren't like they were," Raul said. "Things are changing, Nayima." Like he was scolding her.

Raul lowered the truck's bed door and pulled out the plastic crate. He carried it to her porch. Next, he took down the barrels and rolled them to the house one by one. The heavy barrels thundered across the soil.

When he returned, breathing hard, Nayima was on her feet again, with her gun. She jacked a shell into the chamber.

"You could've shot me before I did all that work," Raul said.

"I'm not shooting you yet," she said. "But any marshals that show up here tomorrow are declaring war. They might bring her, but they could take her at any time. We're all property! I won't give them that power over me. She's better off dead. I'm not afraid to die too."

Raul gave her a forlorn look before he walked past her and slammed the bed of his truck shut. "I was hoping for some eggs, pero maybe mañana."

"I swear to your God, Raul, I will kill anyone who comes to this house."

Raul opened his driver's side door and began to climb back inside, but he stopped to look at her over his shoulder. He had left his truck idling. He had never planned to stay long.

"She doesn't have a name," he said.

"What?"

"Nobody bothered to name her. In the records, she's called Specimen 120. Punto. Some of the researchers call her Chubby for a nickname. Like a pet, Nayima. Our hija."

The weight of the shotgun made Nayima's arms tremble.

"Don't bring anyone here," she said. "Please."

Raul got in the truck and slammed the door. He lurched into reverse, turned the truck away, and drove. Nayima fired once into the air, a roar of rage that echoed across the flatlands. The shotgun kicked in her arms like an angry baby.

After the engine's hum was lost in the open air, the only sound was Nayima's wretched sobs.

* * *

In her front room, Nayima's comm screen flared white, turning itself on. A minder waited in five-by-five on her wall, as though she'd been invited to breakfast. The light haloing her was bright enough to show old acne stars. Makeup had yet to make a comeback, except the enhanced red lips favored by both men and women. Full of life.

"Hello, Nayima," the minder said. Then she corrected herself: "Ms. Dixon."

Nayima nodded cordially. Nayima's grandmother, born in Alabama, had never stood for being called by her first name, and neither did Nayima—an admittedly old-fashioned trait at a time when numbers mattered more than names.

The minder seemed to notice Nayima's puffed eyes, and her polite veneer dulled. "You remember the guidelines?"

Guideline One and Only: She was not to criticize the lab-coats or make it sound as if she had been treated badly. Blah blah blah and so forth. Questions about the embryo—the girl—broiled in Nayima's mind, but she didn't dare bring her up. Maybe the marshals wouldn't come. Maybe she could still get her water credits.

"Yes," Nayima said, testing her thin voice.

"We added younger students this year," the minder said. "Stand by."

Three smaller squares appeared inset beneath the

girl's image—classrooms, the children progressively older in each. The far left square held the image of twelve wriggling, worming children ages about three to six sprawled across a floor with a red mat. A few in the front sat transfixed by her image on what seemed to be a looming screen, high above them. Every child wore tiny, powder blue plastic gloves.

Nayima had to look away from the smallest children. She had not seen children so young in forty years, and the sight of them was acid to her eyes.

Hadn't Raul said the girl was four?

Nayima blinked rapidly, her eyes itching with tears.

Crying, she was certain, was against the guidelines.

Nayima willed herself to look at the young, moony faces, braving memories of tiny bodies rotting on sidewalks, in cars, on the roadways, mummified in closets. These were new children—untouched by Plague. Their parents had been the wealthy, the isolated, the truly Chosen—the infinitesimal number of survivors who were not carriers, who did not have the antibodies, but had simply, somehow, survived.

Nayima leaned closer to her screen. "Boo!" she said.

Young eyes widened with terror. Children scooted away.

But when Nayima smiled, the entire mass of them quivered with laughter, a sea of perfect teeth.

Nayima's teeth were not perfect. She had never replaced the lower front tooth she'd lost to a lab-coat she'd smacked across his nose, drawing blood. He'd strapped her to a table, raped her, and extracted her tooth on the spot, without anesthesia.

Nayima had been offered a dental implant during Reconciliation, but a new tooth felt like a lie, so she had refused. In previous classroom visits, she had answered the question What happened to your tooth? without bitterness—why should she feel contempt for brutes any more than she would a tree dropping leaves?—until a minder pointed out that the anecdote about her extracted tooth violated the guidelines.

The guidelines left Nayima with very little to say. She chose each word with painful care.

These schoolchildren asked the usual questions: why she had survived (genetic predisposition), how many people she had infected (only one personally, as far as she knew), how many carriers were left (fifteen, since most known carriers were "gone now"). By the fourth question, Nayima had lost her will to look at the children's faces. It was harder all the time.

The girl who spoke up next was not yet eight. Her face held a whisper of brown; a girl who might have been hers. And Raul's.

"Do you have any children?" the girl said.

All of Nayima's work, gone. No composure. No smile. A sharp pain in her belly.

"No, I've never had children," she said. "None that survived."

Nayima shot a pointed gaze at the minder, who did not contradict her. Maybe the minder didn't know about Specimen 120. Maybe a bureaucrat had made up the story to tease Raul.

"Okay," the girl said, shrugging, not yet schooled in the art of condolences. "What do you miss the most about the time before the Plague?"

An easy answer came right away, and it almost wasn't a lie. "Halloween."

When she explained what Halloween had been, the children sat literally open-mouthed. She wondered which part of her story most stupefied them. The ready access to sweets? The trust of strangers? The costumes?

The host looked relieved with the children's enchantment and announced that the visit was over. A flurry of waving blue gloves. Nayima waved back. She even smiled again.

"Don't forget my water credits," Nayima said from behind her happy teeth.

But the minder's image had already flashed away.

*　　*　　*

Nayima lined up her contraband on the front table—the sawed-off, a box of shells, an old Colt she'd found in the attic with its full magazine, the baseball bat she kept at her bedside. She'd even found a gas mask she'd bartered for at market. When the marshals came, she would be prepared. In her younger years, she would have boarded up at least her front windows, but her weapons would have to do.

"Raul is the real child," she told Tango and Buster while they watched her work. Buster swatted at a loose shell at the edge of the table, but Nayina caught it before it hit the floor. "He believes every word they say. 'Things are changing,' he says. Believing in miracles. Sending marshals here—to me!"

Tango mewed softly. A question.

"Of course they're not bringing a child here," she said. "A judge's ruling? In favor of carriers? You know the lab-coats would fight to keep her." She shook her head, angry with herself for her weakness. "Besides, there is no child. Babies with carrier genes don't live."

The crate was light enough to lift to the table with only slight pressure in her lower back, gone when she stretched. But she could only roll a barrel slowly, oh-so-slowly, across her threshold. How had Raul managed so easily? She left the second barrel outside. By the time she closed her door again, her lower back pulsed with pain and she felt aged by a decade.

"Lies," Nayima said.

Tango and Buster agreed with frenzied mews.

She would have no Sunday dinner if she died tomorrow, Nayima reminded herself. So she got her cleaver from the kitchen, unwrapped the beef, and began chopping the meat on the table, not caring about dents in the wood. She chopped until she was perspiring and sweat stung her eyes.

Nayima held a chunk with both hands and sank in her teeth. She mostly did not bother with salt in her own cooking, so the taste was overwhelming at first. The cats gnawed at the meat beside her on the table with loud purrs.

"Could there be a child?"

Suppose they'd had a breakthrough, found a way to rewire the genes? But why go through that trouble and expense when other children were being born? The girl must be a failed experiment. A laboratory fluke. Did they need caretakers for a child born with half a brain—was that it? Nayima swore she'd be damned if she'd spend the years she had left tending the lab-coats' mistakes.

"But there is no child," she reminded Tango and Buster. "It's all a lie."

After dark, with her flashlight to guide her, Nayima set her traps for the thief cat with slices of meat and visited the wooden chicken coop Raul had helped her build, as big as her grandmother's backyard shed. She checked the loose wires in the rear, but the hole was still secure. She hadn't collected eggs earlier, so chickens had defecated on some. A few eggs lay entirely crushed, yolks seeping across the straw.

Nayima was exhausted by the time she'd cleaned the nest boxes, scrubbed the surviving eggs, and set them on a bowl on her kitchen for Raul to find later—but she couldn't afford to sleep tonight. The marshals might come at any time.

Nayima fixed herself a cup of black tea from her new water—so fresh!—and sat vigil by her front window with her shotgun, watching the empty pathway. Sometimes her eyes played tricks, animating the darkness. A far-off cat's cry sounded like a baby's, waking Nayima when she dozed.

Just before dawn, bells jingled near the chicken coop. Heart clambering, Nayima ran outside. The food was gone from the first trap she reached, but the door had not properly sprung. Shit.

More frantic jingling came from the trap twenty yards farther. Nayima raced toward it, her light in one hand and her gun in the other.

A pair of eyes glared out at her from beyond the bars.

The cat scrambled to every corner of the cage, desperate to escape while bells mocked him. This was the one. Nayima recognized the monster tabby's unusual size.

"Buddy, you stole the wrong chicken."

Nayima could not remember the last time she had felt so giddy. She carefully lowered her flashlight to the ground, keeping it trained on the trap. Then she raised her shotgun, aiming. She'd blow a hole in her trap this way, but she had caught the one she was looking for.

The cat mewed—not angry, beseeching. With a clear understanding of his situation.

"You started it, not me," Nayima said. "Don't sit there begging now."

The cat's trapped eyes glowed in her bright beam. Another plaintive mew.

"Shut up, you hear me? This is your fault." But her resolve was flagging.

The cat raised his paw, shaking the cage door. How many times had she done the very same thing? How many locks had she tested, searching for freedom?

Could there really be a child?

Nayima sobbed. Her throat was already raw from crying. Never again, she had said. No more tears. No more.

Nayima went to the trap's door and flipped up the latch. The cat hissed at her and raced away like a jaguar, melting into the dark. She hoped he would run for miles, never looking back.

Is my little girl with those zookeepers without even a name?

"But it's all lies," she whispered at the window, as she stroked Tango in her lap. "Isn't it?"

Dawn came and went with the roosters' crowing. Nayima did not move to collect the morning eggs, or to eat any of the beef she and the cats had left, or to empty her bulging bladder. She watched the sky light up her empty pathway, her open gate.

Why hadn't she closed the gate?

Based on the sun high above, it was nearly noon when Nayima finally stood up.

The metallic glint far down the roadway looked imaginary at first. To be sure, Nayima wiped away dust on her windowpane with her shirt, although the spots outside still clouded it. The gleam seemed to vanish, but then it was back, this time with bright cobalt blue lights that looked out of place against the browns and grays of the road. Two sets of blue lights danced in regimented patterns, back and forth.

Nayima's breath fogged her window as she leaned closer, so she wiped it again.

Hoverbikes!

Two large hoverbikes were speeding toward her house, one on each side of the road at a matching pace, blue lights snaking across their underbellies. At least it wasn't an army, unless more were coming. Marshals' hoverbikes were only big enough for two, at most.

"You damn fool, Raul," she whispered again, but she already had forgiven him too.

Nayima was too exhausted to pick up her shotgun. She had failed the test with her cat thief, so what made her think she could fight marshals? Let them take what they wanted. As long as she had Tango and Buster, she could start again. She always did.

As the hoverbikes flew past her gate, Nayima counted one front rider on each bike in the marshals' uniform: black jackets with orange armbands. The second rider on the lead bike was only Raul—his face was hidden behind the black helmet, but she knew his red hickory shirt. His father had worn one just like it, Raul had told her until she wanted to scream.

"Nayima!" Raul called. He flung his helmet to the ground.

The hoverbike Raul was riding hadn't quite slowed to a stop, floating six inches above the ground, so Raul stumbled when he leaped off in a hurry. The marshal grabbed his arm to help hold him steady while the bike bobbing obediently in place.

"Querida, it's me," Raul said. "Don't worry about the marshals. Please open the door."

Nayima stared as both marshals took off their helmets, almost in unison, and rested them in the crooks of their arms. One was a young man, one a woman, neither older than twenty-five. The man was fair-haired and ruddy. The woman's skin was nearly as dark as her own, her hair also trimmed to fuzz. Had she seen this man during an earlier classroom visit? He looked familiar, and he was smiling. They both were. She had never seen a marshal smile.

The marshals wore no protective suits. No masks. They did not hide their faces or draw weapons. Even ten yards away, through a dirty window, Nayima saw their eyes.

Nayima jumped when Raul banged on her door. "Nayima, ella está aquí!"

"I don't see her." Nayima tried to shout, but her throat nearly strangled her breath.

Raul motioned to the woman marshal, and she dismounted her hoverbike. For the first time, Nayima saw her bike's passenger—not standing, but in a backward facing seat. A child stirred as the woman unstrapped her.

It couldn't be. Couldn't be.

Nayima closed her eyes. Had they drugged her meat? Was it a hallucination?

"Do you see, Nayima?" Raul said. "Ven afuera conmigo. Please come."

Raul left her porch to run back to the hoverbike. Freed from her straps, a child reached out for a hand for Raul's help from the seat. Raul made a game of it, lifting the child up high. Curly spirals of dark hair nestled her shoulders. For an instant, the child was silhouetted in the sunlight, larger than life in Raul's sturdy upward grasp.

The girl giggled loudly enough for Nayima to hear her through the windowpane. Raul was a good father. Nayima could see it already.

"Now you're going to meet your mamí," Raul said.

Nayima hid behind her faded draperies as Raul took the girl's hand and walked to the porch with her. When she heard the twin footsteps on her wooden planks, Nayima's world swayed. She ventured a peek and saw the girl's inquisitive face turned toward the window—dear Jesus, this angel had Gram's nose and plump, cheerful cheeks. Raul's lips. Buried treasure was etched in her delicate features.

Jesus. Jesus. Thank you, Dear Lord.

Nayima opened her door.

COVAX

When David Brin graciously offered this Hugo and Locus Award winning story at no cost to support this anthology, I couldn't resist. The WHO is leading the charge to distribute vaccines equitably around the world with their COVAX (COVID-19 Vaccines Global Access) program. No-one is safe until everyone is safe. That's why The World Health Organization's Covid Solidarity Response Fund will receive donations from the proceeds of this book.

The Giving Plague

by David Brin

1.

You think you're going to get me, don't you? Well, you've got another thing coming, 'cause I'm ready for you.

That's why there's a forged card in my wallet saying my blood group is AB negative, and a MedicAlert tag warning that I'm allergic to penicillin, aspirin, and phenylalanine. Another one states that I'm a practicing, devout Christian Scientist. All these tricks ought to slow you down when the time comes, as it's sure to, sometime soon.

Even if it makes the difference between living and dying, there's just no way I'll let anyone stick a transfusion needle into my arm. Never. Not with the blood supply in the state it's in.

And anyway, I've got antibodies. So you just stay the hell away from me, ALAS. I won't be your patsy. I won't be your vector.

I know your weaknesses, you see. You're a fragile, if subtle devil. Unlike TARP, you can't bear exposure to air or heat or cold or acid or alkali. Blood to blood, that's your only route. And what need had you of any other? You thought you'd evolved the perfect technique, didn't you?

What was it Leslie Adgeson called you? The perfect master? The paragon of viruses?

I remember long ago when HIV, the AIDS virus, had

everyone so awed with its subtlety of lethal design. But compared with you, HIV is just a crude butcher. A maniac with a chainsaw, a blunderer that kills its hosts and relies for transmission on habits humans can, with effort, get under control. Oh, old HIV had its tricks, but compared with you? An amateur!

Rhinoviruses and flu are clever, too. They're profligate, and they mutate rapidly. Long ago they learned how to make their hosts drip and wheeze and sneeze, so the victims spread the misery in all directions. Flu viruses are also a lot smarter than AIDS 'cause they don't generally kill their hosts, just make 'em miserable while they hack and spray and inflict fresh infections on their neighbors.

Oh, Les Adgeson was always accusing me of anthropomorphizing our subjects. Whenever he came into my part of the lab, and found me cursing some damned intransigent leukophage in rich, Tex-Mex invective, he'd react predictably. I can just picture him now, raising one eyebrow, commenting dryly in his Winchester accent.

"The virus cannot hear you, Forry. It isn't sentient, nor even alive, strictly speaking. It's only a packet of genes in a protein case, after all."

"Yeah, Les," I'd answer. "But *selfish* genes! Given half a chance, they'll take over a human cell, force it to make armies of new viruses, then burst it apart as they escape to attack others. They may not think. All that behavior may have evolved by blind chance. But doesn't it all *feel* as if it's planned? As if the nasty little things were *guided*, somehow, by somebody out to make us miserable...? Out to make us die?"

"Oh, come now Forry." He would smile at my New World ingenuousness. "You wouldn't be in this field if you didn't find phages beautiful, in their own way."

Good old smug, sanctimonious Les. He never did figure out that viruses fascinated me for quite another reason. In their rapacious insatiability I saw a simple, distilled purity of ambition that exceeded even my own. The fact that it was mindless did little to ease my qualms. I've always imagined we humans over-rated brains, anyway.

We'd first met when Les visited Austin on sabbatical, some years before. He'd had the Boy Genius rep even then, and naturally I played up to him. He invited me to join him back in Oxford, so there I was, having regular amiable arguments over the meaning of disease while the English rain dripped desultorily on the rhododendrons outside.

Les Adgeson. Him with his artsy friends and his pretensions at philosophy—Les was all the time talking about the elegance and beauty of our nasty little subjects. But he didn't fool me. I knew he was just as crazy Nobel-mad as the rest of us. Just as obsessed with the chase, searching for that piece of the Life Puzzle, that bit leading to more grants, more lab space, more techs, more prestige... to money, status and, maybe eventually, Stockholm.

He claimed not to be interested in such things. But he was a smoothie, all right. How else, in the midst of the Thatcher massacre of British science, did his lab keep expanding? And yet, he kept up the pretense.

"Viruses have their good side," Les kept saying. "Sure, they often kill, in the beginning. All new pathogens start that way. But eventually, one of two things happens. Either humanity evolves defenses to eliminate the threat or ..."

Oh, he loved those dramatic pauses.

"Or?" I'd prompt him, as required.

"Or else we come to an accommodation, a compromise... even an alliance."

That's what Les always talked about. *Symbiosis.* He loved to quote Margulis and Thomas, and even Lovelock, for pity's sake! His respect even for vicious, sneaky brutes like HIV was downright scary.

"See how it actually incorporates itself right into the DNA of its victims?" he would muse. "Then it waits, until the victim is later attacked by some *other* disease pathogen. The host T cells prepare to replicate, to drive off the invader, only now some chemical machinery is taken over by the new DNA, and instead of two new T cells, a plethora of new AIDS viruses results."

"So?" I answered. "Except that it's a retrovirus, that's the way nearly all viruses work."

"Yes, but think ahead, Forry. Imagine what's going to happen when, inevitably, the AIDS virus infects someone whose genetic makeup makes him invulnerable!"

"What, you mean his antibody reactions are fast enough to stop it? Or his T cells repel invasion?"

Oh, Les used to sound so damn patronizing when he got excited.

"No, no, think!" he urged. "I mean invulnerable *after* infection. *After* the viral genes have incorporated into his chromosomes. Only in this individual certain *other* genes *prevent* the new DNA from triggering viral synthesis. No new viruses are made. No cellular disruption. The person *is* invulnerable. But now he has all this new DNA...."

"In just a few cells—"

"Yes. But suppose one of these is a sex cell. Then suppose he fathers a child with that gamete. Now *every* one of that child's cells may contain both the trait of invulnerability *and* the new viral genes! Think about it, Forry. You now have a new type of human being! One who cannot be killed by AIDS. And yet he has all the AIDS genes, can make all those strange, marvelous proteins.... Oh, most of them will be unexpressed or useless, of course. But now this child's genome, and his descendants', contains more *variety*...."

I often wondered, when he got carried away this way. Did he actually believe he was explaining this to me for the first time? Much as the Brits respect American science, they do tend to assume we're slackers when it comes to the philosophical side. But I'd seen his interest heading in this direction weeks back and had carefully done some extra reading.

"You mean like the genes responsible for some types of inheritable cancers?" I asked sarcastically. "There's evidence some oncogenes were originally inserted into the human genome by viruses, just as you suggest. Those who inherit the trait for rheumatoid arthritis may also have gotten their gene that way."

"Exactly. Those viruses themselves may be extinct, but their DNA lives on, in ours!"

"Right. And boy have human beings benefited!"

Oh, how I hated that smug expression he'd get. (It got wiped off his face eventually, didn't it?

Les picked up a piece of chalk and drew a figure on the blackboard.

HARMLESS $\rightarrow$ KILLER! $\rightarrow$ SURVIVABLE ILLNESS $\rightarrow$ INCONVENIENCE $\rightarrow$ HARMLESS

"Here's the classic way of looking at how a host species interacts with a new pathogen, especially a virus. Each arrow, of course, represents a stage of mutation and adaptation selection.

"First, a new form of some previously harmless microorganism leaps from its prior host, say a monkey species, over to a new one, say us. Of course, at the beginning we have no adequate defenses. It cuts through us like Syphilis did in Europe in the sixteenth century, killing in days rather than years... in an orgy of cell feeding that's really not a very efficient modus for a pathogen. After all, only a gluttonous parasite kills off its host so quickly.

"What follows, then, is a rough period for both host and parasite as each struggles to adapt to the other. It can be likened to warfare. Or, on the other hand, it might be thought of as a sort of drawn out process of *negotiation*."

I snorted in disgust. "Mystical crap, Les. I'll concede your chart; but the War analogy is the right one. That's why they fund labs like ours. To come up with better weapons for our side."

"Hmm. Possibly. But sometimes the process does look different, Forry." He turned and drew another chart.

HARMLESS $\rightarrow$ KILLER! $\rightarrow$ SURVIVABLE ILLNESS $\rightarrow$ INCONVENIENCE $\rightarrow$ BENIGN PARASITISM $\rightarrow$ SYMBIOSIS

"You can see that this chart is the same as the other, right up to the point where the original disease disappears."

"Or goes into hiding."

"Surely. As E. coli took refuge in our innards. Doubtless long ago the ancestors of E. coli killed a great many of our ancestors before eventually becoming the beneficial symbionts they are now, helping us digest our food.

"The same applies to viruses, I'd wager. Heritable cancers and rheumatoid arthritis are just temporary awkwardnesses. Eventually, those genes will be comfortably incorporated. They'll be part of the genetic diversity that prepares us to meet challenges ahead. Why, I'd wager a large portion of our present genes came about in such a way, entering our cells first as invaders...."

Crazy sonovabitch. Fortunately he didn't try to lead the lab's research effort too far to the right on his magic diagram. Our Boy Genius was plenty savvy about the funding agencies. He knew they weren't interested in paying us to prove we're all partly descended from viruses. They wanted, and wanted *badly*, progress on ways to fight viral infections themselves.

So Les concentrated his team on vectors.

Yeah, you viruses need vectors, don't you. I mean, if you kill a guy, you've got to have a life raft, so you can desert the ship you've sunk, so you can cross over to some *new* hapless victim. Same applies if the host proves tough, and fights you off—gotta move on. Always movin' on.

Hell, even if you've made peace with a human body, like Les suggested, you still want to spread, don't you? Big-time colonizers, you tiny beasties.

Oh, I know. It's just natural selection. Those bugs that accidentally find a good vector spread. Those that don't, don't. But it's so eerie. Sometimes it sure *feels* purposeful....

So the flu makes us sneeze. Salmonella gives us diarrhea. Smallpox causes pustules which dry, flake off and blow away to be inhaled by the patient's loved ones. All good ways to jump ship. To colonize.

Who knows? Did some past virus cause a swelling of the lips that made us want to kiss? Heh. Maybe that's a case of Les's "benign incorporation"... we retain the trait, long after the causative pathogen went extinct! What a concept.

So our lab got this big grant to study vectors. Which is how Les found you, ALAS. He drew this big chart covering all the possible ways an infection might leap from person to person, and set us about checking all of them, one by one.

For himself he reserved straight blood-to-blood infection. There were reasons for that.

First off, Les was an altruist, see. He was concerned about all the panic and unfounded rumors spreading about Britain's blood supply. Some people were putting off necessary surgery. There was talk of starting over here, what some rich folk in the States had begun doing—stockpiling their own blood in silly, expensive efforts to avoid having to use the Blood Banks if they ever needed hospitalization.

All that bothered Les. But even worse was the fact that lots of potential donors were shying away from giving blood because of some stupid rumors that you could get infected that way.

Hell, nobody ever caught anything from *giving* blood... nothing except maybe a little dizziness and perhaps a zit or spot from all the biscuits and sweet tea they feed you afterwards. And as for contracting HIV from *receiving* blood, well, the new antibodies tests soon had that problem under control. Still, the stupid rumors spread.

A nation has to have confidence in its blood supply. Les wanted to eliminate all those silly fears once and for all, with one definitive study. But that wasn't the only reason he wanted the blood-to blood vector for himself.

"Sure, there are some nasty things like AIDS that use that vector. But that's also where I might find the older ones," he said, excitedly. "The viruses that have *almost* finished the process of becoming benign. The ones that have been so well selected that they keep a low profile, and hardly inconvenience their hosts at all. Maybe I can even find one that's commensal! One that actually *helps* the human body."

"An undiscovered human commensal," I sniffed doubtfully.

"And why not? If there's no visible disease, why would anyone have ever looked for it! This could open up a whole new field, Forry!"

In spite of myself, I was impressed. It was how he got to be known as a Boy Genius, after all, this flash of half-crazy insight. How he managed not to have it snuffed out of him at OxBridge, I'll never know, but it was one reason why I'd attached myself to him and his lab, and wrangled mighty hard to get my name attached to his papers.

So I kept watch over his work. It sounded so dubious, so damn stupid. And I knew it just might bear fruit, in the end.

That's why I was ready when Les invited me along to a conference down in Bloomsbury one day. The colloquium itself was routine, but I could tell he was near to bursting with news. Afterwards we walked down Charing Cross Road to a pizza place, one far enough from the university area to be sure there'd be no colleagues anywhere within earshot—just the pretheater crowd, waiting till opening time down at Leicester Square.

Les breathlessly swore me to secrecy. He needed a confidant, you see, and I was only too happy to comply. "I've been interviewing a lot of blood donors lately," he told me after we'd ordered. "It seems that while some people have been scared off from donating, that has been largely made up by increased contributions by a central core of regulars."

"Sounds good," I said. And I meant it. I had no objection to there being an adequate blood supply. Back in Austin I was pleased to see others go to the Red Cross van, just so long as nobody asked me to contribute. I had neither the time nor the interest, so I got out of it by telling everybody I'd had malaria.

"I found one interesting fellow, Forry. Seems he started donating back when he was twenty-five, during the Blitz. Must have contributed thirty-five, forty gallons, by now."

I did a quick mental calculation. "Wait a minute. He's got to be past the age limit by now."

"Exactly right! He admitted the truth, when he was assured of confidentiality. Seems he didn't want to stop donating when he reached sixty-five. He's a hardy old fellow ... had a spot of surgery a few years back, but he's in quite decent shape, overall. So, right after his local Gallon Club threw a big retirement fest for him, he actually moved across the county and registered at a new blood bank, giving a false name and a younger age!"

"Kinky. But it sounds harmless enough. I'd guess he just likes to feel needed. Bet he flirts with the nurses and enjoys the free food... sort of a bimonthly party he can always count on, with friendly, appreciative people."

Hey, just because I'm a selfish bastard doesn't mean I can't extrapolate the behavior of altruists. Like most other user-types, I've got a good instinct for the sort of motivations that drive suckers. People like me need to know such things.

"That's what I thought too, at first," Les said, nodding. "I found a few more like him, and decided to call them 'addicts.' At first I never connected them with the other group, the one I named 'converts.'"

"Converts?"

"Yes, converts. People who suddenly become blood donors—get this—very soon after they've recovered from surgery themselves!"

"Maybe they're paying off part of their hospital bills that way?"

"Mmm, not really. We have nationalized health, remember? And even for private patients, that might account for the first few donations only."

"Gratitude, then?" An alien emotion to me, but I understood it, in principle.

"Perhaps. Some few people might have their consciousnesses raised after a close brush with death, and decide to become better citizens. After all, half an hour at a blood bank, a few times a year, is a small inconvenience in exchange for..."

Sanctimonious twit. Of course he was a donor. Les went on and on about civic duty and such until the waitress arrived with our pizza and two fresh bitters. That shut him up for a moment. But when she left, he leaned forward, eyes shining.

"But no, Forry. It wasn't bill-paying, or even gratitude. Not for some of them, at least. More had happened to these people than having their consciousnesses raised. They were converts, Forry. They began joining Gallon Clubs, and more! It seems almost as if, in each case, a personality change had taken place."

"What do you mean?"

"I mean that a significant fraction of those who have had major surgery during the last five years seem to have changed their entire set of social attitudes! Beyond becoming blood donors, they've increased their contributions to charity, joined parent-teacher organizations and Boy Scout troops, become active in

Greenpeace and Save The Children..."

"The point, Les. What's your point?"

"My point?" He shook his head. "Frankly, some of these people were behaving like addicts... like converted addicts to *altruism*. That's when it occurred to me, Forry, that what we might have here was a new vector."

He said it as simply as that. Naturally I looked at him, blankly.

"A vector!" he whispered, urgently. "Forget about typhus, or smallpox, or flu. They're rank amateurs! Wallies who give the show away with all their sneezing and flaking and shitting. To be sure, AIDS uses blood and sex, but it's so damned savage, it forced us to become aware of it, to develop tests, to begin the long, slow process of isolating it. But ALAS—"

"Alas?"

"A-L-A-S." He grinned. "It's what I've named the new virus I've isolated, Forry. It stands for 'Acquired Lavish Altruism Syndrome.' How do you like it?"

"Hate it. Are you trying to tell me that there's a virus that affects the human *mind*? And in such a compli-cated way?" I was incredulous and, at the same time, scared spitless. I've always had this superstitious feeling about viruses and vectors. Les really had me spooked now.

"No, of course not," he laughed. "But consider a simpler possibility. What if some virus one day stumbled on a way to make people enjoy giving blood?"

I guess I only blinked then, unable to give him any

other reaction.

"Think, Forry! Think about that old man I spoke of earlier. He told me that every two months or so, just before he'd be allowed to donate again, he tends to feel 'all thick inside.' The discomfort only goes away after the next donation!"

I blinked again. "And you're saying that each time he gives blood, he's actually serving his parasite, providing it a vector into new hosts...."

"The new hosts being those who survive surgery because the hospital gave them fresh blood, all because our old man was so generous, yes! They're infected! Only this is a subtle virus, not a greedy bastard, like AIDS, or even the flu. It keeps a low profile. Who knows, maybe it's even reached a level of commensalism with its hosts—attacking invading organisms for them, or..."

He saw the look on my face and waved his hands. "All right, far-fetched, I know. But think about it! Because there are no disease symptoms, nobody has ever looked for this virus, until now."

He's isolated it, I realized, suddenly. And, knowing instantly what this thing could mean, career-wise, I was already scheming, wondering how to get my name onto his paper, when he published this. So absorbed was I that, for a few moments, I lost track of his words.

"... And so now we get to the interesting part. You see, what's a normal, selfish Tory-voter going to think when he finds himself suddenly wanting to go down to the blood bank as often as they'll let him?"

"Um," I shook my head. "That he's been bewitched?

Hypnotized?"

"Nonsense!" Les snorted. "That's not how human psychology works. No, we tend to do lots of things without knowing why. We need excuses, though, so we rationalize! If an obvious reason for our behavior isn't readily available, we invent one, preferably one that helps us think better of ourselves. Ego is powerful stuff, my friend."

Hey, I thought. *Don't teach your grandmother to suck eggs.*

"Altruism," I said aloud. "They find themselves rushing regularly to the blood bank. So they rationalize that it's because they're good people.... They become proud of it. Brag about it...."

"You've got it," Les said. "And because they're proud, even sanctimonious, about their newfound generosity, they tend to extend it, to bring it into other parts of their lives!"

I whispered in hushed awe. "An altruism virus! Jesus, Les, when we announce this..."

I stopped when I saw his sudden frown and instantly thought it was because I'd used that word "we." I should have known better, of course. For Les was always more than willing to share the credit. No, his reservation was far more serious than that.

"Not yet, Forry. We can't publish this yet."

I shook my head. "Why not! This is big, Les! It proves much of what you've been saying all along, about symbiosis and all that. There could even be a Nobel in it!"

I'd been gauche, and spoken aloud of The Ultimate.

But he did not even seem to notice. Damn. If only Les had been like most biologists, driven more than anything else by the lure of Stockholm. But no. You see, Les was a natural. A natural altruist.

It was his fault, you see. Him and his damn virtue, they drove me to first contemplate what I next decided to do.

"Don't you see, Forry? If we publish, they'll develop an antibody test for the ALAS virus. Donors carrying it will be barred from the blood banks, just like those carrying AIDS and syphilis and hepatitis. And that would be incredibly cruel torture to those poor addicts and carriers."

"Screw the carriers!" I almost shouted. Several pizza patrons glanced my way. With a desperate effort I brought my voice down. "Look, Les, the carriers will be classified as diseased, won't they? So they'll go under doctor's care. And if all it takes to make them feel better is to bleed them regularly, well, then we'll give them pet leeches!"

Les smiled. "Clever. But that's not the only, or even my main reason, Forry. No, I'm not going to publish, yet, and that is final. I just can't allow anybody to stop this disease. It's got to spread, to become an epidemic. A pandemic."

I stared, and upon seeing that look in his eyes, I knew that Les was more than an altruist. He had caught that specially insidious of all human ailments, the Messiah Complex. Les wanted to save the world.

"Don't you see?" he said urgently, with the fervor of a proselyte. "Selfishness and greed are destroying the planet, Forry! But nature always finds a way, and this time symbiosis may be giving us our last chance, a final opportunity to become better people, to learn to cooperate before it's too late!

"The things we're most proud of, our prefrontal lobes, those bits of gray matter above the eyes which make us so much smarter than beasts—what good have they done us, Forry? Not a hell of a lot. We aren't going to think our way out of the crises of the twentieth century. Or, at least, thought alone won't do it. We need something else, as well.

"And Forry, I'm convinced that 'something else' is ALAS. We've got to keep this secret, at least until it's so well established in the population that there's no turning back!"

I swallowed. "How long? How long do you want to wait? Until it starts affecting voting patterns? Until after the next election?"

He shrugged. "Oh, at least that long. Five years. Possibly seven. You see, the virus tends to only get into people who've recently had surgery, and they're generally older. Fortunately, they also are often influential. Just the sort who now vote Tory..."

He went on. And on. I listened with half an ear, but already I had come to that fateful realization. A seven-year wait for a goddamn coauthorship would make this discovery next to useless to my career, to my ambitions.

Of course I could blow the secret on Les, now that I knew of it. But that would only embitter him, and he'd easily take all the credit for the discovery anyway. People tend to remember innovators, not whistle-blowers.

We paid our bill and walked toward Charing Cross Station, where we could catch the tube to Paddington, and from there to Oxford. Along the way we ducked out of a sudden downpour at a streetside ice cream vendor. While we waited, I bought us both cones. I remember quite clearly that he had strawberry. I had a raspberry ice.

While Les absentmindedly talked on about his research plans, a small pink smudge colored the corner of his mouth. I pretended to listen, but already my mind had turned to other things, nascent plans and earnest scenarios for committing murder.

2.

It would be the perfect crime, of course.

Those movie detectives are always going on about "motive, means, and opportunity." Well, motive I had in plenty, but it was one so far-fetched, so obscure, that it would surely never occur to anybody.

Means? Hell, I worked in a business rife with means. There were poisons and pathogens galore. We're a very careful profession, but, well, accidents do happen.... The same holds for opportunity.

There was a rub, of course. Such was Boy Genius's reputation that, even if I did succeed in knobbling him, I didn't dare come out immediately with my own announcement. Damn him, everyone would just assume it was his work anyway, or his "leadership" here at the lab, at least, that led to the discovery of ALAS. And besides, too much fame for me right after his demise might lead someone to suspect a motive.

So, I realized. Les was going to get his delay, after

all. Maybe not seven years, but three or four perhaps, during which I'd move back to the States, start a separate line of work, then subtly guide my own research to cover methodically all the bases Les had so recently flown over in flashes of inspiration. I wasn't happy about the delay, but at the end of that time, it would look entirely like my own work. No co-authorship for Forry on this one, nossir!

The beauty of it was that nobody would ever think of connecting me with the tragic death of my colleague and friend, years before. After all, did not his demise set me back in my career, temporarily? "Ah, if only poor Les had lived to see your success!" my competitors would say, suppressing jealous bile as they watched me pack for Stockholm.

Of course none of this appeared on my face or in my words. We both had our normal work to do. But almost every day I also put in long extra hours helping Les in "our" secret project. In its own way it was an exhilarating time, and Les was lavish in his praise of the slow, dull, but methodical way I fleshed out some of his ideas.

I made my arrangements slowly, knowing Les was in no hurry. Together we gathered data. We isolated, and even crystallized the virus, got X-Ray diffractions, did epidemiological studies, all in strictest secrecy.

"Amazing!" Les would cry out, as he uncovered the way the ALAS virus forced its hosts to feel their need to "give." He'd wax eloquent, effusive over elegant mechanisms which he ascribed to random selection but which I could not help superstitiously attributing to some incredibly insidious form of intelligence. The more subtle and effective we found its techniques to be, the more admiring Les became, and the more I found myself loathing those little packets of RNA and protein.

The fact that the virus seemed so harmless—Les thought even commensal—only made me hate it more. It made me glad of what I had planned. Glad that I was going to stymie Les in his scheme to give ALAS free rein.

I was going to save humanity from this would-be puppet master. True, I'd delay my warning to suit my own purposes, but the warning would come, nonetheless, and sooner than my unsuspecting compatriot planned.

Little did Les know that he was doing background for work I'd take credit for. Every flash of insight, his every "Eureka!" was stored away in my private notebook, beside my own columns of boring data. Meanwhile, I sorted through all the means at my disposal.

Finally, I selected for my agent a particularly virulent strain of Dengue Fever.

3.

There's an old saying we have in Texas. "A chicken is just an egg's way of makin' more eggs."

To a biologist, familiar with all those latinized-graecificated words, this saying has a much more "posh" version. Humans are "zygotes," made up of diploid cells containing forty-six paired chromosomes ... except for our haploid sex cells, or "gametes." Males' gametes are sperm and females' are eggs, each containing only twenty-three chromosomes.

So biologists say that "a zygote is only a gamete's way of making more gametes."

Clever, eh? But it does point out just how hard it is, in nature, to pin down a Primal Cause... some center to the puzzle, against which everything else can be calibrated. I mean, which *does* come first, the chicken or the egg?

"Man is the measure of all things," goes another wise old saying. Oh yeah? Tell that to a modern feminist. A guy I once knew who used to read science fiction told me about this story he'd seen, in which it turned out that the whole and entire purpose of humanity, brains and all, was to be the organism that built starships so that *houseflies* could migrate out and colonize the galaxy.

But that idea's nothing compared with what Les Adgeson believed. He spoke of the human animal as if he were describing a veritable United Nations. From the E. coli in our guts, to tiny commensal mites that clean our eyelashes for us, to the mitochondria that energize our cells, all the way to the contents of our very DNA... Les saw it all as a great big hive of compromise, negotiation, *symbiosis*. Most of the contents of our chromosomes came from past invaders, he contended.

Symbiosis? The picture he created in my mind was one of minuscule puppeteers, all yanking and jerking at us with their protein strings, making us marionettes dance to their own tunes, to their own nasty, selfish little agendas.

And you, *you* were the worst! Like most cynics, I had always maintained a secret faith in human nature.

Yes, most people are pigs. I've always known that. And while I may be a user, at least I'm honest enough to admit it. But deep down, we users count on the sappy generosity, the mysterious, puzzling altruism of those others, the kind, inexplicably decent folk... those we superficially sneer at in contempt, but secretly hold in awe.

Then you came along, damn you. You *make* people behave that way. There is no mystery left, after you get finished. No corner remaining impenetrable to cynicism. Damn, how I came to hate you!

As I came to hate Leslie Adgeson. I made my plans, schemed my brilliant campaign against both of you. In those last days of innocence I felt oh, so savagely determined. So deliciously decisive and in control of my own destiny.

In the end it was anticlimactic. I didn't have time to finish my preparations, to arrange that little trap, that sharp bit of glass dipped in just the right mixture of deadly microorganisms. For CAPUC arrived then, just before I could exercise my option as a murderer.

CAPUC changed everything.

Catastrophic Autoimmune PUlmonary Collapse... acronym for the horror that made AIDS look like a minor irritant. And in the beginning it appeared unstoppable. Its vectors were completely unknown, and the causative agent defied isolation for so long.

This time it was no easily identifiable group that came down with the new plague, though it concentrated upon the industrialized world. Schoolchildren in some areas seemed particularly vulnerable. In other places it was secretaries and postal workers.

Naturally, all the major epidemiology labs got involved. Les predicted the pathogen would turn out to be something akin to the prions which cause shingles in sheep, and certain plant diseases... a pseudo-lifeform even simpler than a virus and even harder to track down. It was a heretical, minority view, until the CDC in Atlanta decided out of desperation to try his theories out, and found the very dormant viroids Les predicted—mixed in with the glue used to seal paper milk cartons, envelopes, postage stamps.

Les was a hero, of course. Most of us in the labs were. After all, we'd been the first line of defense. Our own casualty rate had been ghastly.

For a while there, funerals and other public gatherings were discouraged. But an exception was made for Les. The procession behind his cortege was a mile long. I was asked to deliver the eulogy. And when they pleaded with me to take over at the lab, I agreed.

So naturally I tended to forget all about ALAS. The war against CAPUC took everything society had. And while I may be selfish, even a rat can tell when it makes more sense to join in the fight to save a sinking ship... especially when there's no other port in sight.

We learned how to combat CAPUC, eventually. It involved drugs, and a serum based on reversed antibodies force-grown in the patient's own marrow after he's given a dangerous overdose of a vanadium compound I found by trial and error. It worked, most of the time, but the victims suffered great stress and often required a special regime of whole blood transfusions to get across the most dangerous phase.

Blood banks were stretched even thinner than

before. Only now the public responded generously, as in time of war. I should not have been surprised when survivors, after their recovery, volunteered by the thousands. But, of course, I'd forgotten about ALAS by then, hadn't I?

We beat back CAPUC. Its vector proved too unreliable, too easily interrupted once we'd figured it out. The poor little viroid never had a chance to get to Les's "negotiation" stage. Oh well, those are the breaks.

I got all sorts of citations I didn't deserve. The King gave me a KBE for personally saving the Prince of Wales. I had dinner at the White House.

Big deal.

The world had a respite, after that. CAPUC had scared people it seemed, into a new spirit of cooperation. I should have been suspicious, of course. But soon I'd moved over to WHO, and had all sorts of administrative responsibilities in the Final Campaign on Malnutrition.

By that time I had almost entirely forgotten about ALAS.

I forgot about you, didn't I? Oh, the years passed, my star rose, I became famous, respected, revered. I didn't get my Nobel in Stockholm. Ironically, I picked it up in Oslo. Fancy that. Just shows you can fool anybody.

And yet, I don't think I ever *really* forgot about you, ALAS, not at the back of my mind.

Peace treaties were signed. Citizens of the industrial nations voted temporary cuts in their standards of living in order to fight poverty and save the environment. Suddenly, it seemed, we'd all grown up. Other cynics, guys I'd gotten drunk with in the past—and shared dark premonitions about the inevitable fate of filthy, miserable humanity—all gradually deserted the faith, as pessimists seem wont do when the world turns bright—too bright for even the cynical to dismiss as a mere passing phase on the road to Hell.

And yet, my own brooding remained unblemished. For subconsciously I *knew* it wasn't real.

Then the third Mars Expedition returned to worldwide adulation, and brought home with them TARP.

And that was when we all found out just how *friendly* all our home-grown pathogens really had been, all along.

4.

Late at night, stumbling in exhaustion from overwork, I would stop at Les's portrait where I'd ordered it hung in the hall opposite my office door, and stand there cursing him and his damned theories of symbiosis.

Imagine mankind ever reaching a symbiotic association with TARP! That really would be something. Imagine, Les, all those *alien* genes, added to our heritage, to our rich human diversity!

Only TARP did not seem to be much interested in "negotiation." Its wooing was rough, deadly. And its vector was the wind.

The world looked to me, and to my peers, for salvation. In spite of all of my successes and high renown, though, I knew myself for a second-best fraud. I would always know—no matter how much they thanked and praised me—who had been better than me by light years.

Again and again, deep into the night, I would pore through the notes Leslie Adgeson had left behind, seeking inspiration, seeking hope. That's when I stumbled across ALAS once more.

I found *you* again.

Oh, you made us behave better, all right. At least a quarter of the human race must contain your DNA, by now, ALAS. And in their newfound, inexplicable, rationalized altruism, they set the tone followed by all the others.

Everybody behaves so damned *well* in the present calamity. They help each other, they succor the sick, they all *give* so.

Funny thing, though. If you hadn't made us all so bloody cooperative, we'd probably never have made it to bloody Mars, would we? Or if we had, there'd have still been enough paranoia around so we'd have maintained a decent quarantine.

But then, I remind myself, you don't *plan*, do you. You're just a bundle of RNA, packed inside a protein coat, with an incidentally, accidentally acquired trait of making humans want to donate blood. That's all you are, right? So you had no way of knowing that by making us "better" you were also setting us up for TARP, did you? Did you?

5.

We've got some palliatives, now. A few new techniques seem to be doing some good. The latest news is great, in fact. Apparently, we'll be able to save

15 percent or so of the children. Up to half of those may even be fertile.

That's for nations who've had a lot of racial mixing. Heterozygosity and genetic diversity seems to breed better resistance. Those peoples with "pure," narrow bloodlines will be harder to save, but then, racism has its inevitable price.

Too bad about the great apes and horses. At least all this will give the rain forests a chance to grow back.

Meanwhile, everybody perseveres. There is no panic, as one reads about happening in past plagues. We've grown up at last, it seems. We help each other.

But I carry a card in my wallet saying I'm a Christian Scientist, and that my blood group is AB negative, and that I'm allergic to nearly everything. Transfusions are one of the treatments commonly used now, and I'm an important man. But I won't take blood.

I won't.

I *donate*, but I'll never take it. Not even when I drop.

You won't have me, ALAS. You won't.

I am a bad man. I suppose, all told, I've done more good than evil in my life, but that's incidental, a product of happenstance and the bizarre caprices of the world.

I have no control over the world, but I can make my own decisions, at least. As I make this one now.

Down, out of my high research tower, I've come. Into the streets, where the teeming clinics fester and broil. That is where I work now. And it doesn't matter to me that I'm behaving no differently from anyone else today. They are all marionettes. They think they're acting altruistically, but I know they are your puppets,

ALAS.

But I am a *man*, do you hear me? I make my own decisions.

Fever wracks my body now, as I drag myself from bed to bed, holding their hands when they stretch them out to me for comfort, doing what I can to ease their suffering, to save a few.

You'll not have me, ALAS.

This is what *I* choose to do.

When Medicine Is the Illness

In 2015, a study was published showing that hydra (not the mythical monster or the Marvel Universe ultra-fascist terrorist group, but the freshwater creature that eats small crustaceans, insect larvae, and worms) showed signs that it was immune to aging. Perhaps by controlling the aging process in cells, human longevity could be increased infinitely. I had always believed life expectancy to go up through medical advances, and now it seemed like cellular biology might unlock immortality.

The following year the CDC (Center for Disease Control and Prevention) published a study showing that life expectancy in the US had actually started to decline in 2015, for the first time in decades. And the US spends more money per person on Healthcare than any other country in the world. I began to really question the future of Healthcare.

It wasn't clear at first why life expectancy was dropping. But it later became clear. What was being called "Deaths of Despair." Deaths related to alcohol, drugs, and suicide. The Opioid Epidemic central in that diagnosis.

Will multi-billion dollar settlements from drug companies and pharmacy chains curb the greed of pharmaceutical magnates like the Sackler family? An angry public seeks justice.

Grains of Wheat

by Alex Shvartsman

As he lay dying, Bryce Green contemplated the irony of his predicament. He'd spent a lifetime building the world's foremost pharmaceuticals company. Under his leadership, Green Industries had eradicated numerous ailments and made him the world's seventh richest man in the process.

The genetic disease ravaging his body was so rare that it had never made financial sense to look for the cure. And by the time he'd learned that it afflicted him personally, it was far too late. His researchers worked feverishly, yet the breakthrough was months, perhaps years away. The doctors told him he had only a few days left.

"There is a woman asking to see you," said his assistant. "She's Rajan Jethwani's daughter."

All sorts of people sought an audience; bootlickers and sycophants, hoping to remind Bryce of their existence, in case there was somehow room for them in his will. He tolerated precious few visitors, and certainly not the child of a one-time business partner from decades ago.

He tried to wave his arm in dismissal, an IV drip and an array of sensor cables attached to it like marionette strings, but only managed to twitch a few fingers. Instead he whispered, "Send her away."

"She claims that a biotechnology startup she runs in Bangalore has developed medicine that can treat your condition, sir."

A cure? No, it wasn't possible. This woman was playing some angle, telling him what he wanted to hear in order to gain access. Well played. He couldn't afford to refuse her.

"Hello, Uncle Bryce," said the Indian woman in her forties. "It's me, Rohana. You taught me to play chess when I was little, remember?"

Bryce recalled the annoyance of getting stuck watching his business partner's kid while Rajan spent evenings in the lab, so close to their firm's first break-through. Back then they couldn't afford a babysitter.

"We were just about to begin clinical trials on this drug when I heard of your diagnosis," she said. "Naturally, we did everything we could to accelerate the process." She held out a small pill. "This isn't a cure, but one of these per day can alleviate your symptoms and prolong your life by a year or more."

Bryce was skeptical, but he had nothing to lose. With her help, he gulped down the pill.

*   *   *

Every day, Rohana Jethwani would visit and deliver another dose. She never stayed more than a few minutes or said much, but Bryce didn't care because the drug was working. He was getting stronger, feeling better than he had in weeks, beginning to eat solid food. On the seventh day she handed him a sheet of paper along with the pill.

"What's this?" Bryce asked. He was sitting up in bed, reading a quarterly report. He felt strong enough to work again.

"Your bill for the first week."

Aha! Bryce didn't believe in altruism and Rohana's kindness was making him somewhat uncomfortable. He'd gladly pay for treatment. He glanced at the bill and suppressed a chuckle; it was a measly $127. Like her father, Rohana didn't seem to grasp that pharmaceuticals were always a sellers' market, and consumers would reach as deep as they had to into their pockets when it came to their well-being.

"Say, would you consider selling the formula? Or, perhaps, the entire company?"

"I don't think so," said Rohana. "When you taught me chess, you also told me a legend about its creator. Do you remember it?"

Bryce shook his head.

"Some ancient king liked the game so much that he let the creator name his reward. The man wanted wheat: one grain for the first square of the chessboard, then double the amount for each subsequent square. The king agreed, not realizing the enormity of the request."

Rohana stared Bryce in the eye. "You told me that story around the time you 'forgot' to reapply for my father's work visa. He was forced to move back to India, and to sell you his share of the company mere months before you made millions off his research. He died in obscurity a decade ago, but you didn't even know that, did you?"

Bryce tried to say something, but Rohana cut him off.

"You need one pill per day to live, and I'm willing to

supply them. Your first pill was a dollar, the second two dollars, and so forth. It's a pittance now, but your twenty-first pill will cost over a million, and it'll get really expensive after that. In the end, you'll either be dead or I'll own the company you stole from my father. And when I do, you and every other patient will receive care at rates they can afford."

"How dare you blackmail me!" Bryce crumpled the bill in his fist. "I will bring the full resources of Green Industries down on your foolish head."

"This isn't blackmail," said Rohana. "Just a business transaction. Business the way you'd handle it. Going forward, you will wire the money each day and a courier will deliver the pill. Your scientists won't be able to reverse-engineer the formula quickly enough, and if you try anything underhanded, the pills stop for good." She turned to leave. "The next time I see you I'll either be in charge of Green Industries, or attending your funeral. The choice is yours."

She walked away, Bryce still holding the bill in his shaking hand.

When Your Future Catches up to You

An epidemic of isolation. That was and still is the pandemic experience for so many of us. Sometimes Science Fiction makes uncanny predictions—even though it's not necessarily what writers are trying to do. But the pace of technological and political change has made it hard for writers to extrapolate on the present day and imagine a future world. The future you wrote might arrive before your story gets published, turning your futuristic ideas into an alternate history.

Here's what Sally Weiner Grotta says about her story, "One Widow's Healing":

Before we were put in pandemic lockdown, Philadelphia's Thomas Jefferson Hospital asked writers to submit speculative short stories as inspiration for medical professionals to help them imagine and create the health care systems of the future. They called the project 2100 Health Odyssey. Specifically we were instructed to write a positive, hopeful story set in the year 2100. My response was the story "One Widow's Healing," which received an award from Health Odyssey. At the time that I wrote it, I had no idea how relevant it would become.

Sometimes you get lucky and strike a cord. None of us knew how prophetic the story was, even when I accepted it around mid-November of 2019. But now the idea of a dystopian epidemic of isolation isn't just believable, it feels lived.

One Widow's Healing

by Sally Wiener Grotta

Dr. Maria Heilari fidgeted with her avatar's gown, editing it up to the last minute despite the rental agreement that forbade tampering with the design. Regardless what Gabrielle (Chanel's virtual saleswoman) had said, the sequins weren't right. Too fussy. Too many. Especially for a simple nanophysician who lived almost entirely in shorts and t-shirts and rarely wore shoes. At least, the avatar's hair emulated her chin-length grey frizz, and the rounded body approximated Maria's, though with more bust, longer legs and unbent back. But it was all too frivolous just when she needed the world to take her seriously.

Why did I let Gabrielle talk me out of renting white tie and tails?

Maria glanced at the countdown clock; the ceremony was about to begin.

Dolled up and glittery, or sensible and solemn, I'm in the thick of it now.

Zooming out through her desk's holographic projection, Maria tested her avatar controls one last time. Having declined a bodysuit, she wore a mesh headset, gloves and slippers. She turned her head right and left, wiggled her hands, shuffled her feet, and the avatar mimicked her movements.

Initially, Maria had planned to attend in person. What an adventure that would have been. Heck, she'd rarely been outside of Scranton, let alone as far as Europe.

Until recently, Scranton had been enough.

Gazing out her window at the winter-bare trees and granite hills of Nay Aug Park, Maria imagined she could still smell evergreen trees and river spray, mixed with the taste of Doug's flesh on hers. Her mind overlaid years of memories, hand-in-hand strolls along the park's nearly deserted paths, through winter snows, spring blossoms, summer breezes, fallen leaves. On one such autumn walk twenty years ago, a scruffy mutt – Watson – had bounded into their path and their hearts.

Maria hadn't left their one-bedroom apartment in nearly thirteen years, never feeling the wind or touching another creature since Watson died two months after Doug. Not that she was hearth-locked; just that, like most people, she'd no reason to go outside. All information, entertainment or interactions were online. Anything she needed or wanted could be 3D'd or droned.

Physician heal yourself, she thought. *Time to re-enter the real world.*

But within minutes of Maria RSVPing "yes" to the all-expense-paid trip to Sweden, Mark Singh, Whole Life System's Chief Communications Officer, had vidcon'd.

"Congratulations on the Nobel, Dr. Heilari." His voice had oozed sincerity though his avatar's smile had failed to crinkle its eyes. "I'll be your liaison for the ceremony and its aftermath."

He'd proceeded to explain the intricate rules of etiquette: who to bow to, how deeply, proper titles, when to speak, how to speak... too many directives, too tedious to remember.

"I'll do my best to protect you from the crack-pots that'll come out of the woodwork, but I can do nothing about the pressing crowds you'll encounter in Stockholm."

"I think I'll stay home," Maria had decided.

Singh had readily agreed. "I'll arrange for the avatar rental."

Maria glanced at the pictures on either side of her large wall monitor. "Well, Doug," she said to her favorite – the vidcard of Watson and Doug cuddling on the sofa – "I might be there only virtually, but hell... they'll have to listen to me now."

A drumroll from her speakers prompted everyone in the Stockholm Concert Hall to stand for the Swedish Royal Anthem. Then Maria's avatar joined the other honorees on their promenade down the aisle toward their red velvet seats on the royal blue stage. Viewing the crowded auditorium through her avatar's eyes on her holodesk and via the public stream on her wall monitor, Maria had difficulty distinguishing who was physically present and who was a hologram avatar.

Singh had said that Drs. Lamont Mitchell and Kamau Quammen would attend in person. But walking behind Maria's avatar, they resembled their official corporate pictures too closely – perfectly trimmed beards (one pure white, the other grey), neat ear-length hair (exactly the color of their beards), and just the right touch of casual smugness.

If they're not avatars, she wondered, *what does it say about them that they choose to look artificial?*

Maria knew she was no genius, not like Mitchell and Quammen, whose various cybermedical innovations had changed the way medicine was practiced.

She was in Stockholm (virtually) thanks to a mere intuitive leap prompted by a widow's loneliness, backed up retroactively with a decade of data crunching. Yet Mitchell and Quammen had to share their Prize with *her*, since their newest invention was based on her discovery.

Her discovery, dammit. And here on the world stage, WLS would no longer be able to silence her.

Her avatar sat motionless on the stage among the twenty other honorees, while Maria was stuck at her desk in her small living room office, doing nothing. Officials droned on, prizes were awarded, and musical interludes played. At this rate, it could be another forty minutes before her turn.

*   *   *

Maria was jolted out of her reveries by a MedicAlert icon buzzing on her wall screen.

It's not my concern. Not today.

Singh had made that very clear. "Your online actions will be recorded for posterity. If you window away from the ceremony for even a moment, the insult will go viral."

Whatever the emergency, it would be covered by the substitute nanophysician Singh had assigned to handle today's 39 scheduled patients.

Maria had no doubt that the sub would competently follow the routine 10-minute script: check the internal nanites' readings, ask the patient standard questions relevant to the symptoms and test results, then sign off on the prescriptions calculated by the WLS-AI.

But she was worried about Alex Asanti... and Matti Cohn... and Asa Krupp... and...

One by one, names and faces catapulted through her mind. Maria couldn't help herself, even now in the midst of the most momentous event of her life, because *they* were her life.

Maria had been chastised more times than she could count. "You're online to check diagnostics and prescribe, not to engage in social diversions or invade individuals' privacy."

Still, she had overstepped the bounds only when she felt it was necessary, never going far enough for WLS to carry out their threats of dismissal.

Who would fight for her patients if she were sacked?

WLS had changed tactics sometime between her paper's publication and Mitchell and Quammen's unveiling of their Robotic Healing Hands. Nowadays, her supervisors seldom threatened dismissal. Instead, they were outwardly respectful, and generally overlooked her day-to-day infringements. Mostly WLS ignored her, including any of her attempts to explain how and why the cyberhands were a travesty.

Maria wondered if Mitchell or Quammen had even read her paper. Or had an assistant skimmed the abstract and concocted a one-line report, focusing on a few keywords: hands, touch, palpate, heal?

What had she expected? Who read anything longer than a wristpad screen these days?

The MedicAlert kept buzzing. Why was the sub

ignoring it?

Oh, heck, what harm would it do to open a thumb-nail window, while the ceremony continues to stream on the main screen and the holodesk?

But as soon as she read the scrolling inset message – "Joseph Albertson (908.7845:076-3950-9877) small vessel cerebral aneurysms" – Maria went into full vidcon mode.

"Hello Joe. How are you feeling?"

"Not so good, doc. My head hurts awful bad."

"I know, Joe. While I fix it, keep me company. Tell me, who won the *MegaRegatta* today?"

They chatted, while Maria directed Joe's nanites to repair the vessel walls, remove plaque and inflammation, and administer an analgesic.

When she tried to add Nanotros to Joe's daily meds to prevent future aneurysms, an *UNAUTHOR-IZED* warning box strobed on her screen – as she had expected. Nanotros was a high-cost anti-modulator considered unsuitable for the 28% of patients who couldn't afford supplemental plans – the so-called *Lifers* – like Joe.

"Ahhh... that's better. Thanks, doc."

"I'm glad Joe. I'm prescribing auto-repeat treatments as needed. Bye." Maria wished she didn't have to hang up on him so quickly, but she needed to get back to the ceremony.

*   *   *

Dr. Maya Eklund, Director of the Royal Swedish Academy of Science, stepped to the podium. "One of the great mysteries of modern medicine," she said, "has been why otherwise healthy people have been dying at an increasing rate. The Whole Life System provides a consistent standard of life for everyone, combatting the potential for illness and incapacity the moment our internal nanites detect a micro-anomaly, often arresting disease or disability before any symptoms manifest. Yet, mortality rates continue to rise."

A subsistent standard for Lifers, Maria sniped silently. *You think you're doing them a favor giving them base-level nutrition, housing and health care, but Joe deserves better.*

Eklund droned on about Maria's "meticulous analyses of over twenty million patient records." Then, she launched into a gushing description of Mitchell and Quammen's implementation of Maria's discovery with their Robotic Healing Hands.

"Through the dynamic data exchange between these palpating cyberhands and patients' nanites," Eklund said, "we now have the diagnostic missing link that we can expect will reverse mortality rates."

Damn their cherry picking twisting of my discovery. But no more. Tonight, I'll finally tell the world: WLS's accursed cyberhands aren't the answer.

Ekland finished with a flourish. "Dr. Maria Heilari, please step forward to receive the 2100 Nobel Prize for Medicine from her majesty."

*   *   *

At the press conference following the ceremony, Maria's avatar sat with Marshall and Quammen on the stage of an historic wood-paneled lecture hall jam-packed with journalists. Unlike the staid ceremony, the energy in the room was frenetic and nerve-wracking.

A Nobel Foundation spokesperson whose name Maria couldn't remember introduced them. "Drs. Heilari, Marshall and Quammen will speak briefly, then they'll field your questions." She turned toward Maria's avatar. "Dr. Heilari..."

Maria took a deep breath to steady her hands on the avatar controls. It was now or never.

Suddenly, the holofeed from the avatar's "eyes" went black, and the words that came out of her avatar's mouth weren't Maria's uploaded statement!

"Thank you, Ms. Nyman." The avatar nodded to the woman who had introduced it. "I'm honored to share a Nobel Prize with Dr. Marshall and Dr. Quammen, whose humanitarian work I have long admired..."

The avatar had been hijacked!

Maria poked icons and buttons, frantically trying to regain control, to no avail. *I'm a damned fool, letting Singh talk me out of attending in person.* Not knowing what to do, Maria kept hitting the same commands.

Suddenly it was over, and Dr. Marshall was introduced.

Maria crumbled in defeat, slouching deep into her high-backed desk chair, tears of frustration and anger pouring unchecked. But then she noticed a blinking icon in the corner of her wall monitor. Someone at the press conference had beamed a message to her in the seconds before WLS had hacked her avatar.

"Dr. Heilari, I've read your paper," the note said. "I'm

taking the transAtlantic tube to Pennsylvania tonight. Please answer your door tomorrow when I ring. We need to talk. ~ Alex O'Brian, personal assistant to Luna Matheny."

Luna Matheny? What could that eccentric gazillionaire possibly want with her? And had O'Brian really read her paper? Or was he one of those crackpots Singh had warned her about?

Before slumping off to sleep, Maria googled Alex O'Brian. Someone of that name was indeed Matheny's personal assistant.

*   *   *

Maria studied O'Brian on her security monitor. His face might be craggier and his black hair thinner than in his online portrait, but he looked enough like his photo that she opened her door.

"Dr. Heilari, thank you for seeing me."

When he extended his hand, Maria hesitated. She hadn't touched anyone in years, not since Doug's death.

O'Brian's handshake was warm, uncalloused and firm. He wore casual charcoal trousers and a matching turtleneck under a grey tweed blazer. Everything about him radiated wealth and confidence.

Thank goodness I changed from shorts to jeans. Heck, I'm formal. I'm wearing shoes.

"I must admit, Mr. O'Brian, I'm curious. Please come in."

He sat in her desk chair, while she perched on the sofa. Maria hadn't realized how worn the upholstery had become. She absentmindedly wiped dust from the plex coffee table between them.

"I know you're busy, Dr. Heilari, so I'll get right to the point. Mx. Matheny recognizes that WLS is distorting the core of your work; she sent this proposal which I believe you'll prefer to your current situation." He tapped his wristpad to beam a presentation to her wall monitor.

Maria had had enough corporate-speak to last a lifetime. "Close that, Mr. O'Brian. Tell me in your own words what you consider the 'core' of my work."

Another tap and the monitor blacked.

"The core?... Touch... that the survival of humanity depends on physical connections."

"And by 'humanity'...?" she asked.

"That which makes us more than a collection of isolated individuals consuming, linking and reposting. To use an old-fashioned word that Mx. Matheny favors... our soul."

Maria stood abruptly, annoyed that she'd been so naïve as to listen to a religious kook. "I'm sorry, Mr. O'Brian, I have no interest in metaphysics." She gestured to the door.

"My apologies if I've insulted you. Mx. Matheny sincerely wishes..."

"Why should I believe you? Why would the richest person in the solar system be interested in me?"

"Luna Methany?" He shrugged. "Much of her success stems from her delight in pummeling competitors. Yet, she dreams of improving the human condition. My guess is that she sees in you the opportunity for both. Luna told me to ask you... If you had a blank check, how would you create the revolution in medicine that she believes she sees in your paper?"

Maria collapsed onto the creaking sofa.

Just then her wristpad pinged, displaying an automated message. "Four patients in your queue. You're behind schedule."

O'Brian pointed at Maria's wrist and at the vidcam above her monitor. "You do realize they're watching you? They know I'm here, and are probably listening."

Maria stared at the cam, then at O'Brian. *Luna Methany...? A blank check...?* Not knowing what to believe, she shook her head.

"Dr. Heilari, WLS blocked me every other time I've tried to reach you. Has any member of the press talked directly with you, or is WLS purposely keeping you sequestered?"

Her wristpad chimed more loudly, as did the speakers on her various screens.

Maria shuddered. Sure, she'd been angered by WLS's manipulations, but that didn't mean she had any reason to trust O'Brian.

"What proof do you have that Luna Matheny sent you?"

"Give me a moment..." He tapped, then whispered into his wristpad. "I'm with Dr. Heilari. Please tell Luna I need her on the line."

Within moments, Methany's larger-than-life face filled the wall monitor — and it wasn't an avatar. About the same age as Maria, Methany was barefaced, showing every freckle and blotch. Her signature carrot-colored hair was pulled into pigtails that exposed white roots. Maria didn't know whether to be honored that Methany didn't hide behind a digital mask, or insulted that she didn't consider Maria worth the effort.

"Hello, Dr. Heilari. Congratulations on your Nobel Prize."

The screen suddenly scrambled into disorganized pixels. "Luna, they're blocking your signal," O'Brian said into his wristpad.

Luna's voice came over the speakers. "One moment…" Her face reappeared, though at low-res. "Dr. Heilari, we haven't the luxury of time before WLS hacks us… Tell me, what would it take to introduce true healing hands into modern medicine?"

Maria scowled, unable to hide her disappointment. "You're misreading my work, just like WLS. My findings don't relate solely to physical touch, but emotional and social as well."

Luna flicked her hand in dismissal. "Fine, explain."

"Why do you think so many otherwise healthy people are dying at an alarming rate? Because they aren't living! They've all the basic necessities, but nothing that gives them reason or meaning. Yes, we need human touch. But we also need a sense of human connection."

Alex harrumphed. "How, in Heaven's name, do you plan to integrate *that* into an economically feasible health program?"

"By instituting old-fashioned house calls."

"There aren't enough medical professionals," Alex said.

"Not professionals… that's the point. Anyone with a

solid empathy rating could be trained... Lifers preferably because they have the highest mortality rates.
Give them a reason to step outside their homes, to
look forward to living another day, and their quality
of life and longevity will improve... as would those of
their patients.

"They'd use palpating gloves with sensors similar to
those in WLS's cyberhands. But because they'd wear
the gloves only when communicating with the nanites,
the Lifers would be a personal connection, flesh
to flesh, engaging the patient's psyche, increasing
their desire and ability to live longer and more fully...
boosting the patient's immunity system." Remembering the sweetness of Doug's caress, she added,
"They would be touched, and by that touch, healed."

"Done. We'll do that and more," Luna said.

It was happening far too quickly. "No. I'll do it, and
you'll fund it. No corporation will ever again hijack my
life's work."

"You'll need more than money," Luna countered.
"You'll need business-savvy people. But you'll be in
charge of medical strategy, with veto power over..." The
monitor flickered, then blacked. Luna's staticky voice
came through O'Brian's wristpad. "WLS is jamming my
stream."

At the same time, piercing alarms sounded, and
various screens displayed strobing red icons. The
doorbell rang; the security monitor showed two thick-
set men. When they didn't get an immediate response,
they banged on the door.

Alex spoke into his wristpad. "We're trapped, Luna.
I'm going to need extraction." He turned to Maria. "We

can make this happen. Are you coming with me?"

Maria looked around her apartment, filled with memories of her life with Doug, and her many hours of caring for her patients. Then she took down the vidcard of Doug cuddling Watson. "Let's go," she said. "We've got lives to heal."

The Ballad of John Henry

My dad was a folk singer. We held a hootenanny at the house, must have been around my seventh grade year, the year I took my first computer programming class. My parents had divorced long before, and my mom actually was a programmer at this time. Dad sang "The Ballad of John Henry." I'd never heard him sing that song before nor since, but it stuck in my head.

Per the legend, John Henry was a Black American railroad worker who was pitted against a machine to see which was faster. In the song, Henry wins the race only to die from exhaustion, hammer still clutched in his hand.

This has always been my mental image of the human vs. machine trope. As my own interest in software development grew, I thought about how automation has been used to cut jobs. And so, I concluded that the best applications do more than just make people more productive, they take the mundane and repetitive tasks off the plates of humans. Free up people, who tend to make errors, to do what they're good at, like being creative, solving problems, and connecting with other people. This also improves job satisfaction. And let machines do the tasks that they're good at and can do more reliably than humans.

This concept has a name, cognitive offloading. In "The Extended Mind: The Power of Thinking Outside the Brain," Annie Murphy Paul suggests that we have already reached the limits of human cognitive capacity. And part of the solution is to offload some of our cognitive workload to technology.

Many of us have already been doing this, in fact humans have been doing it for ages. Rather than memorizing all your friends' phone numbers, you probably have them stored in your phone. Before that, people used Rolodexes or little black books. Before the printing press, people memorized things far more than we do today.

Nowadays, when I'm in the middle of one task, I tell Google to remind me to do a second task later (or set a timer) so I can focus on the task at hand rather than watching the clock and trying juggle two thoughts. Friends may criticize me when, in the middle of a conversation, I'll Google something in order to answer a question or respond in some detail to a topic of conversation. When I hear an interesting news story on the car radio, I tend to just remember general concepts, enough to look it up later if needed. These are just some of my cognitive offloading strategies, freeing up my brain for more important work.

A few years ago, in the early days of this book's development, I asked a doctor/writer friend of mine what doctors think about the future of medicine. His response reminded of John Henry—they're afraid to be replaced by machines. I was surprised by this, considering that the US currently has a shortage of doctors.

But that has been a Science Fiction trope—instead of doctors, will we have mere technicians who know little or no medicine, trained only to use a machine that treats the patient? If the machine encounters a rare condition it doesn't know how to treat, or if the machine fails, the technician has no recourse. It's a scary proposition.

That's not the only approach, in my opinion not

the best approach, to automation. Of course, it won't be easy to develop the technology that augments doctors and makes them more effective and productive. And Healthcare providers may face a steep learning curve before they can use such technology effectively, because it's not just a matter of using a tool. It's about techniques of cognitive offloading.

Second Generation

by Julie Nováková

"Is our baby going to be okay?"

The tiny human being was almost lost under the monitors and cannulas fastened to her reddened skin with hypoallergenic adhesive tape. One tube went into the mouth, another into the nose. *Was* she going to be okay?

Doctor Sengupta knew to expect the question, but that didn't make the answer any less obscure. There was little she could tell the concerned parents with certainty—likelihoods, confidence intervals, margins of error. On a population level, she could say what the probable outcome would be. On a case-by-case basis, who knew?

"Her condition is not immediately life-threatening, and we'll do everything we can to make her better. We'll keep you updated," she assured them the only way she could and tried to avoid their desperate, pleading gazes. She could see they were still worried, but what could she do other than advise them to discuss everything with the base's therapist?

You should work on your bedside manner, Newton chastised her.

Shut up, she thought. *You're here to analyze, so help me analyze and leave these comments for yourself. They're only part of your damned sim personality anyway. For all I care, they should have left you more machine-like.*

The facts: Nathalie Charbon was six days old. She was also number two second-generation Martian, preceded by her cousin Marc by less than a week. She was also sick, having developed symptoms consistent with the onset of necrotizing enterocolitis, or NEC—in short, as Dr. Sengupta explained to Louis and Amélie Charbon, dying of the bowel. There were traces of blood in her stool, which had barely had time to change from meconium to actual feces. She was lethargic to the extent that she could barely be woken up for feeding and couldn't suckle. She'd lost more than the usual ten percent of birth weight and had barely gained any so far. The ultrasound showed signs of abdominal distention.

A mild stage of NEC was the likeliest verdict, and Dr. Sengupta wasted no time treating the symptoms. What puzzled her, though, was the underlying cause. Nathalie wasn't premature. She hadn't asphyxiated during birth and wasn't born with any heart disease. She'd been breastfed, or at any rate fed breastmilk from a syringe when she couldn't feed herself. There were none of the typically described risk factors. She'd been born a healthy full term infant, her weight slightly above average.

With all probability, introducing intravenous feeding, biopatches and tailored antibiotics, monitoring the infant and keeping her hydrated and warm would within a week or so decrease the symptoms enough to resume feeding her small, increasing doses of probiotics-laced breastmilk.

Still, it was a puzzle, and Dr. Sengupta did not like unresolved puzzles.

*   *   *

Strange buzzing woke her up, and she felt disoriented before a voice in her head said: *There's another one.*

The doctor on call and the nurses already placed the ailing infant in an incubator under monitoring. Dr. Möller turned to her, relieved. "Glad you're here. I've taken blood and stool samples, come look at them. I'm afraid we'll need a biopsy."

"Sono?"

"Doesn't look too good, but take a look yourself. Do we prepare an X-ray?"

Sengupta stared at the newborn boy with a sense of unpleasant déjà vu. Nathalie Charbon lay in her incubator just a few meters away, and now Marc Durand was almost as covered in tubes, tape and monitors as she was. He was slightly bigger and heavier, but otherwise the sight was almost the same. Sengupta turned her gaze to the smart display on the incubator. It showed images and basic analyses of the samples. Blood in the stool: check. Inflammation metabolites: check. Sono: slightly distended bowel.

She drew in a sharp breath. This was no accident. NEC had been rare enough as it was. Even in prematures, its incidence had declined rapidly over the 21st century thanks to more effective prevention and care. In full-term infants, it was almost unheard of... and now, within a few days, they've got *two* with all the initial symptoms.

"Infectious outbreak? Or family?" she muttered under her breath. So far, there was no clear infectious agent suspect. She needed to have a good look at the possible contributing genetic factors. Marc was Nathalie's second cousin. It would make sense. Or something in their shared environment... but that was pretty much identical for everyone in the settlement.

"The parents," Möller said quietly, and at first she thought he was about to add something to her remark. Only then she followed his gaze and saw the worried-looking couple standing in the corner.

"Right," she nodded. *Names and occupations?*

Paula and Robert Durand. Life support engineer and atmospheric physicist, Newton supplied. *I'm surprised you don't already know from the broadcasts. They've just had the first second-generation Martian! They're in the spotlight.*

Sengupta didn't bother to answer that. She didn't care much for gossip stories, and this, in her opinion, fell under that label.

Once she greeted the Durands, she began asking about their son. Paula Durand frowned a little. "We've already told Dr. Möller everything."

"Tell *me* again. When did you first notice something was amiss?"

"He was sleepier in the last two, maybe three days, and when he woke up, he cried. Nursing and carrying him didn't help very much."

"We started worrying that maybe he was in pain for some reason, and then we checked his stool and it looked like it contained blood..." her husband supplied. Sengupta remembered that he studied atmospheric escape and the resulting isotopic fractionation on Mars.

"So we hurried right here." Paula Durand looked up to her, nervously tugging at the zipper of her jacket. "Is he going to be okay?"

That question again.

"We'll do everything we can for him," Sengupta assured them with the traditional sentence she loathed. "He's stable now."

"Can... can we stay?"

"For as long as you'd like. No one is going to try to separate you from your child. But no drinks, food... you know. You can also watch him anytime on camera."

She then explained the need to do a biopsy, as noninvasive as possible. A tiny remote-controlled probe could be sent through the nasogastric tube to do in situ imaging and take samples from selected portions of the gut. "We'll have them in a few minutes' time."

There was so much hope in the Durands' eyes.

Yet the samples confirmed the diagnosis: initial stage of NEC. There was necrotic tissue in the colon. A very preliminary PCR and metabolite analysis showed an almost certain dysbiosis, imbalance of the microbial community in the gut. Pathogen species couldn't be held at bay by the usual community of mutualist and commensal microbes, and these even seemed to behave harmfully.

So: intravenous nutrition, biopatches, selected antibiotics and probiotics, constant monitoring....

Yet that was only treating the symptoms.

With no immediate procedures at hand, Sengupta sat in her office, the breathtaking view of the Martian sunrise above the eastern rim of the Perepelkin Crater before her eyes. There was work to do.

You should eat something, Newton reminded her. *Your blood sugar is low.*

Oh, sod off.

But she still chewed a few dried dates before taking her eyes off the scenery behind her window and diving in. Closing her eyes she increased the bandwidth, plunging into the abyssal depths of big data.

Genetics; epigenetics; proteomics; microbiome; growth; psychomotor development; grades; psychological evaluations; medical history... The data on first-generation Martians such as Louis and Amélie or Paula and Robert was extensive. Each of the babies born on Mars was under close observation; most Earthers could only dream of such scrutiny, or dread it. Every aspect of their condition was recorded in fine detail, almost day by day.

No human could effectively sift through data so big. That was where Newton came in: it did her bidding so that she wouldn't have to construct models manually; it sifted out patterns, looked up data and visualized it in ways a human could comprehend. The AIsistant consisted of multiple interconnected neural networks of varying architecture, loosely akin to regions of the brain. Generalized visual processing, statistical analysis, medical pattern matching... and last but not least of all, the human behavior recognition and mimicking to ease communication, which Sengupta felt ambivalent about.

Now was the time to set any doubts aside and let the thing work. She had Newton scrape every hygiene report from portions of the settlement where the

Charbons and Durands had spent the most time recently, cross-correlate the parents' medical histories and pregnancy outcomes and compare them to the rest of the local population, start searching for any potentially responsible genes, genetic interactions or epigenetic modifications, and analyze their microbiome development. On a sample this size, any nontrivial genetic effects would be next to impossible to discern—but on the other hand, she didn't need significant *p* values and good confidence intervals. She only needed an inkling to pursue.

Point one: shared environment. Both regular and more detailed swipes revealed nothing out of the ordinary anywhere... Her gaze flew across the charts. *Mother's food or medicine intake: nothing....*

Sengupta moved elsewhere in the endless and yet spaceless virtual landscape. Where she needed an inkling, she couldn't find any. Genetics provided no useful clues, and thorough epigenetic data required more information than they had. She finally resurfaced with a budding headache and cramps in her stomach suggesting that eating a handful of dates after a night spent half-awake wasn't enough. With a sigh, she went to the nearest cafeteria.

It was abuzz with people at this hour, just before the main shift and start of school. Looking at the people chatting above breakfast plates, coffee and juice, Sengupta still felt amazement at the existence of this place—not the cafeteria, but what it symbolized. The whole settlement—the fact that there were now enough people on Mars to warrant schools, shops and entertainment. The fact that they could sit and chat here without any regard for physical distance, which would be frowned upon in most places on Earth. For many, the habitat symbolized paradise. And yet, Sengupta had a conflicted view of it. True, she'd come here herself, she saw the appeal of living offworld— but at the same time, she was painfully aware that they weren't, and for a long time wouldn't be, a self-sufficient settlement. They depended on Earth, and yet the very existence and prosperity of the settle-ment made increasingly more Earthers think that they didn't actually *need* the Earth. As if everyone could just resettle on Mars or elsewhere. It was prepos-terous. They didn't see the supply rockets and all the effort channeled just into making this place *survivable*. There were cafeterias, a hall for theatre and cinema, schools—but all of it under thick layers of regolith for radiation protection, equipped with multiple filters and checkpoints to ensure breathable atmosphere.

All of that enabled people to live here... and now, the first two second-generation Martians were seriously ill, and she didn't know why.

No radiation protection in the world would help them if the cases continued.

*   *   *

Marc Durand was slowly improving. Sengupta was relieved. But the state of Nathalie Charbon worried her. The baby girl was getting sicker. Sengupta decided to talk to the parents.

"We may need to begin printing an implant," she went directly to the matter.

The Charbons visibly paled. "But... that takes *weeks*

to do properly—" Amélie Charbon begun. She had dark circles under her eyes. She and Louis both spent most of their time close to their daughter, but were unable to hold her due to the monitors and controlled environment inside her incubator.

"It does. However, unless we can halt and reverse the damage, your daughter might not have any other option. We should start now, while we have some time."

Some time. Less than a week, Sengupta guessed, unless something changed for better or worse. Barely enough time to cultivate the cell layers, not speaking of testing the replacement organ. Even *weeks* were on the optimistic side. But if it came to a choice between almost certain death and using a fast-grown implant....

The next two days went in a haze. Sengupta spent nearly all of her waking time in the infirmary and lab. New biopatches to mitigate the risk of bowel perforation. Increased probiotic doses. Tailored IV and enzyme cocktails to keep the rest of the body as close to healthy as possible. Meanwhile, the tiny human being slept through almost all of it. When she briefly opened her eyes once, the parents wept.

Nathalie's state wasn't improving. It was declining much more slowly than Sengupta had feared, though. There was still time.

The third day, the necrosis spread to nearly half as much tissue as before. 1 p.m. blood check showed that blood gases and platelet count had gotten worse, too.

Newton whispered the chances in her mind, and they did not look good. Still, they changed the IV again.

Administered more healing patches through the tube.

4 p.m. sono showed signs of free air in the abdominal cavity. A probe quickly confirmed the diagnosis: intestinal perforation.

Sengupta felt her heart racing. The implant—if they only had maybe one more day...

We don't, Newton said.

You need not remind me.

The incubator was moved to the operating room while she readied herself. In the corner of her eye, she glimpsed the Charbons behind a glass wall in the adjacent room. Without a further glance there, she put on her VR goggles and haptic gloves. The operating robot's limbs didn't mimic human hands, of course, but its data was translated into human-comprehensible feedback through her AIsistant, Newton. Beside her, Jürgen Möller was putting on his goggles to assist if needed.

The anesthesiologist on call, with the assistance of his AIsistant and Newton, administered the anesthetic. Sengupta made the incision. Removed the gangrenous gut, while Möller assisted in cleaning the cavity. Did the ostomy and closed the incision.

Hoped for the best.

Möller spoke to the parents after the surgery, for which she was grateful. Albeit tired, she could handle immersing herself in monitoring the patient, but not talking to people.

For a few hours, everything was stable. Sengupta allowed herself to hope it would stay that way. Right now, most of Nathalie Charbon's colon was gone, but that wasn't too much of a problem if she got into a state ready for another surgery and could receive the organ bioprinted from her own stem cells.

Möller was replaced by the regular shift doctor. She was considering going to sleep, too. A sleep-deprived doctor was a dangerous doctor.

Then the girl's blood sugar and lactate increased, and her blood pressure started dropping. Heart rate spiked.

Sengupta was on her feet before she could even think. *Sepsis? Change IV, add more antibiotics, increase oxygen, grow blood cultures to make the ATBs more targeted...* She moved with the precision of a machine, her and Newton's insight in perfect sync. Dr. Kuang appeared by her side, and without exchanging a single spoken word, each got on with the steps to assess the baby girl's state. Their AIsistants conversed across a broadened bandwidth, and each task—cultivate several blood samples aerobically and anaerobically, meanwhile do the PCR, increase cardiovascular system monitoring, do a new sono—felt as if all four, the two humans and two AIs, were a single entity with two pairs of hands and feet, and enough computing power to simulate the likely outcomes.

They were not looking good. Early signs of pulmonary edema and kidney failure....

More patches, more IVs, more monitors.

Need to put her on assisted ventilation, the entity thought as one as Charbon's breathing became more rapid and intermittent.

Kuang's hands prepared the neonatal ventilator, while Sengupta began disconnecting the cannulas.

Wireless monitors still fed them data on the newborn girl.

Before she could be placed in the ventilator, the monitors sent an alert: The baby had ceased breathing. Less than twenty seconds later, the heart stopped, too.

2:03 a.m. station time, Nathalie Charbon passed.

*   *   *

Try to revive. Once clearly over, check and double-check everything. Speak to the parents—this time, she wouldn't let anyone else do it. Retreat into the office. Write the report. Then....

Meera Sengupta avoided going to her cabin for as long as she could, but eventually, there was nothing else to keep her away from the fine mist they called a shower here, and her bed. She went through the mist. Put on her pajamas. Dimmed the lights. Turned on music for sleep, and abruptly turned it off.

Sat on the couch in the semi-dark cabin, arms wrapped around her knees, her jaw clenched. Stared into the blank wall.

A voice she could do without spoke: *Not your fault.*

She gritted her teeth. *I know.*

Just thought I should remind you. I understand why you're upset, though.

Oh, do you? Sengupta imagined the intertwined neural networks busy at parsing her human reactions, categorizing them based on the huge datasets they'd learned on. *Let me tell you something: I'm upset because I'm not upset enough. Does that make sense?*

Newton was silent for a brief moment, enough to make her wonder if she really made it "think" harder.

But most likely it was just a learned response to *indicate* deep thought, not a processing requirement. *It does, doesn't it? You're aware that as a human being, you should feel very upset when a baby dies. And you are feeling somewhat upset, your physiological signs are clear. But you think you should be more upset, correct? Because an innocent infant is dead. It's a tragedy. And it happened on your watch. At the same time, though, you see the death as a data point and you realize it hasn't been due to any mistake of yours. You did everything you could. Your lack of proper human reaction makes you upset.*

Now it was her turn to be silent. She was stunned.

Well, fuck you, she thought finally. *If I haven't been scared shitless of you AIs before, I am now.*

Merely because of a correct assessment? Would you feel the same way if a human psychologist made the same observation?

She thought about it for a moment. But Newton wasn't human. Its processing, observation and memory capacity was much greater than a human's, and it was essentially a black box with unknown potential biases, with a hopeful utility function slapped on as an afterthought to keep it leashed. It was prudent to be afraid or at least wary of any such thing.

I can't sleep right now. Let's find out why Nathalie died, she said in the end. *There* must *be something we've overlooked.*

*   *   *

The colony administrator's office was a minimalist room with pearly white walls, an off-white desk with smooth edges and two chairs, one on each side of the desk. Sengupta wondered for a second what would happen if the administrator were supposed to receive more than a single visitor. Perhaps someone would bring in more chairs. One of the walls was covered in epiphytic plants, and behind the desk was a window overlooking the western portion of the Peripelkin Crater, with the central peak visible on the right hand and the top of Alba Mons peeked above the distant crater rim on the left hand. It was a beautiful sight, and Sengupta couldn't help but wonder if Administrator Chiara Carella ever sat on the visitor's chair when she was working alone.

"Please, have a chair." Carella smiled thinly. "I need you to tell me about the situation with the infants."

"You've seen my reports, haven't you?"

"Yes. But I need sitrep from you."

Just like when you ask parents to tell you about their children's trouble in their own words, Newton observed.

Sengupta summarized all as best as she could. All of the parents had given consent to share medical data with the administration until revoked, so she didn't have to dance around anything.

Carella's face was grave. "So we still know nothing?"

"No. We have excluded many potential causes with a great degree of likelihood. Narrowed down the list of suspects, so to speak. The research is ongoing."

"It feels more like shots in the dark than suspects," Carella noted drily.

To her own surprise, Sengupta felt an onrush of anger. Who was this woman to criticize her work, her life-saving—

—except in this case, not life-*saving*—

Calm down. You heart rate just spiked. Newton spoke soothingly in her head. *You know what this is. It has all the signs of a beginning panic attack. Imagine stepping aside and looking at yourself clinically.*

The cursed thing was right. Sengupta forced herself to breathe slowly.

Carella was gazing at her quizzically. "Are you all right, Doctor? Hasn't all of this been too much of a strain to you?"

She's likely trying to frame it as a failure of an overworked physician. Don't give her the excuse.

"No," Sengupta said evenly, though she suddenly wasn't so sure.

It's a publicity nightmare. She probably really cares about the children, but cares about her standing more. A physician's failure is tragic, but acceptable. A mystery killing the colony's children less so.

"What background do you have?" Sengupta asked aloud, though she could have queried Newton first. But she wanted to hear from Carella.

The administrator furrowed her brow. "Economics. Why?"

"Let your AIsistant advise you on the principles of scientific hypotheses, medical testing, confidence intervals—anything else you might need so that you'll see that I cannot give you more at this moment. We're working around the clock here. Earth receives the same data. No one's come up with a definitive answer yet."

Carella bit her lip in an unconscious gesture, visibly taken aback. "Thank you, Doctor," she said coldly then and motioned for Sengupta to leave.

Meera Sengupta started quivering when she was finally out of that pretentiously furnished room. So, it was a question of *publicity* now. She should have expected nothing else with the spotlight aimed at the families of her patients. Everyone was talking about Paula Durand's commendable work on the resilience of life support, or her husband's achievements in outlining the escape of Martian atmosphere throughout the ages and its effects on the planetary environment.... But she was a pediatric gastroenterologist. A physician and a scientist. Settlement politics was beyond her, and she was happier that way. And now...

Do you need to talk about what happened in there? Newton inquired.

Not with you, thank you.

Good. So a therapist?

That gave her a pause. If trying to assess the episode impartially, she had to admit it would probably be the right course of action; certainly if it recurred. The suggestion shouldn't have irked her.

Perhaps it would be reasonable even if she'd seemed okay. Just to talk to someone. Sengupta didn't make friends easily, and had no interest in romance or sex, which drove away many potential acquaintances. She could talk to her colleagues, of course – but not about everything. The autopsy, for instance. She could—and *did*—discuss it with them at length from the medical point of view, but not from the viewpoint of someone who'd had to open the tiny ribcage of a newborn and examine her inner organs before sewing her up again. She'd done it all through the interface, of course, but that somehow made it even worse.

At least Marc Durand got better so that small doses of oral feeds could resume. They started feeding him tiny doses of pumped milk with an added probiotic cocktail. Still, he was far from healthy. His bowel seemed better now that he was receiving treatments, but Sengupta wondered whether he'd remain stable afterwards. Nathalie Charbon's fate was warning enough.

*   *   *

Two may be an accident; three's a pattern. Or, in this case, four.

Meera Sengupta watched the twin infants in their incubators with a dark frown. Same initial symptoms as Nathalie Charbon and Marc Durand. Adia and Aleela Cheywa were born slightly prematurely and with a lower birth weight, as typical for twins, but otherwise didn't seem much at risk of NEC either.

"All second-generation Martians," she murmured. "*Every single one*. But there were more kids born recently...."

Twelve in the previous three months. Out of these, only Charbon, Durand and the Cheywas have both parents who had been born on Mars, Newton supplied.

Can't be an accident. Sengupta bit her lip, deep in thought. The biopsy she'd just conducted showed signs of mucosal necrosis and gut dysbiosis, but there appeared to be no clear infectious cause. Besides, if hygiene had caused the colitis, why would the infection pick only second-generation Martians?

Show me data on all the other newborns, she told Newton.

She closed her eyes and dove into the data landscape. Now, with four patients (or three, since monozygotic twins couldn't really count as two singular data points), one getting healthier and receiving increasing doses of milk after more than two weeks of treatments, she had more to go on.

Perhaps it was foolish to try to do more than treat the symptoms while more capable scientists and AIs here and on Earth worked the problem. But first, she would never—there had to be a common underlying cause, and she'd be damned if she didn't even try to pinpoint it. Second, Carella was probably looking for any excuse to terminate her contract and send her Earth-born ass back to Earth. Sengupta had often wondered whether she'd stay here indefinitely, but she certainly wouldn't leave like that.

She left Newton looking for SNPs in the genome data, and returned to the environmental data. Same for the whole settlement... Same for all human-made settlements on the *planet*.

Second-generation Martians. Nobody else... Mars must have been the answer, of course, but *how*? The gravity? Nonsense; why would it affect second-generation newborns like this? She called up the studies on gravity, human and animal development. Merged the public data into new metastudies. Newton stopped answering for a moment; it was completely busy, as was the department's computer he needed to process the bulk of data. Still—nothing of use came up, no pattern, not even a one-percent chance.

Show me the gut microbiomes again.

The composition was mostly normal. Several strains of Lactobacilli, *E. coli*, several *Citrobacter* and *Klebsiella* species... Their ratios were a little off, but the main problem wasn't their presence, absence or numbers— it was their metabolism. *E. coli* and *Klebsiella* behaved as facultative pathogens when the conditions in the gut were off, and it seemed to be the case here. They began attacking the already weakened bowel tissue... But *why*?

Not gravity. Not the artificial atmosphere. What else? Sengupta was running through all the differences she could think of in her head, while another, wandering part of her mind thought idly about publicity, patients and parents. Then something dawned on her, and she froze for a second.

Mars was no spare Earth. It wasn't just smaller, with a much thinner unbreathable atmosphere, lacking a magnetic field... it had more subtle, invisible differences as well. Each planet had its unique composition of isotopes of different elements – ratios of lighter and heavier carbon, nitrogen, *any* other element, influenced by the planet's size, mass, distance from the Sun, particular history... For Mars, atmospheric escape had played a substantial role. Robert Durand studied that.

"But that would be insane," she murmured aloud. "It was tested, wasn't it?"

What? Newton inquired.

"Influence of, let's say, Martian regolith isotopic

composition on health. The plants and meat cultures we eat were grown on it. We make water, including minerals and salts, out of in situ resources..."

Within seconds, she was looking at the studies. Most were conducted decades ago, before the settlement commenced or at its beginning. No notable influence on plants, animals or humans... But the latter were tested only in the short term. Not across generations.

"Why would it affect the *second* generation?" Sengupta wondered. "Why not the *first*?"

Transgenerational effects should mean either genetics, or epigenetics. Since no suspect mutations had been found, what about epigenetics? Could each Martian parent transfer such epigenetic modification of their DNA to the child that he or she would develop unexpected problems? It wasn't unheard of. Not only for instance did prenatal malnutrition lead to epigenetic changes causing metabolic disorders later on in life—that was easy, because that wasn't really transgenerational. But some influences seemed to persist in later generations, too, although to a lesser extent. Humans, like other mammals, had their epigenetic make-up almost fully reset in each generation. The Överkalix study and several follow-ups suggested that some influences might persist in the next generation. But in humans, it was too difficult to discern the effects of genes, epigenetics, ecology and culture throughout the life of the generation in question. One did not come up with inbred strains of human in strictly controlled environments.

Could, Sengupta mused, *the Martian environment have impacted the 'reprogramming' in the germ line and embryo? All the more in each generation, so that the changes could be transferred?*

There is no data suggesting that, Newton replied. *However, given who has been impacted, we can probably rule out simpler explanations such as impaired enzyme function solely due to the environment. But consider the transgenerational epigenetic influences discovered so far. The effect is observable on the population level, but little. It is highly unlikely that it would impact all four newborns this way.*

Sengupta saw the numbers dancing in her mind. It didn't surprise her that she thought the same. *What if it doesn't impact* them *directly?*

The AIsistant was trained to sound intrigued when deemed appropriate. It did now. *What do you mean?*

She told him, and Newton didn't shoot the idea down. It gave her estimated probabilities, fished out appropriate studies, and suggested possible tests.

It was a feeble construction—one built on several very speculative assumptions and all the more difficult to test. But what if it was *right*? Or, at least, one of more additive factors causing the issues?

Well, before she'd give others false hope, there was nothing easier than to try testing it.

*   *   *

This office wasn't pretentiously furnished or minimalist. It was tiny and cluttered, and now three people sat in it: Sengupta and Möller, to both of whom it belonged, and Emily Gao, a geochemist in charge of the in situ resource utilization of the base. Gao seemed perplexed as to why Sengupta had invited her, but listened to her brief account of the ailing second-generation newborns with interest.

"...and I suspect that isotopic differences between Earth and Mars, projected into the food we eat, the water we drink and the air we breathe, are responsible for triggering the disease. Take heavy water, for instance," Sengupta said. "As opposed to ordinary water, it's got slightly different melting and boiling points, viscosity, dipole—well, anything you can think of. If you ingest too much of it, your enzymes can't work properly, and eventually you die."

"Yes, but that's *water!*" Gao spoke. "It's essential for all cells, all enzymes, and deuterium has twice the mass of normal hydrogen, so the difference in the water molecules is pretty big. The deuterium ratio in our water is negligible—larger than on Earth, but still far, *far* below toxicity. With *no other* element can you even approach—"

Sengupta shrugged. "You don't need to. What if the differences are additive? Take a slightly shifted carbon isotope ratio here, nitrogen there..."

Gao was shaking her head vigorously. "Wouldn't have any substantial impact on human cells."

"How could it not affect us, why only those children?" Möller asked. "We've been here for nearly forty years. This was *tested* right at the beginning, in labs on Earth and here. None of the cultures or animals had such severe problems..."

Tell them, Newton prompted her.

Sengupta smiled mirthlessly. "I wasn't thinking only about *human* cells."

She sent their AIsistants the data she'd been working on for the past few days. "Cell cultures on artificial colon tissue—here on tissues of Earth-like composition, here grown from a sample from one of our patients. And then, each of them seeded with the gut microbiome standard sample and fed either Earth isotopic standard, or Mars standard nutrients. You can see the results."

Even Gao, as a non-physician, could. The Mars-tissue, Mars-nutrients Petri dish was filled with visibly dying tissue. Microscopic images showed dead cells and proliferation of a few bacterial strains.

"I should add that it doesn't take epigenetic effects into consideration," Sengupta noted. "If having two first-generation Martian parents meant additive epigenetic effects in the child, contributing to slightly impaired bowel function, it could in combination with the effect on microbiota lead to the disease.

"Imagine the following scenario: Earth-born humans land on Mars and start living here. They might experience slightly impaired function of some enzymes, and so does the gut microbiota, but it's living in a healthy gut. The effect is so negligible that it's beyond noticing in such a small population.

"First-generation Martians, though, are exposed to it in utero. They probably develop such epigenetic changes that the body 'deems' appropriate based on its 'interpretation' of its cells' inner workings. Who knows—perhaps it manifested akin to a slight malnutrition, perhaps a disease... Still, they are mostly fine.

"But if these epigenetic changes are transferred from *both* parents to the *second* Martian generation, their effect grows, and the discontented, perhaps starving bacteria can just leap at their chance to do damage. Necrosis ensues practically as soon as the gut is colonized."

"That is... imaginable," Möller admitted, still not fully convinced.

That was all right. *Results* were meant to convince; hypotheses were meant to be tested.

Gao narrowed her eyes. "Why am *I* here, then?"

"To help us with the testing. Neither of us is an expert in Martian materials composition and the filtering and sterilization procedures we use. You are."

"Well... Let me try to come up with something."

They would do a few more simple tests, publish the findings, and seek collaborators from Mars- and Earth-based labs and biohacker collectives. There was finally something to do apart from merely treating mysterious symptoms.

Later that night, unable to fall right asleep, Sengupta asked inside her mind: *I realize I may not have been the first person to think of this idea—perhaps just the first that didn't cast it aside as too unlikely, requiring too many improbable steps. But—why haven't you, and the likes of you, thought of it?*

I wasn't trained on such a dataset. The hypothesis you've had required too much of a leap of imagination for me. Even I am not perfect, Newton acknowledged.

Under different circumstances, she might have felt a bit of satisfaction at that concession. Now, though, what mattered was saving the children.

More carefully controlling the isotopic composition

of the IV wasn't too hard. Nor was delivering Earth-like nutrient grown probiotics and small doses of specially reprocessed breastmilk in the gut.

Marc Durand went home within another week.

Merely a week after him, Adia and Aleela Cheywa were back with their parents as well.

*   *   *

That was where people like Carella imagined the story would end in triumph. The cause was, after much heroic work, pinpointed; basic treatment was found and successfully applied; everyone lived happily ever after and could smile at the cameras.

In fact, Sengupta's assertion would require years of thorough testing at least. Several research labs on Mars and Earth leaped at the opportunity, some taking a more theoretical approach, some already working with the taken assumptions to devise a cure. Marc Durand and the Cheywa twins still had to take probiotics daily and complement breastmilk with an Earth-standard nutrient mix. They were slated to receive experimental treatment to heal their bowels and provide a more stable Earth-like environment for their gut microbiota as soon as possible—which could mean a few months as well as many years.

More second-generation Martians still happily in utero would hopefully be able to receive specially designed probiotics and patches to prevent necrosis. Sengupta was in charge of that. Later on, epigenetic drugs were on the menu, should the epigenetic hypothesis withstand much, much more testing.

While the clock for that was ticking ever so fast, the

gazes of reporters slowly moved elsewhere, to newer, more fashionable topics.

But in truth, the work was just beginning.

*   *   *

What are you thinking of?

Meera Sengupta, staring at the bluish Martian dusk from the window of her cabin, suppressed a sneer. *You know that already.*

In abstract thoughts and feelings filtered through our bandwidth. Not in your own words, Newton objected.

All right. She sighed. *Are we doomed? We're still fucking up the Earth, even after a century of trying not to. If there ever was something to show us there is no easy Plan B, this was it. We've always imagined cruising the universe from one planet to another... and an isotopic imbalance can so easily throw us off balance. Anywhere we go, we'll depend on so much tech that if something goes wrong... so do we.*

Newton's voice in her head sounded soothing, or perhaps she just imagined that. *You've found out about it pretty quickly, all things considered. Research is being undertaken and treatments developed. You'll find a way.*

Right; another 'easy fix'. A patch atop another patch. *And you'll be there for the ride, am I right?*

True to your habit, you are. Always by your side all the way to the stars. Per aspera ad astra.

How many aspera, she wondered absently. How many obstacles would they face?

The blue-tinted horizon seemed to offer no answer.

Decoding Bias

I used to think we did a pretty good job of combating racism with our lending practices at a financial institution where I worked in the '90s and '00s. While loan officers had a little leeway, and they could get a manager to approve an exception, the human element had been removed from much of the loan approval process.

We used the FICO score, a number developed by the Fair, Isaac and Company, which took into account a borrower's payment history, the amount and types of loans they had payed on, etc. We even used a second product by Fair Isaac, a custom score, which used additional data from our loan application and analyzed how past borrowers with those values had paid on their loans to us. This took into account their loyalty to our institution (i.e., maybe they would pay us even if they didn't pay their other creditors—and we wanted to reward that loyalty). Combining these two scores, which were based on very sophisticated statistical analysis of mounds of data, with their actual ability to pay (i.e., their income in comparison to all their debt payments, or their debt-to-income ratio) and you had an approval matrix that was supposedly "color blind."

Fair Isaac is always analyzing their FICO score and trying to improve how predictive it is. They receive new data monthly from creditors. But we didn't send them all our loan applications every month, so our custom score got stale, less predictive over time. We reached a point where our loan officers were overriding the matrix more frequently, and when they did, those borrowers were still paying on time. We'd call that a good lending decision, but it relied more on the human factor, and potential human biases.

It was my job to extract data from our systems and provide it to Fair Isaac so they could come up with a new custom score for us. Flying with my bosses up to Fair Isaac's headquarters in Northern California, I was impressed with their process, their insight into our data, the ability to tweak the variables in our score, and quickly re-test the score's predictiveness.

But the problem is in the data. Maybe it's better to say it's *not* in the data, because the data is incomplete. Individuals from marginalized demographics are less likely to have accumulated wealth over past generations and face obstacles that white members of the community either don't face or are less likely to face.

And there are a host of things like rent, utilities, etc., that require monthly payment, but landlords, utilities, and cell phone companies don't send payment history to Fair Isaac because they are not "creditors." This often makes it harder for people of color to build their credit, and the FICO score is less predictive of their future payment habits.

At least since 2010, Fair Isaac has provided a way for rent payments to get included in your FICO score. However, the onus is usually on the renter to ask their landlord to start reporting their rent payments. Or, for an additional fee, the renter can pay their rent through one of several third-party services that report to the credit bureaus. A small step in the right direction, maybe, but the additional effort and fees involved are still obstacles.

Health studies have also neglected people of color, and women. Some studies have made great effort to correct this, although success in those efforts is sometimes limited. There's a lot of well-earned mistrust to overcome, too. The healthcare field has perpetrated some atrocities against non-white communities, and Covid has shown a spotlight on inequities in healthcare today. Stereotypes about non-White patients being less sensitive to pain, still persist.

But health scientists must learn how to bridge that chasm. Drawing conclusions from incomplete information leads to faulty conclusions, to bad science.

And using technology, like the automated calculation of the FICO score and the custom credit score I provided the data for, not only perpetuates racial injustice, but can amplify it. Like the AI that was taught to recognize the difference between a husky and a wolf, but actually just flagged any picture with snow in the background as being a picture of a wolf.

It might be true that wolves spend more time in the snow than huskies (my own pet husky in Southern California has only been in snow a few times in his life). But the presence of snow is an inappropriate indicator of whether a canine is a husky or a wolf. Another Machine learning experiment identified any person who was cooking as a woman.

Electronic Health Records (EHR) systems are starting to incorporate machine learning, prompting doctors on possible diagnoses, using models to predict when a patient might be about to have a serious health event. The models have even been used for Covid patients to automatically alert physicians that a patient may be getting worse, allowing them to provide care before a patient's condition deteriorates further. So, machines are limited to the data we give them, and automation is not going to correct racial inequities.

Hundreds of local and state governments in the US have now declared racism to be a public health emergency. Not just a factor, or a problem, but an actual crisis. Acknowledging this is an important first step. But we clearly have a long road ahead of us to curb bias in healthcare.

In "The Algorithm Will See You Now," Justin C. Key, himself a Black psychiatrist, imagines how a Black psychiatric provider in the future contends with bias embedded in the technology she uses.

The Algorithm Will See You Now

by Justin C. Key

Alaina Harris didn't look depressed. The twenty-eight-year-old Black woman smiled at our receptionist and showed bright interest in the paintings on the waiting room wall. Why was she here? The algorithm assessment of her neural scans from her primary care doctor were unhelpful. Her referral note simply read: "odd presentation, in need of therapy, no medical issues." I sighed. 'Odd' wasn't a treatable disorder.

I pulled up my own emotional calibration app on my phone, brought my heartrate down a few beats, and flattened my anxiety curves. They spiked whenever a Black woman like myself came through our door for a new appointment. The noise cleared. I called her in.

"Dr. Hairston." Alaina offered a warm, light handshake. "You're Black."

"Last time I checked."

"I'm sorry. It's just, this is great. I didn't know what to expect and . . . oh god, I'm rambling."

"It's nice to meet you, too," I said.

There was so much to gather from that first human interaction. From how she addressed me, to where she sat in the room, to her palpable energy. She wore a sweater despite us being at the height of summer. She took in what seemed to me every corner of my office, noting the decor, checking for the windows and the doors. Cautiously curious. She paused at her neural display gracing the wall behind her seat. A patient's response to this was also informative.

"So," I said. "What brings you to see a psychiatrist?"

Off that one question, she told me about growing up in the city, her parent's loveless marriage, her difficulties in college, the way her mind often worked against her. An open book, she was yet uninterpretable. The way she described her childhood in vague, distant terms suggested a repressed trauma. I didn't expect to get there in the first session.

She finally sat back and sighed. "I just feel like everything is hard, you know? Work is hard, friends are hard, living is hard." She glanced at me, as if just remembering where she was. "Not that hard, though. Don't get me wrong. I love life."

I smiled. She relaxed.

"You mentioned things at home being stressful," I said. "Tell me about that."

"I live with my best friend. Lauren. We've been besties since college, and I love her. I really do."

"I sense a 'but' coming on."

Blues shifted to orange in some of her neural clusters. I focused on her body language, which spoke a similar message. The change in position. The nervous smile. This was the topic.

"We're very different people," she said. "I love her. I need her. I just … I don't know if she's a good friend for me, you know? If I'm good for her. Seems I can never do enough."

"You feel as if you're not being a good friend?"

"She says I'm not." She laughed, not pleasantly.

"Lauren always ends arguments by going on one of her drives. And when she's upset she's probably drunk or high or both and . . . it's just not smart. It's selfish."

A faint blue light flashed in the bottom corner of Alaina's display. I shifted to hide my distraction and tapped the side of my chair twice.

Are you sure you want to disregard this clinical warning?

I tapped again. Yes.

"That sounds really hard to deal with," I said.

"It is. Because I try. Really hard. It's a lonely place to be. I'm never alone, though, not really. I'm always the one listening. Except here, I guess."

"I'm glad you're having the chance to be heard," I said. A beat of silence hung between us. "There may be times where you feel differently in our sessions. Alone, unheard. If that happens, I invite you to let me know. It could be important for us to work through."

We finished. I didn't mention interventions. Frankly, I wasn't sure she needed it and, if she did, I didn't yet know what we would be treating.

Once she was gone, I skimmed the automated intake draft, which included all the essentials for billing and legal purposes. Most of the data—like eye movement analysis—only needed review when flagged for significant abnormalities. The meat was in the formulation, diagnosis, and proposed treatment. I frowned. The algorithm honed in on abnormalities in the brain's language and emotional centers and interpreted this as a psychotic process, which was clearly wrong. The algorithm could be way off base, especially with Black patients. I deleted the assessment and wrote my own, spending some extra time noting that the benefits of continuing with her as a patient outweighed the risk of the compatibility flag.

I checked my emotional state readout. I was slightly angry and anxious, foreign attributes in my own office. I recalibrated myself, went out to our reception area, and poured myself some herbal tea to enhance the calming effect.

"A tough new?" Michael said from his doorway. We had started the practice together out of residency, decades ago, right as the cluster-based treatment revolution swept through psychiatry. We were some of the only private psychiatrists left who still did face-to-face interactions.

"Straight forward, actually," I said. "Algorithm pegged her as psychotic, but she's definitely not. Just some depression and anxiety."

"The algorithm conflated psychosis and trauma with one of my patients the other day."

He gestured towards the blue warning lights through the office door I'd failed to completely close. "You want me to take her? I have space on my panel."

"Oh, that? No, nothing significant. She's African American."

Michael nodded and left it alone. The blue indicator warned of a potentially undesirable result from a patient's neural network paired against the provider's. Subconscious biases, uncanny similarities, all could theoretically interfere with a healthy therapeutic alliance. For years the algorithm had conflated race with shared experience. The latest iterations supposedly addressed this, but old glitches died hard, and Black patients were still underrepresented in data pools because of continuing disparities in mental healthcare access and engagement.

Regardless, some things we didn't challenge each other on. We knew where my Blackness ended and his Whiteness began. It's why we'd always worked well together.

Back in my office, I replayed the part of the intake that sparked the warning: Alaina recalling Lauren's criticism. The printout identified neuronal clusters indicating shared experience, similar neuroanatomy, and a high percentage of paired firing between our respective mirror neurons. The computer essentially posited that our brains were too much alike to achieve a successful balance of objectivity and subjectivity. Specifically, the algorithm predicted that I would deter her from getting ablation therapy despite analysis showing it to be the most beneficial treatment long-term.

I read it over again to be sure.

I considered Michael's offer. The International Psychiatric Association hadn't released any official recommendations since the seminal study on the pairing technology showed a clear parabolic correlation between therapist-patient neural pairings and outcomes. Like many things, the algorithm gave no insight into the 'how'. Many speculated that the lack of boundary setting, regression, and poorer physician decision making contributed to this phenomena.

But handing over her case was the last thing I

wanted to do. Because, for the first time in years, I was intrigued.

*　　*　　*

The ride home was a good in-between time to reflect, rediscover, and digest the day's patients. Today, though, I needed some me-time to recalibrate.

I waited until I was on the freeway to run the anxiety module. I gritted my teeth against the pressure emanating from my temporal implant and swiped through the files that came up on the car's display, sorted by emotional state, impact, and then date. Ah, there it was. I frowned at the algorithm's attempt at a title: Fear of Misdiagnosis.

"Play back, quantity thirty." My fingertips dug into the well-earned grooves in the main passenger seat's armrest as the machine soaked my brain in the sensory input that provoked anxiety.

It's all your fault.

A woman with brown, fluffy hair and dazzling hoop earrings sat in the seat beside me. When I looked at her, she was gone.

I gasped and reflexively yanked off the probe.

What the hell had happened?

A notification blinked on the frozen display.

Origin of emotional dysregulation identified. Would you like to link to it?

Yes. A crude representation of my own neural network materialized in a faint hologram that zoomed into a black, foggy void with only scant, roaming particulates. I'd seen this many times before, but never in myself. The visual representation of an ablated past.

The ablation procedure had been pivotal in my development and making it through the second half of college. But, what else was there? I blinked. I couldn't recall. First generation, on scholarship, my family's expectation of *'there goes Dr. Hairston!'* followed me from childhood to college. Neural Cluster Ablation had only just entered clinical trials. The procedure hoped to magnetically target select neuronal clusters correlated with distress and remove them permanently. The study gave me my first neural probe, a device now ubiquitous for neural self-regulation, especially amongst mental health workers.

You were never good enough. Not then, not now.

Softer now. The faintest shadow of a woman's image lingered and then disappeared with a blink. I began to reach out and then stopped.

Sensory hallucinations were known artifacts from memory recalibration. My connection with Alaina had somehow stirred up a random remnant from that black void. The ghost of a past I decided not to think about. I *paid* not to think about.

I shut off the program.

*   *   *

Alaina was early to her next appointment. I turned off my neural upload as she walked into my office. She wore a sweater similar to the week before.

"I've been thinking about your situation with your roommate," I said after we had settled. "How was it talking about her?"

"Exhausting," she said. "We're just different people. 'If you can't do anything about it, then why worry?' That's what my dad used to say, at least."

"It's obviously been affecting you."

"Sometimes I get really upset about the things Lauren says. I try not to let her see that it gets to me."

"You must let it out somehow."

"I'll go for a walk. Play the piano. Sometimes I snack a little. Well, a lot, if I get stressed enough. But that's a whole thing." She waved a hand. "Mostly, I just deal."

"This relationship means a lot to you."

She smiled, then sobered herself. "It does. Me and Lauren always been like *this*. We helped each other through some shit coming up." Scant blue and orange lines cascaded through Alaina's limbic system. "I screwed up. And I can't leave it like that, you know?"

"How did you screw up?" I said.

She shifted. Distress grew.

"Can we talk about something else?"

My usual response would be to explore this resistance. The real work of therapy happened in these moments. But I, too, was uncomfortable. And I was afraid of losing the patient's trust. What if she didn't come back to her next appointment?

I didn't press. We spent the rest of the session talking about whether she would call her mother for her birthday even though they hadn't spoken since her mother cursed her out for forgetting her birthday the year before.

I cancelled my next patient and ran provider analysis on Alaina's session. My heart rate and temperature had peaked several times. The suggestion to change topics threw me, yes, but what else caused a response? I zoomed in on one of the spaces. When Alaina said *I messed up*, my parameters leapt.

Would you like to flag these for future sessions?

I closed the app.

*   *   *

Tunde worked with an investment company based overseas. His days started as mine ended. I entered quietly, changed into evening clothes, and found myself in the kitchen. Nini, our house's virtual assistant, suggested a vegan salad with light dressing from *The Rude Girl*, a new place just down the street. I no longer wondered how the machines came to their decisions, much less if they were right. The algorithm knew my blood markers, genetic risk, the daily change in body composition, and a slew of other factors that, when put together, predicted this specific meal would give me the best chance to live until I was old enough to regret living. How could I argue with that?

After his work, right when I was beginning to doze beneath the now-warm sheets, Tunde slid into bed beside me. The hum of some television series leaked from his earbuds. I stirred. A soft *click* as Tunde switched to his reading app.

I noticed a long time ago that Tunde feigned reading financial periodicals around me. I'd looked for couple's therapy but gave up when I couldn't work in both our schedules. Hell, what had that been? A year ago now?

My hand went to my phone and the regulation app. Instead, I put it aside.

"Can't sleep?" Tunde said.

"Why do you always read in bed?"

"Because reading in the shower would be silly."

"Is talking to me not enough stimulation for you? Am I not enough?"

Before Tunde could respond I got out of bed, took some sheets from the closet, and went to sleep on the couch.

*   *   *

I continued to see Alaina weekly. Our topics ranged from her loving but misguided single father, her fluctuating motivation to execute on a long-standing business idea, and wondering if life out in the country would 'be much simpler.'

Branching lines sprouted and thickened after every session, a testament to the connections made. I felt genuine joy when Alaina, who had come to me without experience expressing herself or her emotions, began to consciously make these connections.

"Maybe that's why I let this Lauren thing bother me so much," she said after recounting a best friend who moved away in the third grade. Alaina glanced back at her neural map and lightly traced the new, thin tendril as it branched out from her current cognitive state to the memory cluster highlighted on that very first session. "Because I'm afraid of being alone, see? I just wish I could make things right."

I didn't speak. Many things—good and bad—were born in silence.

"She was dating this guy. They were engaged. He was an asshole. The type who hit on her friends when she wasn't in the room. She must have known about it. In fact, I'm sure she did. He tried to kiss me while she was throwing up in her bathroom. I *had* to say something. She confronted him, and he broke it off."

"She blamed you?"

Alaina wiped her eyes and then laughed at her wet fingers. "Not at first. She started dating again and seemed genuinely happy. She was definitely a lot better. Stopped drinking, too. Then those relationships didn't work. She'd say little things here and there. 'Another Saturday night, me and you, just like you wanted.' Drinking got bad again, and then we'd argue about that."

"Does she drink a lot?"

"Not anymore. Just when she gets really upset. Then she goes for her drives."

I made a mental note to return to one of Lauren's 'drives'. "You mentioned rectifying the relationship. What do you think that would look like?"

"Being here, for one. It was her idea. She thinks that if I get help, her life will be easier. That, and I quote, she'll be able to 'live.'"

"So it's your responsibility to make her happy?"

Alaina smiled. "Aren't we all a little bit responsible for someone's happiness?"

*   *   *

Tunde and I committed to a home-cooked meal one night a week. Our calendar chose the day well in advance, and it usually coincided with Tunde's sometimes erratically scheduled days off. I got home later than usual. Tunde sat on the couch, reading his periodicals. A dirtied dinner plate rested beside him.

"You ate already?" I said.

"Was I not supposed to?" I put the plate in the sink and, as I left, Tunde rose. "I didn't know when you would be home. You didn't send me any—"

I closed the door behind me. No one yelled. No one threw anything. I often heard of those types of antics when patients talked of their childhood. For us, only silence.

Sometimes, I wondered if that was worse.

*　　*　　*

"Insurance notice," Michael said one morning. Both of our nine o'clocks had downgraded their in-person sessions to neural upload review and treat. He flicked the notification over to my device. "That new one you've been seeing. You going to take her on pro-bono?"

"You know we can't afford that." I quickly read the notice. I'd expected this, sooner or later. Had it already been twelve sessions?

"I want to explore your relationship with Lauren," I said once Alaina was situated in my office.

"I don't want to talk about her today. She gets on my last nerves."

"I think it would be beneficial to bring her into the room with us." At Alaina's look—and her reddening neural map—I spoke quickly. "Not the real her. Just your experience of her to help us get to the root of the issue."

"The issue is she's stubborn as a rock. Will it hurt?"

"It won't hurt," I said. "It'll be emotionally uncomfortable. But that's the point. Discomfort, we can work with."

I picked up the remote to the neural simulator and held it for her to see. "May I?"

She nodded. There were no probes to place. The same functional-MRI sensors used to create her neural map could tell the molecular structure of the nutrient from her breakfast that made it across her blood-brain barrier.

"Think about your last altercation with Lauren. Try to remember it exactly as it happened."

As the patient explored her own memory, I ran the Neural Amplification and Recreation Protocol. The system used Alaina's sensory input and neural response data to create a personalized 'key' that could reverse engineer experience from Alaina's memories.

A soft triple beep warned of impending output. Then, a new voice came to life.

"It's all your fault," a woman said. The tone was incongruently friendly. "If you had just minded your own business everything would be fine. You always thought you knew best."

The NAR protocol was one of the most jarring experiences for patients in any setting. It essentially took one's memories and thoughts and brought them out into the open. So I expected a reaction. Only not this one. Because Alaina wasn't frightened or surprised or scared. Alaina was angry.

"He wasn't good for you," she said.

"Is anyone?" the NAR produced. I moved to turn the program off, then stopped myself. "You just want me to be alone. Like you."

"Leave, then. Go back to him. You two deserve each other."

"I will."

I stopped the protocol.

"How—" I cleared my throat, took a deep breath. "Excuse me. How is it hearing that?"

"Hard," she said.

"How often does that come up with her?"

"Daily."

I can't leave because I'm all you have. Without me you'd probably kill yourself.

I spilled my tea fumbling for the controller. "Sorry, I thought I had turned that . . ." But the NAR was off. Alaina hadn't spoken. What's more, the voice wasn't quite the same as Lauren's.

"She says that all the time. That I'd be alone without her."

"You heard that, just now?" I said.

"Of course I did," she said. "Am I not supposed to?"

"No, you are, it's just . . ." I shifted. "It sounds like there's a lot of conflict with her. You really value this relationship. That's why it's taking such a toll on you."

As I said the last my mind tallied up the truth of it, what I had been gradually noticing over the last several sessions. The way Alaina's clothes hung loose, something I noticed because she wore the same weeks before. The steady decline in weight every week. The picking of her fingers. The soft rock back and forth in her chair. Alaina wasn't doing well. Perhaps the insurance was right to push me.

"Treatment can help," I said.

"I thought this was treatment."

"It is. But it may not be enough."

"I don't want pills."

I smiled. "No pills. We've come a long way."

I pulled up her display and showed her the highlighted area in her amygdala linked to the cluster of memory and association cells that represented Lauren.

"This is your friend. This is the effect your friend has on you." Thankfully, there were still strong positive associations that connected to pleasure and joy. I focused on these first. "You would still have your positive responses to her. All the things you enjoy about your relationship. It's these areas, where you're experiencing anxiety and distress, that we can dampen."

"To make me numb?"

"No, not numb. More resilient."

"Is this what you did?"

I frowned before I could stop myself.

"There are other, stronger treatments, but I don't think you need them right now. The dampening process is a lot less invasive. It basically takes all of the data we've gathered here in therapy, the work we've done, and multiplies the benefit a hundred-fold."

"I don't want to care less," she said. "I just need to be better."

I tried another angle. "You think Lauren's criticisms are valid?"

"I do."

We agreed on no treatment for that day. I noted that I was still assessing the need for intervention and uploaded a small clip of our in-session conversation, which I knew insurance would request. I marked the NAR protocol as a procedure. I hoped to delay the conversation of out of pocket payment as long as possible. Insurance often cared little about my hopes.

That done, I considered replaying the moment of the unexpected voice. *I can't leave because I'm all you have.* Did I really need to? *Without me you'd probably kill yourself.* No. The explanation was simple: NAR often created echoes in a patient's mind as part of the neuronal intervention.

Why, then, had I heard it as well?

*　　*　　*

The algorithms responded to some change in me. Nini suggested food with more carbs and eliminated some morning and evening workouts to increase my sleep. Self-regulation increased. I checked my regulation app constantly, adjusting as soon as it swayed from normal. I did this so often that security asked me to verify my identity to make sure the app hadn't been hacked.

Tunde and I were intimate for the first time in years. Afterwards I felt a sense of emptiness, like giving someone deprived of sugar just a taste of some blandly sweet thing, a shadow of what used to be.

"Something's on your mind," he said as I got up to shower and get ready for work.

More like something was *in* my mind. The voice inspired by Alaina's neural recording was full and near constant now. What's more, it had evolved from the original stranger to something more familiar, something from my past.

"If you could remove your worst memories, would you?" I said.

"Is this a philosophical problem or a practical one?"

"I'm asking you, would you?"

"If I needed it, I would," he said.

"You don't know this, but I overheard you talking about it back in college. You said it was like killing a part of yourself. You compared it to The Ship of Theseus."

A pause that he tried to cover with a cough. He should know better.

"Hey, you needed it. You did what was best for you. What was best for us. As for the ship, I'd rather ride around in one with a few stand-out patches than rotting wood." He put his tablet screen-down on the bed. "What brought this on, babe?"

I ignored the algorithm's pre-set outfit choice for the day, neatly centered in my closet, and picked out an older blouse in need of ironing. "Nothing."

*   *   *

"You seem distracted," Alaina said in the middle of our session, less than two hours later.

She was right. My mind was elsewhere. I brought my full attention back to Alaina and smiled. This was what I trained for.

"You're right, I am a little distracted. I've had a couple rough nights lately, and it's harder to keep my mind from wandering. How does it make you feel, thinking that I'm not listening?"

"It feels like criticism. Like you have better things to do, and I'm a waste of time."

"I wonder where you've learned such a reaction?"

After some thought, Alaina talked about Lauren's drinking and driving. The session was back on track. I offered to see her a second time that week on Thursday. She obliged.

Although handled well, in truth Alaina's observation annoyed me to no end. I unsuccessfully attempted to adjust my modulation many times that night. After another bout of unfulfilling intercourse, I used Tunde's snoring as cover and went into the den to access my patient records. I pulled up the moment of distraction with Alaina, viewed it from her perspective, and cursed. My eyes were glassy, my gaze off. And when she called me on it I looked less in control and more like a pupil being reprimanded.

The computer flagged this section for 'embarrassment', 'resentment', and 'doubt'. I selected 'doubt', saw a cluster of neurons glow in the frontal lobe, and then connect to another cluster in the thalamus.

I looked up. "Babe?"

Soft snoring answered. I pulled up the security system. All entryways were locked and there was no recent spike in noise levels.

Two voices. Whispering. Far away, but clear. I crept out of the den and into the kitchen.

You're drunk.

No shit. A good friend would take the keys. But not you. You only act like you care.

The closer I got to the door leading out to the garage,

the louder they grew.

Give me the keys, then, Laura.

Don't be concerned now.

I crept up to the door. Soon I'd be leaning against it. The voices were clear now. I knew they came from inside me somehow, but that didn't make them feel any less real. I touched the reinforced metal and flinched at the initial, wood-like feel of it.

Slam!

I jumped. Something behind me shattered. The voices stopped. I didn't go to the app to analyze my emotions or cluster connections. I just left the kitchen as fast as I could without panicking. As the door closed behind me, underneath the slide of metal was the faintest rev of a gas-powered engine.

*   *   *

I didn't sleep more than twenty minutes that night. Thankfully, the next day was one of my virtual algorithm consultant days, a gig I picked up that paid well and offered some intellectual curiosity in a sea of monotony. I reviewed algorithm assessments and briefly checked in with patients. At times there were glaring errors, like recommendations based on misgendering, but mostly I was just there to give a human face to medicine.

A light ping startled me as I turned off the monitor. Just my secretary. On an adjacent display, her likeness materialized in a hologram.

"Zachary Parker called. He's demanding an earlier appointment because his 'life is falling apart'." My schedule appeared under her.

I responded to such requests with a five-minute video call to explore boundaries and ultimately deny. But after a night of phantom memories and tortured dreams, I took the easy way out.

"Give him Alaina's Thursday slot," I said.

I immediately knew what was happening. Alaina had gotten to me, I'd failed at hiding it, and now I was punishing her for it. She was evoking in me the role that Lauren played in her life.

I dialed my secretary.

"Let's keep Alaina's appointment."

"Oh. Dr. Hairston, I already rescheduled her for next week."

"I see. How'd she take it?"

"Fine," she said. "She wasn't upset or anything."

The week went on at a crawl. Zachary Parker didn't make it to his appointment. I cleared the hour after Alaina's next visit so that we could spill over past our time if the topic allowed.

But Alaina never came. She was a no show.

*   *   *

She didn't show up the next couple of weeks. My secretary called at first, and then me. Voicemail. I considered calling from either a blocked number or pretending to be someone else, but quickly shot down both ideas. That was crossing the line. Patients fell off all the time.

*   *   *

Self-recalibration increased; I surrendered some of the settings to automatic adjustments. Sleep came easier. Home disagreements quieted. My thoughts were once again clear. I distracted myself with work. Helping others with their problems allowed me to postpone the need to address my own.

If scheduled outpatient appointments were a kind of cruise control, then working in the emergency room reminded of the power and the stakes of being active behind the wheel. It also reminded of the cost of hospitalizing someone. I made sure to do at least one shift a month.

I put out a call to the community hospitals with my hourly rate and requested length of work. Of the several options that appeared almost immediately, I chose Michelle Obama Memorial. With fewer resources, the work would naturally be more involved. As a Black provider, the unique patient experience often made it worth it.

I started with clearing out the holdovers from overnight. Individuals in need of sobering up, others contemplating the knife or the phone until the early morning, and the manic episodes that seemed immune to treatment. Each had a computer read-out that aggregated data from all their medical care across the country and analyzed them against a global database of various clinical presentations, treatments, and outcomes. This produced a nice little table of risks, scores, and suggested interventions.

I only looked to the notes for guidance on the last three. One I discharged because their craving for death had been induced by alcohol, another I marked for admission to a sister hospital with open beds, and the third I set up for in-house guided psychedelic therapy.

This last patient, a social media influencer, recently lost half his followers after his now ex-partner posted a video of his candid, transphobic rant. His elaborate plan for suicide included a livestream.

Inpatient admission, the algorithm suggested. Though he was a clear candidate for guided psychedelic therapy, the algorithm considered available resources in its calculations, and Obama Memorial didn't have any licensed therapists. It would be way too much at my hourly rate for me to sit and do it, so I called a video service I contracted with. After a six-hour trip I could reassess him on my way out and, if I was right, potentially discharge him.

"Busy morning," I said as I entered the shared work-room just outside the overcrowded emergency department.

The senior emergency medicine resident sighed. "Always. Air quality's been low the last week. Lot of algorithm-induced anxiety around lung cancer predictions. So a lot of these 'shortness of breath' should be in and out."

"What you got for me?" A purple tag—psychiatric services—marked several of the triage bay video feeds.

"I discharged a few. Secondary gain, most of them. Their suicidal thoughts magically resolved when they heard we didn't have a guide."

I leaned forward and tapped the icon in blue, still pending evaluation. Lauren Roberson, Room Three. "And this one?"

"Young Black woman picked up by the Community Response Team. Crashed her car into the guardrail, got out, and tried to enter passing cars. They found an empty bottle of liquor in the car. She reeked of the stuff."

I was already looking over the drug screen, which included analysis of blood and urine. "Alcohol level is zero."

"Crazy, right? No pun intended. No drugs in her system, bizarre when I talked to her, rambling, kept going on about some issue with her friends. Seems like the real deal."

"They're all the real deal," I said, not unkindly. I expanded her room's live feed. She was in the standard hospital gown; a blue sweater lay across the foot of the bed. Red lines ran the length of both forearms. I squinted, though there was no need. With the video quality, she might as well have been right in front of me.

"Did she come in with some other name?"

"Huh?" the resident said.

"Like Alaina or something like that?"

"No. Is that a psychotic thing?"

I reviewed the video uploaded by the Community Response Team. Shortly after contact she rushed at the main responder, yelling *Where is she? Where is Lauren?*

"It is, isn't it? I thought it was weird she was screaming her own name when the CRT picked her up. You're thinking multiple personalities?"

Blue and red lights flashed in the background of the feed. A characteristic siren just touched the audio.

"Why did they send the police to get her?" I said.

The resident frowned and leaned forward. "That's

the CRT."

"That was definitely police. See." I rewound the video. "Huh. Weird. I thought there were lights—never mind."

I continued to watch. The community responder pulled out a gun as Alaina closed the gap. I blinked. No, not a gun. I closed my eyes.

Get on the ground! Get on the fucking ground!

Pain in my knee and wrist. The smell of hot tires and spent gas.

I paused the playback, checked to make sure the resident couldn't see, double-tapped, and then circled my neural chip to mitigate the anxious thoughts.

My pulse and my breath slowed. I resumed the playback. There was no gun. There were no police. The response team restrained my patient and safely got her into the padded car.

"She's drunk," one of the responders said after.

"No shit. Let's take her to MOM. They'll know what to do with her."

I watched it again and then sat back. It looked like Alaina. Sounded like Alaina. If I checked her neural print against Alaina's, it would be one and the same. But Alaina wasn't homeless and Alaina wasn't psychotic. What was she, then?

"Uh oh. She's not happy."

Alaina approached the front of her room, which was off screen. She screamed soundlessly and waved her arms.

"First cranial pulse of the day, you think?" the resident said.

"Not yet. Charge it up, but wait." At the resident's baffled look, I clarified. "I know her. She's one of my private patients."

When I arrived, Alaina stood on the opposite side of Room Three in full defensive stance. She wielded one of her shoes while two orderlies tried to talk her down.

"Alaina," I said. Her eyes widened and then welled with tears. She dropped her shoe, sat back on the bare bed, and began to weep.

"She got me good," one of the orderlies said. He had a long, thick scratch down the middle of his arm. "I wouldn't get too close."

I nodded and pulled a chair up to the side of her bed.

"You heard it, too, huh?" she said.

"Heard what?" I said, though I wasn't surprised at the accusation.

"I have to know if Lauren's here. If she's okay. Did she tell you where she was going?"

"Why would she tell me?"

"Because you heard her, that day in the office. You didn't ignore her like everyone else."

"I work here," I said. "No one told me to come."

"Yeah, okay," she said. "I know when I'm being lied to. I don't fucking like being lied to."

Anger: a newcomer in our therapeutic relationship. I wished we were in my office. I felt blind without the insights of the neural mapping. She must have taken something that wouldn't show up on the drug screen. With a change so quick, there really was no other explanation. But if I went that route, I might lose her.

"You checked in under Lauren's name," I said. "Why?"

"Because *she* should be here. Not me!"

I looked away, let the air cool.

"What happened between you two?"

"She ran off again because I wasn't going to take her shit. I was looking for her, and they brought me here. I don't know what she wants." She put her head in her hands, massaged her temples, then squeezed. "What do you want?"

On a whim, I asked, "Is Lauren here right now?

Alaina laughed. "You're really trying to play me. She's not here, even if she should be."

"Can I talk to Lauren? Do you have her number?"

Alaina shook her head.

"No, I can't talk to her or no, you don't have her number?"

"She doesn't have a number. She doesn't need one. I don't want to talk about this." She shook her head, looked around, and shrank. "Are you keeping me here?"

"Do you want to stay?"

"You ask like I have a choice."

"Because you do." I could easily petition for a Treatment Despite Refusal claim. Given her presentation so far, the lack of drugs, and already what would be considered a violent act, the algorithm would grant me permission to force a wide range of treatments. "You're on a hold now, yes, but I can release that hold."

"What do you think I should do?"

"Spend a night or two in the hospital. Get some rest. Figure some things out."

"Will you be here?"

"No. But they . . ." They what? Would take good care of her? They'd offer her a bunch of treatment options that would all seem scary and big, and she'd leave the hospital in a couple days never wanting to see a psychiatrist again. Though studies on neural overlaps between provider and patient showed clear negatives, there were less discussed positives. The automatic rapport between two Black individuals, for example, present from our very first handshake and laughter of relief. I was her only mental health provider, and this was her first emergency department visit. I didn't yet know what to make of her symptoms, but if it was something long-term, it probably wouldn't be her last. I couldn't abandon her to the mercy of the system.

"I think you can go home," I said. "But I'm worried about you. I want to see you in my office this Thursday. And we should start treatment. More treatment."

Her eyes widened. "You think I need it?"

"You're stressed. And whatever reason it may be, whether some imbalance in your brain or you ate something that didn't quite agree with you, I think it's time for some relief."

She considered in silence. I let her.

"I'll think about it," she said finally, her voice a little more sure. "If I can go home, I'll think about it."

"Where will you stay tonight?" I said.

"Family. I'll stay with family."

I debated with myself. I needed to know more, and this wasn't the setting to do it.

"I need to talk to Lauren."

"I told you, she's hard to contact."

"Let me be the judge of that. I'll sign the discharge papers and drop the hold, I just need a little assurance here. Give me her full name."

"Lauren," she said. "Lauren Daniels."

"Birthday?"

"January twenty-fourth, two thousand forty."

I went back to the workroom. The resident was finishing a call. When he saw me, he checked the video feed.

"I knew they taught psychs magic," he said. "I swore she was going to swing on you."

"Sometimes patients just need a little talking to."

"You said she was yours. I didn't know you treated psychotic patients."

"I don't," I said.

"Should I put in admission orders?"

"No. Discharge."

The resident lifted an eyebrow.

"No hospital's going to take a psychotic patient refusing treatment, so she'd likely be here all night. You're working a twenty-four, correct?"

He lifted his hands. "Discharge it is. You know I'm with it."

I sat at the computer to see if I could track down this Lauren Daniels. I put in her name and the DOB. Nothing. I tried just the name. There were a few matches. I picked one in proximity to Alaina's age. I opened her chart.

A warning popped up. Ice went down my spine.

It's your fault.

I turned. "What did you say?"

"Nothing," the resident said. Then he laughed. "Careful, or I'll have to admit you."

"Then maybe I could get some rest," I said, going with it.

I went back to the warning. *This patient is deceased. D.O.D 01/24/2040. Are you sure you want to open their chart?*

Was I sure?

I opened it and, while I waited for it to load, checked the transcript of my interview with Alaina. I'd heard two-thousand fourteen but, no, she said forty.

My insides turned to stone as I read the details about the motor vehicle accident that had taken Lauren's life seven years ago.

"Get Acute Ablation Therapy ready for Room Three," I said. I repeated it, this time louder.

"Is it a little soon? He just got here."

I sat up, scrambled at the controls, and brought up Room Three. A man with lazy eyes in need of sobering occupied my patient's bed.

"Where's Alaina?" I said.

"Who?"

"Alaina. Lauren. The damn woman who was in Room Three!"

"She left."

"What?"

"You told me to discharge her."

I ran out of the room, down the hall, and threw open

the back fire escape door and went out into the night. I yelled for her, but it was of no use.

Alaina was gone.

*   *   *

The rest of my shift was uneventful.

*   *   *

Tunde and I rented a private boat off the coast of Playa del Rey and were well out into the ocean just in time for sunset. I left my dampener in the car. Whatever I felt was far from pleasant, but it was necessary. The rest of the shift had been uneventful.

"Something's on your mind," Tunde said as we walked out onto the deck. Dinner had been quiet. He ordered his usual at seafood restaurants: crab legs and coleslaw. I tried something new, the seared scallops, and hated them.

"I had a rough shift," I said.

"Not just today," Tunde said. He looked out to the sea. Judging from the nervous tilt in his voice, he hadn't self-regulated in a while. "When you're with me it feels like your mind is someplace else. Or wants to be. Part of me wonders if you've had any inappropriate relationships lately."

I laughed. Sneaking in an affair while trying to figure out Alaina and the effect she had on me? Absurd. "I should be offended."

"Offended is good," Tunde said. He laughed out toward the darkening horizon. "I'll take offended."

"Something *has* been going on," I said. I continued to smile to keep my husband at ease. "Does the name

Lauren mean anything to you?" I saw the lie forming behind his eyes. "Whatever it is, it's out there already. I didn't know my ablation therapy included a memory wipe. I guess that was the point, though, huh? Who was Lauren?"

"Laura," Tunde said. "You were roommates. In college."

"Laura. Laura Chisholm." I tasted the name, felt its tremble on my lips. I hadn't spoken it in decades. "She always had the big hoop earrings and the hair everyone wanted."

"That's her. Everyone knew Laura."

"Did she die?" I said.

"Yes."

"Car crash?"

"You remember a lot more than you should."

I shook my head. "I don't remember."

"You lost me."

"One of my patients. Her best friend died in a car crash seven years ago. The friend's name was Lauren. She was intoxicated."

"Jesus," Tunde said. "Laura was killed by a drunk driver. That's definitely too close to home. You're going to stop seeing her, right?"

"Yeah," I said. "Definitely."

Silence. Whatever Tunde and I had become, he knew when I was lying.

"You used to tell me about your cousin having schizophrenia," I said. "That it came on after she lost someone. You told her story sometimes when my path got hard, and I thought about giving up."

"I remember," Tunde said.

"I don't recall you ever having a cousin." I turned to him. There were no sensors. No displays. Just the two of us under the dying light. "Was it me? When you talk about this phantom cousin, are you just talking about me?"

"You inspired me," Tunde said after some time. "You inspired us both. You got help. And look how far you've come."

A dorsal fin briefly broke the surface some hundred yards away. I waited for the rest of the dolphin's pod to show. None did.

"What was I like?" I said. "Before?"

"Smart. Beautiful. Creative. All the things you are now."

"Liar," I said.

"It's no lie." Tunde shifted. "You were suffering. Before Lauren died, it was manageable. You had a light episode every now and then, but we got through it. No one knew, unless they needed to know. Lauren's death was . . . tragic, for the whole school, but for you it kept happening over and over because you still heard her." He shivered. "The stuff her voice would say . . . You have to stop seeing this patient. It's taking a toll on you."

The last of the day's rays warm on my skin, I leaned over and kissed my husband. Our lips lingered long enough to let sparks fly between us, like all those decades ago when he proposed as we watched an ocean sunset. But, alas, nothing but stubble and cognition.

"That's why I need to keep seeing her."

*   *   *

Though the *why* of anything in life was complex, the *how* of the situation was clear. I had developed symptoms consistent with mild schizophrenia shortly upon college matriculation. My once benign psychosis dramatically worsened after the tragic death of my college roommate. The ablation therapy did its job, and core memories surrounding the psychosis—including Laura—had been purged. Decades later, the pairing of my cognition with Alaina's facilitated a free stream of emotions between the two of us. Her experience gave life to dormant parts of my past, similar to the classic case studies describing late-stage dementia patients showing transient moments of awareness and memory. I hallucinated because the awakened part of my brain also facilitated bouts of false sensory information decades ago.

Alaina and I started in very much the same place. If I wasn't specially equipped to help her, who was?

*   *   *

I came into the office two hours early to prepare for Alaina's next appointment.. I went over her files, algorithms, and used the cognition extraction technology to see an emulation of my own logic analyze the details of her case.

Alaina was fifteen minutes late. She wore the same baggy sweater from the hospital three days before. She stank of insomnia.

"You look how I feel," she said.

"We both had a rough week. I wanted to bring up a sensitive topic. How did Lauren die?"

"She told you she was dead?" Alaina said.

"I saw it in her records." I leaned slightly forward. "What goes through your mind when I say that? When I mention her dying?"

"She's manipulating you. To get what she wants. Everyone thinks she's dead. Everyone gives her sympathy." Alaina huffed disgust. "She wasn't ready to go. And she didn't. I keep her alive."

"Maybe that's true. But do you think she wants to live at your expense?"

Alaina began to cry. I handed her a tissue. When she was done, I showed her where Lauren's voices lived in her brain. Delusions—or fixed beliefs—were the hardest things to combat in psychiatry. For some people, showing their physical derivatives went a long way.

"This is the sensory part of your brain lighting up when I talk. It comes all the way from the nerve anchored in your eardrum and links back to here, where memories are." I switched from live feed to a previous recording. "See, here, that's your sensory portion lighting up independently. No input from the outside nerves. It does, however, have an intimate connection with this cluster, where your memory of Lauren lives."

I turned off the recording. "Do you hear her now?"

"I only hear you." She kept my gaze for only a few moments before looking past me. Her neural read shifted.

I leaned forward. "I am not here to judge but to explore."

"She needs me."

"She's gone," I said. I turned off the session recording device. "I had a friend, too. She died in a car accident after one of our arguments, like Lauren. I can help you be at peace. I think she would have wanted that."

I clipped the earpiece behind her ear.

"You think I'm crazy," Alaina said.

"Oh, no. No, no, no." I shook my head. "I think you need help. And I have help."

"Will I be like you?"

I shifted. "I don't understand."

She took the earpiece off and gestured around her. "All this, just to function. I see you dampening yourself and dampening yourself. Do you even feel anything anymore?"

"Alaina, I know this is upsetting, but—"

"You're broken," she said. "And I'm whole. It might be a rotting whole, but it's my whole, and it's all there right now. You had a piece of you taken. And now you have to depend on technology just to get through the day. I've seen you!"

For the first time in our many sessions, I was unintentionally silent. Alaina looked to me for the same therapeutic expertise I had shown before to make this moment into something productive, but I had nothing.

"I'm sorry, I—" Alaina began to say.

I held up a hand. "It's fine."

*   *   *

Alaina missed her next three appointments. I took on more shifts at Obama Memorial and kept an eye out for her. She popped up from time to time in the medical charts. Still presenting under different names, still refusing treatment, still looking for her friend, Lauren.

Three months later I had another ablation treatment. Not only to eradicate any resurfacing remnants of Laura but to also clear my memory of Alaina.

I made sure my notes on her were airtight in case of any unlikely future litigation. As I waited for the machine to do its work I took the final chance to reflect on Alaina's words. The Ship of Theseus was replaced piece by piece until it was something completely new. Was I the same person as before the ablation? Of course I wasn't. Would I have become a doctor?

Alaina's choice bothered me the most. We were so alike and yet chose completely differently at the most pivotal junctions in our lives.

Why?

No answer came, only ignorance, and therefore, bliss.

Sex Education

The prevailing theory in the '90s, when I took Intro to Physical Anthropology (i.e., the biological branch of the field), considered sex as binary, and female the default. Two X chromosomes, and you were female. The presence of a Y chromosome made you male.

This was based on observations of rare genetic conditions. Although, perhaps not so rare as we believed. We didn't really test the genomes of that many people. Now, some estimate that Differences of Sex Development, or DSDs, may be as common as 1 in 100 individuals.

There are cases where an individual only inherits one X chromosome (Turner Syndrome), three X chromosomes, XYY, Klinefelter syndrome (individuals with one Y and multiple X chromosomes), or a mosaic of X and Y chromosomes. Perhaps we might not expect Anthropology, a field united by the "biocultural theory," a holistic view of humanity that takes both biology and culture into account, to embrace the dichotomy of sex so wholeheartedly, but that's what I was taught.

It wasn't until the 2000s that WNT4, and other genes that play an active role in sex traits, were discovered, and thereby disproved the notion that sex determination in humans was so simple and binary.

Culturally, however, and even in the '90s, Anthropology did recognize more than two genders, a topic I explored as a field study project for both my Intro to Socio-Cultural Anthropology and my

Cross-Cultural Communication Studies classes. I had the opportunity to work with a research partner who is gay, although he said he felt like an outsider in the community of single gay men because he'd been in a commited relationship for a decade - this was about 15 years before same-sex marriage was legal here in California.

We conducted surveys, interviews, and participant observation in the local gay community, specifically with regard to whether members of gay and lesbian couples adopted "traditional" gender role patterns of sexual division of labor. I'll always be grateful to my research partner and others in the gay community who let me enter their social space and allowed me to get to know them on their own terms. What struck me most was seeing how people I knew from outside the gay community become so much more relaxed, more willing to let their true selves show, in those safe spaces where they were they were the majority.

Biology continues to reveal the false dichotomy of binary gender in the natural world in 2021. Not one, but two new studies are currently battling it out in the peer-review journals, both showing that domesticated betta fish have evolved a sex gene, similar to the X/Y chromosome in humans, that wild betta fish don't have. While adult female beta fish have often been observed to transform into males and to successfully reproduce viable offspring, a single gene has been observed to determine sex in 90% of domesticate betta fish, even though the same gene in wild betta fish does not determine an individual's sex so reliably.

What is clear is that sex determination in the natural world is not as simple as male vs. female. So, should we be surprised to see a spectrum of sexuality and gender in humans? Medical science, and the social sciences, still have so much to learn about human sexuallty and gender.

The following story, first published in the Spanish Women of Wonder anthology from 2016. "Sea Changes," by Lola Robles and translated by Lawrence Schimel, imagines a future planet where the medical science of human sexuality is so advanced that medical interventions can match a person's physical state to almost any possible gender identity.

As a content alert, please note that the story uses the term "hermaphrodite." Current medical nomenclature acknowledges that a true gonadal intersex condition, what historically may have been called true hermaphroditism, is extremely rare in humans, and considered "intersex." The author and translator, in this case, have chosen to use both terms as having distinct meanings, and we respect the author's artistic choice here. We appreciate that "intersex" is a somewhat broader term, and the language, especially in translation, may not currently be adequate to describe this far-future scenario.

I hope you enjoy and find "Sea Changes" as thought-provoking as I do.

Sea Changes

by Lola Robles
translated by Lawrence Schimel

Day 44 of the First Cycle of Spring Jalmannui Year 1202

"I welcome all of you to Jalawdri, the Archipelago World, the planet of the hundred thousand islands and the seas that change color.

My name is Martin, I will be your guide and companion, your friend and brother. I understand very well how you feel. I see your faces full of light, of fear and of yearning. I know that you have made a long journey – that the vertigo of Deep Space has overwhelmed you – and that you have marveled before the cold sidereal beauties that in reality are incandescent suns. I know that some of you had to work very hard, in legal or illegal trades, in order to reach here. I have lived all of this before. Three cycles ago I arrived in this spaceport. You are on Lance Island, from where a medical boat will take us to Central Island. The ship's crew is at your disposal. If you've written a diary, we shall read it with great interest. Here our hands are open".

Georgina's Diary
Day 148 of the journey of the starship Marco Polo

I wanted to get away from Earth as fast as possible – but I enjoyed watching that deep blue sphere streaked with clouds and continents from the Marco Polo.

The ship, although comfortable and quick, is not a transgalactic cruiser, and thus the journey has been long and tiresome, though we've had plenty of time to rest. The relationships between the passengers have not always been easy, we are one hundred and fifty people stuck in an area that's only slightly larger than a submarine. For five months. Fortunately, the psychologists have helped us greatly, and we've formed good groups and friendships.

From time to time, taking it in turns, we could look at the stars. To me it felt like finding myself lost in the middle of the ocean, on a tiny ship, on a moonless night, with the entire celestial sphere above me. Or in the desert, after a scorching day which has now turned cold, contemplating the cosmos from the sand with the same awe that Early Man must have felt in the shadows of an enormous world that was still untamed. Constellations like jewels – gems of golden light, diamonds of blue brilliance, crimson pearls. These are metaphors that I invent, for I have never seen any of those treasures.

When I made out Jalawdri for the first time, its perfect sphere in the distance with intense green seas, I also thought of that crystalline mineral called Emerald, or of exuberantly lush forests, or suboceanic waters. Behind the planet was a yellow sun, shining like a shield.

At my side, Lily and Juan were also silent. Juan is a believer –– a Christian –– and offered a prayer to a god whom I shall never know; a god imagined as loving and generous. Later we celebrated our friendship and the end of the journey drinking wine in secret.

We have scrupulously followed all the rules up until this moment: not to taste alcohol, nor tobacco nor drugs; to write our diaries (though I have waited until the last few days to do so); to use our official names (something that the three of us loathe doing).

We don't like to talk of Fatherlands either, we who have had to remove ourselves from our world of origin, who live exiled, in bodies that feel foreign to us.

But now perhaps we find ourselves before our real home. Our Promised Land.

Day 44 of the First Cycle of Spring Jalmannui Year 1202

After finishing his welcome speech for the passengers of the ship *Eurydice*, Martin contemplated the sea in the distance, beyond the spaceport's landing strips. Dawn was breaking, and soon the light would filter through the waiting room's large windows. The ocean, calm as usual, had acquired reflections of mercury with the dawn. As the sun climbed, the tonalities of the waters would remain shades of cold colors until becoming an almost unbearable blue, beneath clouds like icebergs stuck close to the marine surface.

Lance Island was located in Jalawdri's northern hemisphere, quite close to the Pole, though the water never froze. The island was large enough and sufficiently distant from any other, that it had been possible to establish the spaceport there. It wasn't easy to land a disembarkment module from a transgalactic spaceship with a good number of passengers – it wasn't as simple as descending from a plane or guiding a large ship into port. The chances of missing the precise landing point on terra firma were high, and in that eventuality it was better to have a touchdown spot that wouldn't threaten any inhabited areas.

Cygnus wore a black sealskin jacket, comfortable trousers and boots. His long blond hair, combed back, seemed metallic. Martin considered him to be a person of notable elegance. He was tall and athletic with wide shoulders, and Martin had always seen him dressed in men's clothes and with a masculine appearance. Although his gestures were excessively languid, and over the years it was possible that his face would become increasingly more ambiguous. He used male pronouns for himself, so Martin treated him the same way, even though he knew that Cygnus was an *ak-jalmannui*, a "hommon"(that is to say, "strict") hermaphrodite.

"Have you breakfasted?" Cygnus asked, with a pleasant smile. Receiving a shake of the head in response, he continued: "Coffee and some cakes? You must be starving. Getting up so early always leaves me with a voracious appetite."

Martin nodded, trying to smile. The ak-jalmannui served the hot liquid into two porcelain cups imported from Earth and then, from two little jugs, a bit of liquid chocolate and almond milk frothed to an immaculate white foam, sprinkling cinnamon from Earth over everything. He stuck a rolled wafer into the thick cloud. On another plate he placed three cakes, which he sliced in half with a small finely-sharpened blade. Martin tasted the coffee. It was Turkish – aromatic and delicate. The cakes had been made by Cygnus himself, who loved cooking. As they drank, Martin watched the other's hands, as large and strong as they were smooth and white. All of Cygnus' skin was extremely clear, though no longer so tight, especially across his face, marred by more than a few wrinkles. This deterioration, which was faster than that of other inhabitants of the planet, as well as the blond hair, pale blue eyes and scarlet lips – to say nothing of the tall stature – were characteristics of hommon hermaphrodites. One of the waiters in the room, a dark-complexioned man with a smooth-shorn chin, knew this very well, and when Cygnus asked him to bring them some small crystal glasses he hurried to obey, frequently bowing his head.

"Try this liqueur," Cygnus suggested, serving a cherry-colored drink into the transparent little glasses.

At first it was rough on the palette, then it left a cool aftertaste that invited repetition.

"Delicious," Martin approved.

Now seated, Cygnus smiled again. Before arriving on Jalawdri, Martin had read that the hermaphrodites, in addition to lacking a libido, had neither emotions nor the capacity for empathy. This had proved to be only partly true. Cygnus loved music, good food, elegant clothes, beautiful objects from other times and worlds, and had the grandest and most spectacular home that Martin had ever seen on this planet, full of imported antiquities. Whenever Cygnus had invited the Earthman to his magnificent mansion, he was a supremely courteous host, asking about the most diverse aspects of his nascent World. He was likewise a good listener, letting the speaker talk without bombarding them with questions, not minding if his interlocutor digressed a bit, only bringing the conversation back on track from time to time with a few brief sentences.

Martin no longer thought Cygnus to be a selfish traitor to his own kind, nor a future shark who wanted to travel to Earth to study capitalism in depth and import it to Jalawdri, to despoil a pristine world. No, despite what Gabrielle had always said, Martin no longer believed in this ak-jalmannui's reputed evil intentions. He might well be nonbinary in his thoughts as well as in his body, and therefore judged that progress for his planet truly did depend on technological advancement.

With his lovely countertenor voice, Cygnus now asked:

"So, have you made a decision? We haven't much time left. Neither you, nor I."

Georgina's Diary
Day 55 of the Third Cycle of Summer Jalmannui Year 1201

I'm writing this as I wait for them to come for me, to take me to the surgery. These are the final pages of this diary because, if everything works out right, within a few days I will be able to begin another, leaving behind this stupid name and using my real one instead – the one I have chosen: Martin.

I am afraid. Lito came to visit me a little while ago. He wants to encourage me with his happiness. He has decided not to make the full change, not to remove his uterus and ovaries; they'll just reduce his breasts and rebalance his endocrine system, so that over time his physicality will become more outwardly male, what is here called a fliek-jalmannui. He even thinks to keep calling himself Lito sometimes, and at other times Lily, whenever he feels like it. He was very handsome today – he always has been – with his short brown hair and hooked nose, his glowing complexion and all his vibrant energy; an eternal youngster. During our arduous journey to becoming ourselves, we made love a few times on the ship, and it comforted us. I've been told that Joanna is doing very well, though she won't emerge from recovery for another two days. In her case it must be due to prior health issues, because the operation went perfectly.

I asked Lito to help me shave myself bare. Afterward, he left.

I caress my buzzed scalp. I've always liked the feel of hair cut so short, there is something sensual in that roughness. I touch my face, bony and unquestionably ugly, as I've been told far too often. My cheeks. As a girl, I locked myself in the bathroom of my parents' house and lathered my face with shaving cream, taking the razor, without a blade, and imitating the movements of shaving myself. I pass one of my fingers over the line of my lips. I like my mouth, my lovers have always said that it's carnal and sweet.

"We'll celebrate our first beards with champagne!" Lito declared before leaving, laughing a lot. "We'll sing The Song of the Bearded Star Pirates. *Gabrielle can join us, we'll tell her to let her beard grow too."*

"I sing awfully," I told my friend. "Besides, my voice is a soprano, and I'd like to be a baritone. You at least could be a tenor, even now."

"But our voices will change. Maybe yours won't stretch to a baritone but it will at least become a tenor. Something is something. Think about it."

I lightly touch my breasts, which will be reduced to a minimum, even though mine have never been very large. Perhaps my wanting to be other impeded this. I'll have a male torso and my muscles and bone structure will become stronger as my own body becomes able to produce more testosterone. I'll have my penis and testicles, and above all – yes, above all, – they'll remove my uterus and my ovaries. And that dark blood, so painful and smelly, will at last stop flowing. My monstrous menstrual cycle. Unlike Lito, it's not enough for me for those organs to stay there like a dried-up fountain, in menopause. I want them completely gone. But removing them requires an antiquated surgery, even here on Jalawdri: a scalpel will cut my flesh with cold precision; doctors will dig in my entrails; there will be blood and pain, despite the analgesics. It is not the first time I'll pass through an operating room. I know the defenselessness of nakedness, the helplessness on the operating table, the glacial fear of that darkness the anaesthesia brings, the muddled confusion of awakening and the discomfort that grips your stomach.

Gabriella spent all of yesterday and last night with me, and only left a few hours ago. She is friendly, efficient; she cleared up all the practical issues, for me as well as for Joanna and Lito. Though she is very serious, from time to time she'll let loose with some *ironic statement that proves she doesn't lack a sense of humor. I think she is an honest and upright person, albeit a bit rigid and distant. She is an ouk-jalmannui, an intersex person in whom the feminine is predominant. She has dark blonde hair down to her shoulders, well-defined cheekbones, very green eyes; she must have been very pretty when she was young, in fact she still is. I think she must be around fifty – that undefined age in which one is neither young nor old. She has a woman's breasts and curves but a fine coat of hair covers her upper lip and chin, so if she were to let it grow, in just a few weeks she could indeed sing The Song of the Bearded Star Pirates with Lito and me. As my own surgery draws nearer, what lies beneath her undergarments is speculative distraction. Without a doubt she must have a uterus and a vagina, perhaps some atrophied testicles, and a micropenis that might also be an enlarged clitoris. I use language that is too crude, but after all Gabrielle will never read this diary, we aren't going to be friends. She is someone who is too cold for me, I feel, and I'm used to letting myself be guided by my intuitions. It's a good inheritance of my femininity. In any event, I must explain that Gabrielle isn't her real name. Lito and I have chosen that name because it is the closest-sounding Earth name to her original one, which is unpronounceable for us. It will be very difficult for us to learn this language, which is much more complicated, phonetically, than our own or Inter. Gabrielle, however, speaks Inter with better than acceptable fluency and has a broad knowledge of the history, countries, societies, culture and life on Earth.*

As for the term ouk-jalmannui, the latter part is comprised of two lexemes: "jal" – ocean, which also appears in the planet's name, and "mannui" – inhabitant. Thus the Jalmannui are the inhabitants of the ocean, for that's how this world is considered, even though it isn't really an oceanic planet; it was one many millions of years ago, and then became an archipelago planet as the islands emerged from the marine surface. The prefix "k" refers to humans who have both sexes to one degree or another. From the ak-jalmannui or full hermaphrodites, to the fliek-jalmannui – in whom the male genotype and phenotype is predominant, though not completely so. And people like Gabrielle, the ouk, where the feminine is predominant. The ouk and the fliek are also called "intermediates", what I would call "intersex" in my native tongue; they're infertile, like the hermaphrodites or aks, in whom the genotypic characteristics of both sexes appear equally.

*   *   *

Gabrielle is going to arrive now. She will accompany me to the operating room. I am grateful to her, although I can't manage to get rid of this sensation of helplessness. I'd like to fall asleep, with the warm, if somewhat restless, sleep of other nights. A normal sleep, not this dark nothingness they inject into a vein and which you can remember nothing of. Gabrielle told me she will be at my side when I wake. Then I'll see Lito. The door opens. It is time.

Day 28 of the First Cycle of Spring Jalmannui Year 1202

After closing the door to the silent house, Martin breathed a sigh of relief. Lito's absence allowed him to relax for a while without answering too many questions.

In his bedroom he unpacked his knapsack, arranging everything, and took off his clothes. Home, sweet home.

It took a while to fill the bathtub because he wanted the water to be really hot and he had to boil many liters. A luxury, now that nobody could see him, but he needed it. His bones ached from many hours of lying on the hard bed, trying to sleep. He lathered himself thoroughly with the deep cleansing but hydrating soap. He needed to cut his hair before the arrival of the *Eurydice*. But not his beard, no — it was sparse and thin, like that of a teenager. It seemed incredible that Lito had a beard so thick and black, and such a virile voice, whereas he had barely managed to achieve this peachy fuzz, despite having undergone the complete change. This comparison between the two of them was a game that was fun — up to a certain point. Lito showed him his well-developed muscles, and Martin challenged him to face him and lose on the chessboard, saying that *he* trained his intelligence rather than his biceps. And after comparing themselves with each other, they drank a meka beer, coppery and bitter, with lots of foam. Meka was the most abundant grain on the high islands of the northern hemisphere. Bread and pasta were also made from it. In the tropical islands to the south, which were almost clusters of shallow lakes in the middle of plains of dazzling green, the almost-black rice called *awal* grew better. A liquor was distilled from awal that had such a high alcohol content that drinking it was like swallowing a burning firebrand.

Yes, it was curious that his friend, without having wanted to surrender his uterus and ovaries, was now so masculine in his appearance and attitudes, whereas he, Martin, continued to appear so androgynous, so feminine – so much so that on Earth his gender reassignment might have amounted to nothing – though it was true that he no longer cared, that increasingly he advocated ambiguity, malleability, liquidity, being permanently in transit. And Lito, what was he now? A warrior up for anything, even killing?

Martin emerged from the water and, wrapped in a towel, went to his bedroom and got into bed. The house, made of stone, was cold – ideal for summers but in other seasons one had to light the fire or bundle up.

He thought of looking for Gabrielle's last letter, as he usually did every morning and at night before going to bed. Perhaps that would be too painful.

But in the end, he stretched out a hand and took the letter from a shelf. He extracted it from the envelope and unfolded the sheet of paper. It was much more brief than the previous ones; written in almost-perfect Inter, though with the curious syntax of the ouk-jalmannui, with frequent anacolutha. None had ever been as long as the ones he had written. The sentences didn't say anything of note, just ref

erences to daily life. That banality was the worst offense, the most humiliating insult. He tore the sheet into tiny bits.

Up and dressed now, he entered the room that was both kitchen and dining area. On a table he saw meka noodles, with blue seaweed and fresh vegetables. In the sink, in a box filled with water, was a large fish. So, Khorfu had come to visit.

From the terrace he could contemplate the varied panorama that surrounded the town – the tall, blue mountains in the distance, snow still crowning their peaks. The forests of *shudras* (a conifer very like Earth cedars, which gave the island its name) and cultivated fields of meka. The sea couldn't be seen from the house. An indigo sea, at those latitudes. He breathed, like always, an air as pure as native silver. He was happy there.

On a stretch of ground, beneath the terrace, he found Khorfu and Lito, both dressed in wide trousers with their torsos and feet bare. They fought with *zartus*, scimitars with fearfully sharp edges, which flashed in the sunlight. They shouted, panted, moved at startling speeds, weapons clashing or cutting at the air, now absent of the rival that had avoided the attack.

Khorfu was shorter than the Earthman but more robust. His lustrous black hair fell down to his waist, but was now pulled back into a half-braided ponytail. His skin was dark, deep tan, and a solid beard shadowed his face. Shadowed it, because though his skin shone warmly in its darkness, his face almost always bore a dour look, like a sky that foretells a storm.

Today seemed to be a day for noticing paradoxes. Here was another – that this *kaft-jalmannui*, this hommon male, standing now solemn and stiff as if his dorsal fin were a rock, should have become such friends with a foreigner, Lito, who bent over laughing at both his own mistakes and those of others during training sessions. When he first met them, Khorfu had made a stiff bow but remained at a meter's distance, for he considered that the foreigners came to corrupt the purity of his native world.

And yet for over a cycle now, Khorfu had fished and cooked for Lito, showing him how to use the zartu. They often spent the afternoon together, and the visitor made drawings of very athletic men – naked or dressed in various uniforms – which the other young man described for him, drawing his inspiration from the ancient armies of Earth. They spent many hours discussing how they could block the arrival of capitalism on Jalawdri. Martin joined them then. Khorfu never showed him the least friendliness, but even Martin was able to recognize that Lito's companion was an excellent link between the resistance groups of the different islands and an unmatchable spy.

At last they noticed him. Lito greeted him by raising his arms; the other didn't move a muscle.

Until they had eaten, a delicious meal which Martin praised Khorfu for, they hardly spoke. It was only as Lito set down his chopsticks on the plate that he asked, "So, Martin, did your first meeting with Cygnus go as we planned? Do you think he will fall into our nets like a careless fish?"

Letter from Gabrielle to Martin

Desolation Island
Day 72 of the Second Cycle of Autumn
Jalmannui Year 1201

Dear Martin,

I am glad to learn your good news – and that of Lito. Sometimes Joanna writes to me as well. It is wonderful that your health is improving. I told you, it's a question of time. And more must still pass before the production of hormones balances itself, and your body changes as you desire. Have patience. The next plastic surgeries you must undergo will be minor compared to the earlier ones.

Of course, I also think it is wonderful that you and Lito are so happy on your island. Not many people who come from more developed worlds can adjust to living here. Without a doubt, at first the beauty of nature here seduces them. So many islands and all of them so lovely... The sea, which is almost always calm, like the peaceful inhabitants who almost never get angry, although of course the day they do, no one will ever forget it.

You, for example, come from an overpopulated planet, full of cities and technological advances. It would be understandable for you to wind up growing bored of so much beautiful landscape, of eating just fish and only occasionally lamb, lots of fruit and lots of meka, with few delicacies. Even writing letters by hand that take days to reach their recipient must seem difficult and strange to you, having had at your disposal instantaneous means of communication – your computers and your telephones.

Jalawdri is very backward in many aspects when compared to Earth, for example. However, many of us have been very content here. This is not the case for others, especially since Contact. For them, knowing that there are more inhabited worlds, that the sidereals scattered all of us throughout time and space, was a shock. Our first visitors told of the marvels of their distant planets. This perhaps wouldn't have been a problem, if we'd been a people of fishers and gatherers hardly beyond the Age of Metals, or simply a pre-industrial, pre-technological and pre-scientific society. In that case, we would have viewed you as unreachable gods.

But no, we had advanced greatly in specific fields such as the medicine of gender. Why? Because for centuries, the hommon men and women, overwhelmed by the burden of reproduction and nourishment, since they had to conceive, give birth to and raise children – and in addition fish, grow crops and cook for themselves and for others – often preferred to become ouk, fliek or ak-jalmannui; conditions which were no longer considered anomalies for they had become established over the centuries, even though they continued to be minorities.

The social system of this planet has been for a long time a pyramid controlled by a minority, as occurs so often on so many worlds, with the ak at the apex. They were the oligarchy holding the economic, political and religious power. For their part, the ouks and flieks devoted themselves to commerce, to services, to the growing industry based on electricity and coal, the *health services and teaching... And below them all, the most numerous but the most subjected, were the fully-reproductive Jalmannui: the mustaft and the kaft. With the exception of the tribes of the Virginal Islands, who are thought to have been our original nucleus. They are completely patriarchal pirate warriors, where it is the men, the kaft, who dominate the rest. For me and for many others, returning to this state would be a clear involution. It would even be so for a fundamentalist like young Khorfu.*

Of course, we also don't wish to follow the path of technological development imported from other worlds, as Cygnus advocates. Many of us prefer to continue traveling in ships powered by steam, sails, or oars – in electric cars or on foot, instead of planes, ocean cruisers or fast automobiles. We don't need them. If we offer people from other planets the possibility of coming to Jalawdri in order to transform their bodies, it is out of ideological convictions, not as a means of capturing Inter Credits. And what people like Cygnus will try to do is to transform our medicine into a galaxy-spanning business, without being concerned that our basic intention is to propose to those who arrive that what they really need to do is not necessarily to change their bodies, so much as their minds.

I understand your decision. I know you needed that complete transformation because you felt yourself truly male and not a woman, otherwise you wouldn't have gone through a surgical intervention whose results are unquestionably more perfect than the same operation on Earth, though just as painful. We've already spoken of this: sometimes it is necessary, and other times not, to change your genitals in order to live in a specific way.

We must be free to choose our identity, our behavior, and, of course, what we do with our own bodies as well.

The problem lies in the fact that if the Jalmannui begin to traffic on a large scale with our medicine, as Cygnus proposes we do, others will turn up in search of other forms of enriching themselves. Doubtlessly, beneath our sea beds sleeps that viscous black substance that seems to move everything, which your people are lacking and yearn for so strongly.

Imagine what that would entail for this planet. For its waters and its atmosphere, its islands. In short, what you call its ecology. After half a century of contact with other inhabited worlds, we've managed to still preserve our own. But perhaps we won't be able to continue doing so.

It is very good that Lito, Joanna and yourself have decided to join our resistance. It will be a great help.

Write to me whenever you want.

Gabrielle

Letter from Martin to Joanna
Shudras Island
Day 55 of the Third Cycle of Autumn
Jalmannui Year 1201

Dearest Joanna,

You don't know how happy your last letter made me. Everything you wrote in it, knowing that you are well. And you can't imagine what it means for me to be able to write to you and to be frank with you. I can't do that with anyone else, not even with Lito. And you'll understand why as you keep reading.

But first, and so as not to begin with so much heart-break, I must tell you that no, I don't dream of toasting myself on the thin sands of your volcanic island. Just hearing the name Island of Flames makes me break out in a sweat and start to feel overwhelmed.

The temperature is ideal for me here on my island, though winter is near, and the first snows have begun to fall. I think that there is nothing lovelier than that whiteness which slowly thickens. Icicles hang from the leaves of the shudras trees. There are droplets and crystals that resemble the purest quartz.

I always speak of pureness, don't I? I don't refer to the absence of sin, of course, nor even to grand ideals. Our friend Lito has made a very strange friend here, whom we call Khorfu, that's what his name sounds like to us. He says he is descended from the warrior pirates of the wild tribes of the Virgin Islands and all that. He is a hommon male. To me he is a fundamentalist and a tradi-tionalist; absolutely convinced that any person or thing that comes from outside might contaminate this world. If he accepts Lito and me it is because we are converts to his ways. It is not that pureness, either, that I speak of. Though sometimes I envy Khorfu, his magnificent and virile body, his pride and foolish rigidity, his lack of compassion. I tell myself that I'm envious because I still don't consider myself a "real" man. Other times I suspect that I don't really want to be one. I came to Jalawdri to transform myself into a male, thinking that this would be the only way for me to feel good about myself, to find peace and a certain joy. It turns out that isn't so; that neither my penis nor my beard have given me anything new, though I do not regret my decision of having finally succeeded in becoming Martin.

The hope I've found is something else – that of making this world into my home. Because, as is true for you and Lito, nobody is waiting for me on Earth. And anywhere else it's very likely that I would continue to be a monster, a physical and moral aberration, for my altered and intermediated body.

There is another hope that I shall speak to you about. We've been here since the third cycle of summer, though it seems like it has been much longer, no doubt because the seasons with their three cycles of ninety days each seem so long to us.

Joanna, I've fallen in love with Gabrielle. I don't under-stand how this has happened to me. You know that at first I didn't like her at all, she seemed so hard and distant to me. But little by little, I wound up feeling more and more tenderness toward her. Perhaps because she was always keeping an eye on my recovery, perhaps because of her integrity, the coherence I see in her defense of Jalawdri's ecology, and because she's nonetheless chosen to open this world to those of us who needed its medical knowledge. I felt she was so devoted to those causes that she woke in me both admiration and the same faith, a matching passion for those same convictions. She is a leader, a great leader. She seems to me a valiant Antigone. I would like to become her paladin.

Moreover, I don't think that Gabrielle is as hard as she seems. From things she has written to me or told me, and from things I merely intuit, I suspect that she has a fragile heart hidden behind a wall, like a fortress. My *guess is that she was hurt deeply in some old relationship, and I think that my love and tenderness might cure her. Without a doubt, it would cure me as well. The perseverance of my affection might manage to overcome her distance and coldness. She would understand that she didn't have to defend herself against me, that my love is sincere and pure. That is the pureness I was talking about. It is not just a spiritual love, it is also one of the flesh – of trembling unhappy flesh that would embrace her own.*

I have not yet said anything to Gabrielle, and I do not think she suspects. Nobody knows about this except for you. My secret forms part of my love. I don't want everyone else's opinions about it. I keep it locked in a safe, a coffer, a closed attic, in the tangled vines of dreams before sleep, in the lies I tell so that no one discovers it. You know that I love Lito very much but you also know how his humour is sometimes very wounding. He will laugh about this, and I won't be able to handle that very well.

This love has taken root in me the way a tree digs into the earth, or perhaps it is a cancer. I've bet everything on it and can't allow the possibility of failure, I won't permit it. I love Gabrielle, and I feed that affection at all hours, with a degree of intensity that you couldn't imagine.

A few weeks ago I was on Desolation Island to see her. I had to tell her about some decisions made by our island's resistance group. She welcomed me into her home. There we have had meetings of representatives from the different groups of our organization. I know, Joanna, that you understand fully how important it is for me to feel welcomed within a circle, a sort of family. Our groups are that for me; their solidarity implies a tie as strong as blood, even stronger, because it is chosen freely – it is a decision of the soul.

The day of my visit something very curious happened. Gabrielle was waiting for me in the entrance, thoughtful and contemplating the sea, which is violet and frothy there, with high waves that beat against the coast of naked rock, the black reefs and cliffs. I have always seen her as a woman, and it is as such that I like her. She is elegant, she wears a long dress but also sportswear. I love her earrings and those jewels she wears around her neck. I love that neck of hers, I desire it as a vampire would. I want to embrace, to caress, to kiss her body, to bury myself within it like taking refuge in a cave.

But that day, the day of my visit, she was alone. Jerome, the cook who helps her in her house, had just left. Her beard had grown a little, she wore her hair loose, a sweater and trousers. And suddenly in the violet air of the afternoon, I saw a man. I was perplexed and unsure what to feel at first. I am not attracted to men, or rather, I have sometimes been able to desire their bodies but they've never awoken any affection in me. However, there in front of Gabrielle, who was a she and a he at the same time, I loved her like that, I thought that I could always love her, completely and unconditionally. Even if she didn't feel the same way about me. I am certain, however, that she does feel something. I am important, necessary for her, as a friend, as a comrade. Sometimes we write a letter every day. I have all of them in my bedroom, I re-read them daily. We speak of her world, of mine, of the future. We share too many things to not be joined together by a very special bond...

In any event, sometimes I think that it's enough for me to love her. Because, I think, so long as one loves with all one's heart – without reserve, without fear – there will be salvation for me. For that soul of mine that surrenders itself. That is the pureness I speak of, my dear Joanna.

With all my affection,

Martin

Day 26 of the First Cycle of Spring Jalmannui Year of 1202

When the sun reached the marine horizon, Martin closed his umbrella. He'd had to use it every time he went out onto the deck, because the heat and the light were very intense. He put on dark glasses brought from Earth, to protect his eyes from solar reflections. These kinds of glasses were unknown on Jalawdri, and, as a result, visual problems were quite common.

He still sweated copiously because the climate in this region of the planet was remarkably sultry. In the Wet Tropical Islands, between Spring and Autumn, it rained an average of 500 out of the 1080 days of the year; in the end one had the sensation of being an amphibian rather than human.

He watched the sunset as they arrived at the port of Bay Island. Twilights on Jalmannui became grandiose spectacles in the tropical zones. The sky, from which a cooling breeze began to blow, and the sea with its waves beating gently against the ship's hull, blended into a single color that changed from minute to minute. It happened so quickly that if you weren't paying attention, or if you found yourself below deck, you could easily wind up missing it. At those moments Martin missed not having a camera to photograph or record those dazzling sunsets. But he didn't have one. Thus it was an ephemeral beauty, perhaps even greater because of its fleetingness, though perhaps the Terrans, with their cameras ever ready to record every moment, were the ones who lost out precisely because of their obstinacy in capturing things instead of the direct pleasure of contemplating them at the moment.

Sea and sky had acquired an indigo blue, crossed by green and magenta flashes and sheens, much like the aurora borealis on Earth. The colors didn't melt into, but superimposed themselves on one another with absolute vividness. Then the sun, which seemed to hide itself shyly, overcome by the night, suddenly recovered its golden brilliance – shooting lances of light up toward the celestial heights and into the suboceanic depths. It turned into a flaming red, like the carnations that Martin had seen so often on his native planet, and then pink. Finally, scarlet embers would remain, turning darker and darker, until they dissipated into the near-complete nocturnal blackness.

He disembarked from the ship, and headed toward Cygnus' house.

The door was opened by Fjowla, the housekeeper – a chubby mustaft-jalmannui, friendly and kind-hearted. She had told Martin she had five children:

three mustaft, one kaft and one ouk.

Cygnus had always received Martin in his library, a room whose floor, ceiling and furniture were made of wood, very comfortable and warm in the winter. The owner of the house had many books, published with a very primitive printing system, bound in leather and voluminous, with thick and yellowish pages. Martin couldn't read them because he knew very little of the Jalmannui alphabet, though his ability to speak the language was improving. Almost all of the authors belonged to the caste of the hermaphrodites or intermediates.

But now Fjowla led him to a new room, some 30 square meters in size, where everything except the floor, which was adobe, was made of glass or crystal. The walls, ceiling, table, chairs, clock, utensils. On seeing the guest's look of shock and fear, Fjowla laughed loudly.

"Don't worry, we'll bring you a wicker chair so you feel more comfortable. The master will come in a moment. He told me that he is certain you won't break anything."

Martin wandered slowly through the room contemplating that transparent and fragile environment. Needless to say, he didn't dare touch a thing.

The ak-jalmannui had "hired" him in a rather informal way to teach him some of the languages of Earth. Although Cygnus had never treated him as an inferior, the Terran always noticed a slight patronizing attitude. But soon he also realized that Cygnus' true goal was to interrogate him in full detail about his planet of origin. Martin had thought that this placed him in a superior position with regards to the hermaphrodite. Besides, he could easily get information about the ak's interests and transmit them to his comrades-in-struggle. That's why they had approved of his "employment" on Bay Island, because it allowed him to work as a spy.

How could he have been so simple-minded? Thinking himself cleverer than Cygnus... He played at being a hero so that his friends, and above all Gabrielle, would love and admire him. In fact, she had congratulated him effusively on various occasions for his accomplishments, and suggested subjects about which it would be advantageous for them to learn more. He hadn't understood how fooled he had been until the day when Cygnus told him the truth about Gabrielle.

Cygnus arrived wearing an elegant ivory-colored suit, a white shirt, and a tie, which sported a pin with a natural pearl that on Earth would have been worth a fortune. The suit seemed to jar a bit with his naked feet, shod in open sandals, but they were in Jalawdri.

"Do you like this curious extravagance?" he asked, indicating their surroundings.

The visitor made a movement with his head which was difficult to interpret. Fjowla appeared with a crystal tray, bearing glass cups and a pot containing a dark red tea. Another servant carried in a wicker armchair. The Lord of the House invited his guest to sit, then settled himself onto a crystal chair.

Through one of the room's walls, Martin could see a good part of the bay that gave the island its name, and a full moon over the waters that meekly died upon the sandy shore. There were children bathing.

Cygnus began to ask Martin about his journey on

the ship, since the Jalmannui, with the exception of Khorfu, considered it to be rude to go straight to the point. The Terran's answers were so dry and short that in the end he himself preferred to say:

"Cygnus, forgive my lack of courtesy but I would prefer for us to address the issue you summoned me to discuss."

The other aborted the beginning of a disdainful grimace with his mouth, which had the effect of temporarily disfiguring his face; a face which Martin had always found very attractive, despite knowing that on Jalawdri people with dark features were considered attractive, especially those individuals who were clearly sexed.

"I was very concerned after your last visit," the ak-jalmannui said. "You seemed extremely affected when you left."

"I am better," Martin replied. His hands clenched the wicker armrests of his chair.

"I'm glad. May I speak to you frankly, Martin?"

The guest nodded his head brusquely.

"At first I didn't understand why you went so pale when I told you that I had discovered that Gabrielle had an amorous relationship with her cook, Jerome – who had worked for me beforehand, and who I had fired precisely when I discovered that he couldn't be trusted because of his sympathies toward those who, let us say, are defenders of the current status of Jalawdri. It took me a few days to fully interpret your reaction. In any event, I preferred to verify it with a few investigations, and I have managed to discover some very interesting things. The first is that you and your companion

Lito are a very active part of that resistance organization. I deduced that if you came here so assiduously it was very likely because one of your missions was to keep an eye on me. I suppose that it was Gabrielle who gave you this instruction?"

"No, not at all. It was my idea," Martin responded energetically.

"But she thought your initiative was very worthwhile, didn't she? That's how someone who leads from the shadows must act, making the rest believe that they are the ones who decide. I know her well, your leader. Very well. Dear Martin, deep down you are an ingénue. Not so much for being in love as because of your youth. Most leaders are manipulators, whether they are aware of it or not. Perhaps Gabrielle didn't use you in an intentionally selfish and perverse way. Maybe she just does that with everyone around her. She and I are very alike. We place a good deal of our energy, our time, into making the world be just how we believe it should be. The problem, especially for the world, is that we have conflicting goals. Until now you have only heard the perspective of Gabrielle and her friends. According to that version, I am the enemy – the one who is trying to restore the oligarchy of the ak-jalmannui, to turn this planet into a sex-change theme park. I am the one who will allow our oceans to be contaminated with oil wells. That's what they've told you. But you don't know everything. Do you know what the life expectancy is on the Remote Islands? Less than 40 years. Perhaps you don't know that three out of every ten mustaft-jalmannui across the planet die in childbirth, and that two or even three of every ten babies born don't reach their first birthday. That our illiteracy rates are astronomical. We've advanced tremendously in the medicine of the sexes and are making even greater strides in this area now that it entails a significant source of Inter Credits – but we ignore other problems. We enjoy a freedom you don't have on other worlds with regard to gender identity but that is not enough. I only want for my people and my planet what you have on Earth."

"And you think that what we have is so enviable?"

"We should be the ones to decide that. I won't philosophize any more. You suffer. You suffer greatly because you love Gabrielle, and you've discovered that she has given herself to another. It seems that misfortune is something that never runs out, doesn't it? It is not that difficult to move from the most sublime of loves to the fiercest of resentments, isn't that also true? It is difficult to keep loving when that love is not returned, when they prefer another, when they humiliate you. We feel spiteful, wounded – and wounded people are dangerous. I think that I have spoken enough."

"Yes, that is enough."

"I am going to make you a proposition, Martin. Or rather, another one. Some time ago I offered you the possibility of returning to Earth to be my guide and aide on a trip that I will be undertaking. The most opportune moment was when the ship *Eurydice* returned home after leaving its passengers here. But you quickly answered that you were quite happy here on Jalawdri. Perhaps now you think otherwise. If that is not the case, I will propose something else. I can force Jerome, Gabrielle's lover, to come with me on that ship. Jerome is the son of one of my servants who has debts of honor with me. His father will order him to accompany me, and Jerome cannot refuse because obedience to one's parents is still a basic moral law on Jalawdri."

"And what would I achieve with that?"

"Revenge."

The Terran made no response.

"Logically, I want something from you in exchange. I want to know what you're planning against me, you and your friends."

Martin looked out at the dark night surrounding the crystal urn where they were.

"The plan was to prevent your trip to Earth at any cost. Well, not at any cost. Khorfu was in favor of killing you, but Lito and I managed to convince him that it would be sufficient to highjack your ship when you were going to board the *Eurydice*."

"Oh, thank you both very much. I suppose that is something I owe you thanks for."

"As for... Jerome, I ask you to give me a few days to think about it."

"We'll see each another again in the spaceport when the *Eurydice* lands and you welcome the passengers. You can tell me then what you have decided."

Day 66 of the First Cycle of Spring Jalmannui Year of 1202

The *Eurydice*'s ship-to-planet transport vehicle rose into the dawn sky, leaving behind a wake glittering with light. Stars could still be seen above the spaceport. Martin was seated on a cement step that had become very cold during the nocturnal hours. He took another sip from the bottle of awal liquor.

"What's up, man?" Joanna asked him. "Are you trying to turn into a human volcano?"

"You're the loveliest apparition I've seen in a long time, my dear. Sit down here. I also have an exquisite Earth wine to share. That won't burn your throat."

"And if you treat me so well, why are you treating yourself so badly?"

"Oh, don't start to sound like some self-help manual."

"I've turned up a bit late because your SOS letter arrived with a bit of a delay, so you'll have to update me as to what I've missed."

"When I got home after my interview with Cygnus, I told Lito and Khorfu that I had betrayed them. That same afternoon I wrote to Gabrielle to explain my conversation with the ak-jalmannui."

"And?"

"Well, Khorfu wanted to strangle me. Lito didn't let him but later told me that he could no longer live under the same roof as me. I think he prefers Khorfu's company anyway, and I think that there is something more than warrior brotherhood between them. Gabrielle thanked me, asked me not to return to "her" resistance group and wished me luck after assuring me that she was nonetheless glad to have met me. And journeying on the *Eurydice* is Cygnus – but not Jerome."

"And what do you plan to do now?"

"No idea."

"What was your experience like as a guide and companion to those who came to change their bodies?"

"Very good."

"Well then, you've already got something to devote yourself to on Jalawdri."

Martin shrugged his shoulders. He thought: *When will we all come together again? Lito – my friend, my brother. Gabrielle – my beloved, my brave Antigone. Joanna and I. When will we again walk together? In the depths of my soul there is still love for all of you. Nothing is as pure now as this pain I feel.*

They stood up. The man adjusted his tie, buttoned his long black coat, and shook his feet within their shiny boots. Joanna wore a red jacket, winter leggings, and heels which, to her companion, looked impossible to use. The woman took his arm.

They walked toward the island's port, where the mailboat waited every morning, on its route from island to island, across the ocean.

Choose Your Own Adventure!

I loved the CYOA gamebooks when I was a kid in the '80s—for a while at least. At one point I just started reading a book straight through because I wanted to know all the parts of the story I was missing. Also, I felt like reading only one of the narrative threads was a waste. Buying a whole book and only reading part of it?

I contemplated the complexity of linking all the choices together and creating such an intricate work, or series of related works, a quantum multiverse—although it was a few more years before I was introduced to quantum mechanics and that concept. I wanted to just read it cover to cover and assemble all the stories in my head, but that was overwhelming, so I gave up on gamebooks.

The US Healthcare system is even more complex and more overwhelming to try and understand all the moving parts in one's head. "Even Doctors Can't Navigate our 'Broken Health Care System'" proclaims a Kaiser Health News article from May 2019.

Being sick or injured is stressful, discouraging, even depressing. Some patients feel so overwhelmed by the healthcare system that they delay care.

Or they forgo care because of the cost. Or fear of what the cost might be - it's impossible to know the price tag for a procedure, even though average costs are now listed online. Not every surgery is exactly the same. And costs can vary wildly from hospital to hospital for the same procedure, and for no apparent reason.

Now there are medical bill advocates, a new profession that can be found at some employers, to help people navigate this costly and confusing system.

So much money and effort goes into convincing Americans that our system is the best system that we can have. That single-payer systems, what some call "socialized medicine," won't work here. The lies that marketing genius Wendell Potter told the US about the Canadian health-care system in the '90s (e.g., patients dying in hallways waiting for treatment) are lies that are slow to die.

This isn't to say that other countries' health-care systems are perfect. The UK's system is at least as vulnerable to ransomware as systems in the United States. The EU took longer to approve vaccines. Australia and Japan have struggled to roll out their vaccines. And we desperately need to distribute vaccines in developing countries. But the United States holds the distinction as most expensive in the world, by far. And we're not getting our money's worth by a long shot.

Welcome to the Medical Clinic at the Interplanetary Relay Station | Hours Since the Last Patient Death: 0

by Caroline M. Yoachim

A. You take a shortcut through the hydroponics bay on your way to work, and notice that the tomato plants are covered in tiny crawling insects that look like miniature beetles. One of the insects skitters up your leg, so you reach down and brush it off. It bites your hand. The area around the bite turns purple and swollen.

You run down a long metal hallway to the Medical Clinic, grateful for the artificially-generated gravity that defies the laws of physics and yet is surprisingly common in fictional space stations. The sign on the clinic door says "hours since the last patient death:" The number currently posted on the sign is zero. If you enter the clinic anyway, go to C. If you seek medical care elsewhere, go to B.

B. You are in a relay station in orbit halfway between Saturn and Uranus. There is no other medical care available. Proceed to C.

Why are you still reading this? You're supposed to go to C. Are you sure you won't go into the clinic? No? Fine. You return to your quarters and search the station's database to find a cure for the raised purple scabs that are now spreading up your arm.

Most of the database entries recommend amputation. The rash looks pretty serious, and you probably ought to go to C, but if you absolutely refuse to go to the clinic, go to Z and die a horrible, painful death.

C. Inside the clinic, a message plays over the loudspeakers: "Welcome to the Medical Clinic at the Interplanetary Relay Station, please sign your name on the clipboard. Patients will be seen in the order that they arrive. If this is an emergency, we're sorry— you're probably screwed. The current wait time is six hours." The message is on endless repeat, cycling through dozens of different languages.

The clipboard is covered in green mucus, probably from a Saturnian slug-monkey. They are exceedingly rude creatures, always hungry and extremely temperamental. You wipe away the slime with the sleeve of your shirt and enter your information. The clipboard chirps in a cheerful voice, "you are number 283. If you leave the waiting room, you will be moved to the end of the queue. If your physiology is incompatible with long waiting room stays, you may request a mobile tracker and wait in one of our satellite rooms. The current wait for a mobile tracker is four hours."

If you decide to wait in the waiting room, go to D. If you request a mobile tracker, go to D anyway, because there is no chance you will get one.

D. You hand the clipboard to the patient behind you, a Tarmandian Spacemite from the mining colonies. As you hand it off, you realize the clipboard is printing a receipt. The sound of the printer triggers the spacemite's predatory response, and it eats the clipboard.

"Attention patients, the clipboard has been lost. Patients will be seen in the order they arrived. Please line up using the number listed on your receipt. If you do not have a receipt, you will need to wait and sign in when a new clipboard is assembled."

If you wait for the new clipboard, go back to C. If you are smart enough to recognize that going back to C will result in a loop that does not advance the story, proceed to E.

E. Instead of waiting in line, you take advantage of the waiting room chaos to go to the nurses' station and demand treatment. There are two nurses at the station, a tired-looking human and a Uranian Doodoo. The Doodoo is approximately twice your size, covered in dark brown fur, and speaks a language that only contains the letters, d, t, b, p, and o. If you talk to the human nurse, go to F. If you talk to the big brown Doodoo from Uranus, go to G. Also, stop snickering. The planet is pronounced "urine iss" not "your anus."

F. The human nurse sees the nasty purple rash on your arm and demands that you quarantine yourself in your quarters. If you accept this advice, go back to B. Have you noticed all the loops in this story? The loops simulate the ultimate futility of attempting to get medical care. What are you still doing here? Go back to B. Next time you get to the nurses' station, remember to pick the non-human nurse.

G. You approach the Uranian nurse and babble a bunch of words that end in "oo" which is your best approx- imation of Doodoo language. Honestly, the attempt is kind of offensive. The Doodoos are a civilization older than humankind with a nuanced language steeped in a complex alien culture. Why would you expect a random assortment of words ending in "oo" to communicate something meaningful?

Thankfully, the nurse does not respond to your blatant mockery of its language, so you hold out your arm and point to the purple rash. In a single bite, it eats your entire arm, cauterizing the wound with its highly acidic saliva. The rash is gone. If you consider yourself cured, proceed to Y. If you stay at the clinic in hopes of getting a prosthetic arm, go to H.

H. You approach the human nurse and ask about the availability of prosthetic limbs. He hands you a stack of twenty-four forms to fill out. The Doodoo nurse has eaten the hand you usually write with. If you fill out all the forms with your remaining hand, go to I. If you fill out only the top form and leave the rest blank, hoping that no one will notice, go to I.

I. The nurse takes your paperwork and shoves it into a folder. He leads you down a hallway to an exam room filled with an assortment of syringes and dissection tools. "Take off all your clothes and put on this gown," the nurse instructs, "and someone will be in to see you soon." If you do what the nurse says, go to J. If you keep your clothes on, go to K.

J. The exam room is cold and the gown is three sizes too small and paper thin. You sit down, only to notice that the tissue paper that covers the exam table hasn't been changed and is covered in tiny crawling insects that look like miniature beetles.

Sitting down is a decision that has literally come back to bite you in the ass. If you leap up screaming and brush the insects off your bare skin, go to L. If you calmly brush the insects away and then yell for someone to come in and clean the room, go to L.

K. Three hours later, the doctor arrives. You are relieved to see that she is human. You ask her if she can issue you a prosthetic limb. She says no, mumbles something about resource allocation forms, and leaves. If you accept her refusal and decide to consider yourself cured, go to Y. If you scream down the hall at the departing doctor that you must have a new arm, go to L.

L. A security officer comes, attracted by the sound of your screams. Clinic security is handled by a 6-foot-tall Tarmandian Spacemite with poisonous venom, sharp teeth, and a fondness for US tax law. If you run, go to M. If you are secretly a trained warrior and decide to kill the Tarmandian Spacemite with your bare hands so you can eat its head, go to N. If you sit very still and hope the Tarmandian Spacemite goes away, go to O.

M. Running triggers the predatory instincts of the Tarmandian Spacemite. Go to Z.

N. You use your completely unforeshadowed (but useful!) fighting skills to overpower the security officer. The head of the Tarmandian Spacemite is a delicious delicacy, salty and crunchy and full of delightful worms that squiggle all the way down your throat. Unfortunately, you forgot to remove the venomous fangs. Go to Z.

O. You sit perfectly still on the exam table, and tiny

insects that resemble miniature beetles crawl into your pants and bite you repeatedly, leaving a clump of purple bumps that look suspiciously similar to the scabby rash you had on your arm when you arrived at the clinic. When you're sure the Tarmandian Spacemite is gone, go to P.

P. You have lost an arm and the lower half of your torso is covered in a purple rash. If you decide to cut your losses and consider yourself cured, go to R. If you rummage through the cabinets in the exam room, go to S.

Q. There is nothing in the story that directs you to this section, so if you are reading this, you have failed to follow instructions. Go directly to Z and die your horrible, painful death. Or skip to somewhere else, since you clearly aren't playing by the rules anyway.

R. You sneak out of the clinic and return to your quarters. You search the station database for treatments for your beetle-induced purple rash. There is no known cure, although some patients have had luck with amputation of the affected areas. Sadly, you are incapable of amputating your own ass. Even if you go back to the clinic, the rash is now too widespread to be treated. Go to Z. Or, if you want to see what would have happened if you'd opted to search through the exam room cabinets, go to S. But remember, going to S is only to see what hypothetically would have happened. Your true fate is Z.

S. You rummage through the cabinets and find an assortment of ointments and lotions. If you read the instructions on all the bottles, go to T. If you select a few bottles at random and slather them on your rash, go to T. Have you noticed how often you end up in the same place no matter what you chose? In the clinic, as in life, decisions that seem important are often ultimately meaningless. In the end, all of us will die and none of this will matter. Now seriously, go to T.

T. None of the ointments or lotions do anything for your rash. The Uranian nurse comes in to clean the room and discovers you. If you pretend to work at the clinic, go to U. If you ask for help with your rash, go to V. If you run away, go to W.

   (There is no U, much as there is no hope for patients of the clinic. The nurse would have recognized you anyway. Go to V.)

V. The Doodoo from Uranus (seriously, are you in third grade? Stop pronouncing the planet as "your anus") examines your rash and amputates the affected areas by eating them, neatly cauterizing the wound with the acid in its saliva. You are now a head with approximately half a torso. If you consider yourself cured, go to X. Otherwise, go to Z.

W. You flee from the Uranian nurse but slip on a puddle of slimy green mucous excreted by another patient, probably that idiot slug-monkey that slimed the clipboard. You crash into the wall, and before you can get back up, the Uranian nurse amputates the areas affected by the rash by eating them, neatly cauterizing the wound with the acid in its saliva. You are now a head with approximately half a torso. If you consider yourself cured, go to X. Otherwise go to Z.

X. You are not cured. You are a head with half a torso, and missing several internal organs. Go to Z.

Y. Congratulations, you have survived your trip to the Medical Clinic at the Interplanetary Relay Station! All you have to do now is fill out your discharge papers. You start filling out the forms with your one remaining hand, but you accidentally drop the pen onto the oozing foot of the Saturnian slug-monkey waiting in line behind you. This is undoubtedly the idiot that slimed the sign-in clipboard. You cuss the slug-monkey out with some choice words in French. Choice words because it was rude to leave slime all over the clipboard. French because you know better than to make a slug-monkey angry. You've watched enough education vids to know that slug-monkeys are always hungry, which makes them temperamental.

Unfortunately for you, Saturnian slug-monkeys are far better educated than arrogant humans give them credit for. This one is fluent in several languages, including French. It eats you. Go to Z.

Z. You die a horrible, painful death. But at least you won't have to deal with your insurance company!

Ring of Fire

Moments ago, nearing midnight on this Sunday, I got an emergency notification on my cell phone from the county fire department. Mandatory evacuation due to a wildfire north of thus-and-such boulevard. Why am I still typing these words into the computer?

Aside from the fact I'm a night-owl, of course.

Fortunately, the fire is actually several miles away, on the other side of the neighboring city, and across an eight-lane highway (we call it a freeway here in Southern California). In fact, the evacuation order doesn't apply to my neighborhood, I'm probably just connected to a cell tower near that area. Further, it's raining, and the winds are very still. So, I deem this a low risk.

We've had evacuation orders before, and real close calls with wildfires in recent years. We saw lightning earlier, which could cause a fire—it was my first thought when we saw it. So, I do take such things seriously. And I'm practiced at looking out for fires and understand the risks.

Oh, look at that. About ten minutes later, the county Sheriff has rescinded the order. Says it was sent in error.

But wait! Another five minutes, and the Sheriff has issued a warning of mudslides for the burn scar area, essentially the area that burned so badly last year. Also, that doesn't affect my neighborhood. Those fires were on the mountainside across the valley from me. I could see them well. Watched with my binoculars at night, but the flames could easily be seen with the naked eye.

Those tragic fires, two that merged, one started by a gender reveal celebration gone awry, were blown mostly away from us. But they were huge, and we still got plenty of smoke.

Climate change increases extreme weather. The heat and drought. The rains that cause flash floods and mudslides. The water rolls along too fast, too fast to collect it and restore underground reserves.

As someone with asthma living in the wildfire-prone western US, I can feel the effects of climate change in my own chest. And it's hard to sleep when you're worried that the wind might change and carry the fire toward your house in the night.

The climate is changing faster than many species can adapt. Humans have the advantage of technology, and perhaps technology can alleviate the impact of climate change, or help solve the problem. But what about those who cannot afford to live in communities that are far from polluting diesel truck traffic, those who cannot afford HEPA filters to clean wildfire smoke from the air in their homes, or cannot afford air conditioning when it's over 100 degrees Fahrenheit?

Could our own bodies adapt faster? But what if someone from the present day was transported to the future, how would their body react to a changed climate?

A Passing Sickness

by Paolo Bacigalupi

At first, the headaches weren't so bad. I put them down to the natural dysphoria of being an Arrival. Adapting to the pace of the people, the shifted culture, the technology of a future that I hadn't grown up in, and that now engulfed me; the stress of losing loved ones in an instant, the shock of friends become old while I remained young, all of it.

So of course I wasn't feeling myself. I was twenty-years-into-the-future not myself, and that was even before Amina convinced me to get the Implant.

I met Amina soon after I'd Arrived (or Returned, as Amina called our shocking appearance in the skies over SFO after disappearing for twenty years). She'd recognized me from the news coverage, an anomaly, and as a physics researcher at Berkeley she joined one of the many teams that examined us.

She freely admitted that she'd initially thought of me as her own pet quantum lab rat, and then been surprised to find that she actually liked me. It didn't hurt that we both shared overlapping fields of study, even if I was decades behind in the research.

"How was I supposed to know that you'd turn out to so... quaint?" she said later, laughing.

She called me an old man in a young man's body, but my confused adaptation to her world triggered an unexpected surge of empathy, which in turn triggered a series of less scientific experiments as she tried to teach me the intricacies of thriving in her world.

I'd say something like, "But why would anyone want to do that to their bodies?" as I stared, gawp-jawed, at the woman who now managed my finances, a woman who'd grown her ears to sharp elfin points, sculpted her teeth to fangs, and given herself a twitching cat's tail. And Amina would laugh and shake her finger at me and say, "And why can't these meddling kids stay off my lawn!"

"That's at least two different cultural references, you know."

Unfazed, she'd shrug. "Not anymore, old man."

She called me "old man," but I didn't mind, because she held my hand when she said it.

One of the biggest conversations we had was about the Implant.

"It a minor surgery, Ali. It's got almost a quarter century of testing behind it, so stop being squeamish. I've had mine since I was twelve."

"I just don't like the idea of something in my brain like that. Wires..." I shivered. "I just don't think I want my brain messed with."

"Christ, Ali. Even the really old Millennials have figured out how to use it. You can't have a simpler interface."

"The 'really old' Millennials? Really?"

"I'm just saying riding a bike is harder."

"I'm just saying I don't like the sound of it. It squicks me out."

She muttered something about stubborn old people—and this time she didn't hold my hand.

So I got the Implant.

For the record, I'm man enough to admit that I was wrong; the Implant was all she'd described and more. After two hours of minor surgery and calibration practice at an integrationist's office, I was the proud owner of a NeuralPulse Augmented Living Device, but really, I was suddenly a god. Most people called the devices Implants, despite a plethora of companies and manufacturers. A little stud of an antenna in the earlobe, and an astonishing nano-charged quantum computer drilled through my skill and nestled up against against my brainstem.

And the world came alive.

Before, I'd always been impressed at how much I could accomplish with my phone. We'd all joked when I was growing up that we had Star Trek's tricorders, and wasn't that cool. But now, all that was inside my head, and more. All of it, whenever I wanted it, powered by the electrical pulses of my heart and body. I could talk to anyone I wanted, whenever I wanted. I could whisper with friends across the world while attending the most boring parties, or while watching Amina's bizarre television shows. Exercise trainers materialized before me and worked with me as I got into shape. When I saw some new shirt, or pair of pants, or hat, or backpack, I didn't need to remember the label and look it up, my Implant told me what it was. It simply labeled the item, still on another person's back, and in that second, I bought and shipped it home, the act as quick and triumphant as stripping the pelt from a big game animal.

When I played a videogame, I lived inside a VR world,

every one of my my physical movements tracked and interpolated into the game, the entire world around me become an augmented game zone, full of trolls to battle, castles to explore... With the NeuralPulse feeding experiences straight into my brain, I immersed in new worlds of smells, tastes. I wandered savannah, climbed mountains, excavated ruins.

And the learning! I could pore through novels at a speed that became ever more dizzying, I caught up on the newest physics research from my field. Information poured into my mind, and the more I practiced with it, the more I found I could learn. I learned Hindi in few weeks, and found that I could speak with Amina's grandparents when they called.

Of course, it still took some work to learn, but not in any way that I'd ever understood it. And as the world opened up to me, I saw the people around me differently as well. We were something different. More human than we'd been before. Astonishing power, not at my fingertips, but at the edge of thought.

Everyone around me took it for granted, but I saw the difference. I saw the magic.

"We're so much more than we used to be!" I exclaimed, after having sat in a virtual room with Amina and her parents, all of us comfortably conversing despite the fact that they were in Bangalore, Mumbai and London, and we were in San Francisco.

Amina watched it all with indulgent amusement. "I told you so."

But then the headaches started.

At first, they were small. Sharp shocks of pain right behind my eyes when I looked too long at someone's clothing, trying to find the cheapest price, or when I called a car to my house for a drive into the city, a sudden nausea, manifesting as soon as I tried to make the reservation.

It was intermittent at first, the pain, and I put it down to my own failure to adapt. Everyone else used the Implants all the time, and if they could handle these minor side effects, well, wasn't that the way of all technology? Technology was always advertised as providing utopia, and—inevitably—there were downsides, not discussed.

I'm no technophobe, but I've bought enough shiny tech toys over the years to know that the seductive promise of a magical new tablet is always more luscious than the pedestrian reality of trying to find a power outlet when a battery runs low.

Well, maybe you don't remember that problem, but I still do. Get off my lawn.

So, there were occasional headaches, occasional body twinges, strange sweating hot flashes. A tradeoff for being able to learn Hindi in three weeks. I'm not one to complain, so I pushed through. The discomforts were fleeting, and I wasn't even sure that the Implant was the cause. Just Arriving in the new present was stressful enough to trigger panic attacks and migraines.

Once, at one of our support meetings, I asked the other Arrivals about it.

We met, less than we had initially, but still regularly, all of us bonded by our strange Arrival in this new future. Expatriates from the past, all out of water and confused. I had never known a more disparate group who I suddenly felt kinship with. Our frustrations, our confusions with our families who had moved on without us. We met in person in the beginning, ten or twelve of us, sometimes fewer, sometimes a few more, a rotating cast of others, and, as we got our Implants, too, talking to one another at other times as well, keeping a channel of support where we could meet up and vent about the insanity and glory and loss that we felt having skipped twenty years of time.

"Is anyone else having headaches, when they call a ride share?" I asked.

"I get panic attacks," Avery said, shrugging. "My wife. I see her sometimes and I..." he shrugged again. His wife was old, had a second husband, also old. John lived with them, and one of their adult children who had failed to leave the nest. "No headaches though."

A few others did have headaches, but nothing that seemed connected to car shares. The others were all fine with the device in their heads.

"What about shopping?" I asked.

"I go shopping with my daughters every weekend," Selma said. Her daughters, who lived in Seattle and Mexico City, all of them meeting up to try on clothes in a virtual mall in a virtual Dubai. "It doesn't bother me a bit."

Others agreed. They shopped, chatted, organized, studied, arranged their lives with the new device and never felt a twinge.

"Are you following all the integrationist instructions?" Selma asked, when I described the pain I'd felt when I'd banked a check from my employer.

"Well... I skipped a couple tutorials."

"Probably it's that," Avery said. "You should be glad you've got a job still. I'm having a hell of a time getting employed. If it weren't for Milly, I'd be homeless."

"I think they're doing it for the PR," I said. "But yeah. I just wish I could figure out how to do the banking."

I resolved to go back to the drawing board and follow all the early practice tutorials, all the guidelines and warnings of the integrationist more completely. Not to overuse the device. To make sure that I was calibrating my eyes and movements with the device correctly. I've never shied away from hard work, so I resolved to work harder at practicing with my mind to use the new tool.

But the pains kept coming, and few were as painful as each time I cashed my company paycheck. Seismic Research, LLC, had been kind enough to keep me/re-hire me after my Arrival, but it was impossibly difficult to do work for them. Banking a paycheck was nauseating, but so were other activities, the basic research I was doing, communicating with others in the company at drill analysis sites. Migraines were becoming a daily reality, every time I logged into their offices with my Implant.

On one particular occasion the pain was so great that I actually hallucinated, becoming so disembodied that I found myself fragmenting. I found myself standing next to myself, a long chain of me, one grabbing onto the next, onto the next, stretching from the past, all the way into the future. But more than that, these selves were sickened and ghostly version of me, haggard, and undying and miserable and each one lurked behind other people who seemed to resemble me, and who as I writhed on the floor, in pain and hallucinatory shock, morphed and became children, mixes of myself and... Amina, oddly enough. *My* children? *My* grandchildren, beyond them. And me, clinging to them, weighing them down, riding atop their backs, like some demonic homunculus. It gave me a sickening feeling, seeing myself, hanging upon the backs of my following generations, violating their lives.

I found myself standing next to myself, a long chain of me, one grabbing onto the next.

It happened twice like that, the hallucination, and after that and I couldn't do my job anymore. I quit and found a job pulling coffee in a local coffee shop. That, at least, was something I was equipped to do and it didn't require NeuralPulse to do it, at least not as much. Espresso, despite refinements, was still much as it had always been. A physical act, and a physical experience. It became a comfort for me to come to work every day and pull shots, to watch crema pour forth, thick and perfect. This, at least, was unchanging.

I was lucky in that I'd had investments that had grown, untouched for twenty years while I was gone, so I had some breathing space to figure out my new role and new place, and Amina approved of me doing something easy while I learned the innovations of business, the law, the culture, and tried to adapt to her world.

But the headaches persisted, and the hallucinations also got worse. When I bought my new UrbanSack backpack, pleased that I would be able to blend in better with the people at the coffee shop who I found myself calling the "cool kids," I experienced a trembling pain that ran from my back, down to my feet, and an ache in my leg muscles that made me feel as if I'd been working at the coffee shop for days, instead of hours. I nearly fell over.

A doctor diagnosed my pains as a stress reaction to Arrival, and with a few taps on an emotional regulator, he guided my NeuralPulse to adjust the drug cocktail of my mind, thereby calming my sense of disorientation. Good drugs, regulated through the Implant, my own brain spitting out necessary balancing chemistry that once would have required dangerous and imprecise pills.

But the symptoms kept coming.

Calling rideshares became excruciating, and they also started generating those same horrifying hallucinations of myself scabbed upon the backs of my unborn children, pressing them down, smothering them.

And now the pain began hitting me in grocery stores as well. One day when I bought a mango, I collapsed, finding myself a few minutes later with concerned people looming over, myself on the floor, sweating, gasping, all my muscles aching.

I began avoiding cars, and all sorts of powered transport also began to make me feel vaguely uncomfortable. Even public transport weighed on my body. The only thing that really provided relief was biking. I found a second-hand bike, bought it with the fist-bump transaction that was now traditional for purchases between Implanted people, and started riding that everywhere. I also stopped using the Implant to shop off other people's bodies, and instead hunted for all my clothes from thrift stores. The older the clothes were, the better, I found. No physical reactions at all for that. Nor for nice, physical barter.

Which was how I switched jobs from pulling coffee to working at Salvation Army. Over time, even cashing my coffee shop paychecks had become uncomfortable, a vague uneasiness that had slowly built.

The new job—despite paying almost nothing—worked better for me, plus providing me with first pick opportunities amongst the mountains of clothes that arrived weekly in undifferentiated bags. I burrowed into those masses of throwaways, and there, I found a womb of comfort. A bit of the past, now lingering in the present, much like myself.

I tried to hide how dissociated I felt from the world, but Amina finally noticed something wrong with me.

"Old man?" she asked one day, as I cooked eggs from a couple of chickens that I'd been raising in my apartment.

"Mm?"

"What are you wearing?"

I looked down at my shirt. "This? It's flannel. I got it at the store today." It had a rust and brown check pattern, with a small tear in the sleeve, but still entirely serviceable. "You like it? I think there were some others. I can get one for you. It's hard to find flannel these days. Have you never seen flannel before?"

"Huh."

"What?"

"It's a little... old."

"It's not old. It's vintage. Any way, old things come around. Just like me."

"No. I mean... it's like, musty-man old, not, like, vintage Millennial hipster old."

Admittedly, the tear in the sleeve wasn't really great. "I'll sew the sleeve. Then it'll look new again."

"Ali... old man... I can't really help you fit in, if you don't at least try."

"What's that supposed to mean?"

"You can't wear clothes that look like they're twenty years old."

"Well, I'm from twenty years ago. That's me. If you don't like it—"

"You're different." She was studying me.

"I'm not. I'm the same as I always was. Maybe you're just finally realizing that dating an Arrival is a little more complicated than running a physics experiment."

"No." She was frowning. "You've always been weird. Anachronistic, sure. But now you look like a bum. You barely go anywhere, except on that bike, or unless you can bum a ride from someone else. And this garden you have in the living room... and the chickens now...."

"I like the chickens! They're calming."

"Why didn't you ever buy that new tablet you wanted?"

I looked away. "It's expensive. Anyway, I don't need it. Like you said, Implants do all of that now."

"But you said before that you wanted something you could hold." She was studying me. "Go ahead. Buy one. Try it."

"I don't want to."

"Is it the money? I'll give you the money."

I glared at her. There had been a tablet, light, foldable. I craved having a keyboard to write, something physical. I knew just the one I wanted. "Fine." In an instant, I reached out with the Implant and purchased it.

I sank to my knees, groaning.

"Ali? What's wrong?"

The nauseating feeling of living forever, of pressing down and smothering my unborn children, followed immediately by a tightness in my lungs, pains in my leg, my back, pains shooting upwards…. I shook with the pain, struggled to move. The pain was everywhere in me.

I couldn't even crawl. I whimpered, shaking and immobile. Huddled on the floor. Amina's eyes widened. "Ohhhh. Ali….."

"Wh- what? Wh- why are you looking at me like that?"

"We need to get you to a hospital, right now." She was already glancing away from me, using her Implant to call a ride.

Outside the apartment windows, I could see the empty electric vehicle coming up to the curb. Amina dragged me out. The pain was receding, but my body still shook with the residual fear and memory of it.

"What's going on?" I asked.

"Have you still been having those headaches?"

"Not as many, actually."

"Any hallucinations?" She stuffed me into the car,

and climbed in after. The car pulled away from the curb, smoothly joining the flow of automated traffic. "Any hallucinations?" she pressed again. I looked away. Feeling uncomfortable admitting it. Feeling a failure. A feeling that I didn't belong in this gleaming place where carbon diamond bridges spanned the bay, a crystal palace that I wasn't meant to be a part of.

Amina stared at me, hard. "Have you been having hallucinations, Ali?"

The miserable expression on my face answered her question. To my surprise, her expression softened. "Oh. You poor boy. You poor baby boy." She pulled me close, cradling me against her. She kissed me my cheeks, my forehead. "It's all right. I'll fix this. Why didn't you say anything? Why didn't you tell me?"

I looked away. "So, you don't have... some of these... these pains?"

"Pain? God no! Hallucinations? You think we're crazy in the future? Who would want that in their heads?"

"I thought technology always gets oversold!" I protested. "I assumed that you all just accepted it! Or there was something wrong with me, and I just needed to... to..."

"Just needed to tough it out."

"I don't like to complain," I said miserably.

She rolled her eyes. "Nice going, macho man."

"I'm not macho."

"You didn't tell me you were in pain!"

"I was embarrassed."

She sighed and hugged me again. "Just so you know, no, it's not normal. None of this is normal."

The car was pulling up at the hospital. She helped me out, supporting me. A few minutes later we were in with Dr. Ethan Jarrett, Neural Integration Specialist.

"Hard time shopping?" Dr. Jarrett peered into my eyes with a small pen light.

"Not always?" I ventured.

He and Amina exchanged significant looks. "Where do you work?"

"Salvation Army."

Another significant look passed between them.

"What did you do before working in a thrift store?"

"I was a seismic analyst for a geology research company."

"What kind of work is that?"

"I helped them create algorithms to analyze geological layers, and identify natural gas zones, and to follow frack results, for better flow control."

Dr. Jarrett's eyebrows went up. "So you worked for a mining company?"

"Well, we did data analysis for a number of resource companies, natural gas and oil among them."

"Mm hmm." He sounded pleased. He plugged a device into the tiny port behind my ear. "Can you grant me access to your Implant please?"

I closed my eyes, and suddenly he was inside my head. I was with him. Amina joined us, too, holding my hand. Dr. Jarrett was studying what appeared to be a library of physical books, poking at them, pulling down volumes as they connected and stretched and shifted into one another. It was disorienting.

"Well, the good news is, you've got a virus," he announced.

"That's good news?"

"I knew it!" Amina said.

Dr. Jarrett smiled. "You should be grateful to your girlfriend. From the looks of it," he said as he pulled out more volumes, all of them sticky with cobwebs, "It's been rewiring you for quite some time."

"Rewiring?"

"The Implant integrates into a number of sensory pathways in the body. It can give pleasure, and also discomfort. There are safety parameters to not overwhelm the mind, but the the access routes are powerful, regardless. And, in their own way, habit-forming. It can trigger sensations, as I'm sure you're aware from your experience of gaming and the feedback loops of fast-learning."

He crouched down and started digging through my mind. "Ah. Here." He pulled up a shimmering snaggle of data, flows of 0s and 1s twisting, worm-like in his hands. "It used to be harder to root out, but now..." He smashed his hands together, crushing it, turning it to dust. "It's an old virus. Mostly obsolete. You must have missed a firmware upgrade on install. Shoddy work, whoever did it." He shook the digital dust off his hands.

Almost immediately, I felt lighter.

"Better?" He smiled.

"What was it?"

"Well, the original code wasn't intended as a virus at all. It was originally an Estonian art/tech installation, very avant-garde, called Blue Marble. Intended as a sort of gamified system of experiencing various buying behaviors.

"Its genius was that it used modern data mining to track the impacts of a user's economic behaviors. It drew from a variety of publicly available databases to assess products: their sourcing, their carbon impacts, distances traveled in their supply chain, chemical additives, fair labor practices. It used everything from social media to ratings of political oppression and labor abuses in different countries to environmental standards, to news of government fines and class action lawsuits to create impact scores. It then pushed those "costs" onto the purchaser, but did so as a physical experience. So... if you buy a tablet and it requires rare-earths from a mine in Mongolia, you might end up sweating and worn down physically from the slave labor involved. Or if the carbon costs of a purchase—or of the work you do—will have long-term impacts, lasting for generationally long periods of time, you will experience hallucinations of—"

"Weighing down your children." I shivered at the nauseating memory.

"Precisely. Unfortunately, the code got into the wild. Several Blue Marble variants swept the globe at one point, piggybacking on the original art design of the first: Long View, Guiltifer... there were others. You can look it up, and get all the details. In any case, it's a barbaric abuse of the Implant. A vicious sort of Puritanism, as you experienced." He made a face of disgust. "That said, you don't need to worry. We should be able to adjust most of this, and get you back to normal."

"*Most* of it can be adjusted?"

Dr. Jarrett looked pained. "From what I can see, you've been living with the virus far longer than most people would have reasonably tolerated. Most infected people immediately recognized there was something wrong and had it excised. When the code was first released as a living art exhibit, most people tried it for a day or two and then shut it down.

"You, on the other hand, have been living with this... beastly thing... for almost six months. It's done some damage. Essentially, you've been living under the influence of a virtual Skinner Box for the last half a year, feeling pleasure at certain behaviors, pain because of others.... Your brain may never fully recover. You've been abusively trained, and getting the responses out fully, well," he shrugged, "it won't be easy."

"You have to be able to do something," Amina insisted. "He's barely functional."

"No no. Don't get me wrong. He'll be much better. He's already better, yes? And when I'm done, he'll be a new man. Now, off to sleep with you now. Let's see if we can get this to... work...."

A few hours later, I came out from under the anesthesia to find Amina holding my hand.

"How are you feeling?" she asked.

I felt light. Unburdened by anything. I hadn't realized what the virus had been doing to me.

"I feel good. Really good." I couldn't help smiling. "It's like having bricks lifted off me."

"Why don't you try ordering a car?"

I hesitated.

"Go on."

I imagined the car, my destination. Ok'd the trans-action with the Implant. No pain. No weight. No hallucination. Just an instant of desire, followed by gratification.

Magic.

*   *   *

I'm much better these days. Learning to use the Implant again. It still takes a little effort to get past the fear, but every day it improves, and now, after a year, I've made real progress. I hadn't realized how deeply the virus wormed its way into my brain. How it had burdened even my smallest decisions.

Now I can order what I want. Go where I like. Enjoy the fruits of this wild new civilization, full of bursting optimism, big data, and technology. Amina approves once more of my clothing choices. No more thrift store shirts with holes in the sleeves.

We also have a child now, a daughter.

Life is good. Really good.

But sometimes, I catch myself on the verge of buying something, wondering how much it would hurt if the Long View virus were still policing me. Would it now take into account the existence of my daughter, Maya? Would its hallucinations now include her? Would I see myself dragging down her future, when I purchased an Indonesian sofa, or a flight to New Zealand, or a mango from Mexico?

A pound of carbon released into the atmosphere lasts for a thousand years, the echo of a present moment, rippling far out into the future. It's a truth we don't often come to grips with—the idea that we all live on inside the future, even after we're gone. Much like myself, transported into this future time. Myself, an echo from the past, echoing into the future, always present, never-ending, never to be escaped by my descendants. Some part of Maya will never escape me. But isn't that true for all parents and their children? And in the meantime, this present moment is full of glittering excitement, full of luxuries and learning and the bustle of daily life. So many good things are all around us.

But sometimes, I can't shake a trickle of fear. The fear that Long View put into me, the fear that the things I do today are not as gleaming and glorious as their packaging would appear. The fear that the things I do today are indeed freighted with consequences, and others pay their costs.

On most days, I'm able to stifle that fear, and the virus hardly has any hold on me.

In a few more years, I probably won't feel it at all.

See Eye to Eye

My third-grade class had some great guest speakers that I remember to this day. The musicologist who visited multiple times to teach us the history of Rock Music, the biologist who brought tarantulas and taught us not to fear them by letting them walk across our hands, and the young blind man. We learned about braille, how he used a white cane, and how to guide a blind person if they need your assistance.

Braille seemed hard to learn. But today there are audiobooks and text-to-speech/speech-to-text software, there are screen readers to browse the web in audio format, and we can interact with digital assistants (Siri, Alexa, Google Assistant) by speaking to them. For people with impaired vision, the world continues to present obstacles, but is more accessible than ever before.

Still, loss of vision is the greatest health-related fear in the US, according to multiple studies conducted before the pandemic. Loss of memory, loss of speech, broken bones, all take a back seat to vision. And technology is starting to restore vision itself, at least partial vision, for some.

There are several retinal implants being developed, and they may be used to treat common conditions such as macular degeneration, which often occurs in people over 50 and causes blurriness and blindness in the center of the field of vision.

Such implants could one day be used as a computer interface for Augmented Reality. What happens when people with implants literally see the world differently than others?

Color The World

by Congyun "Mu Ming" Gu
translated by Sarah Huang

*A*nd now am I come to shore, as thou seest, with ship and crew, sailing over the wine-dark sea, unto men of strange speech, even to Temesa.

I was eleven when I first read *The Odyssey*. Athena brought to Telemachus the news that his father Odysseus had returned from Troy. Butcher's elegant translation was full of troublesome Greek names and foreign inflections, but one word jumped out at me.

"What is wine-dark?" I asked Mom.

She winked at me. "What do you think?"

"I think Homer was using it as a metaphor." Rhetoric lessons at school came to mind. "The sea's blue, isn't it?"

"Homer was blind," Mom let out a sigh. "And the sea isn't always so blue. The word blue didn't exist in Ancient Greek. Remember the beach in Long Island? How did the ocean look at sunset?"

I tried to recall those summer days when I rode by the beach. The sky would be turquoise-green, like the water, but it turned violet and agate-colored where it met the sea. On the horizon, milky white clouds shaped themselves into an Olympian palace while crimson-gold rays, like heavenly rivers, poured into a darkening sea.

I liked summer vacations. During those months, I was surrounded by seagulls' cries and the sea breezes' murmurs instead of my classmates' knowing whispers.

To be honest, I didn't find ancient poetry and oil paints all that bad. When I was even younger, I used to sit in a stroller and watch as Mom painted—she would often lose track of time until I began to bawl. But by the age of eleven, I had understood that life wasn't about verses and pigments.

I had learned this the hard way.

"I don't know what wine-dark is," I shrugged.

Mom was quiet for a while. "Homer used the same word, *oinpos*, to describe bulls. In the *Iliad* he talked about how 'two *wine-dark* oxen both strain their utmost at the plow, which they are drawing in a fallow field...'"

"It's okay, Mom," I cut her off, "You can just say that you don't know, either. For all I care, you can say that Homer got Retinal Adjustors. Who cares? Everybody has them—everybody except me."

Mom closed the book. "Amy, I hope you will at least wait until—"

"No, Mom! Why can't I get RA like everyone else?"

"But you're still so young..."

"Mom, you just don't get it!"

Mom knew five ancient languages and could recite page after page of epic poetry. She understood the minute differences among dead words from extinct tongues, but she didn't speak a language that could describe the world we lived in.

I didn't understand why she was so against Retinal Adjustors. She made me too self-conscious to even invite my classmates over. I was already the weird kid with no RA, and the bizarre gray painting hanging above the fireplace would confirm that the weird kid had a weird Mom.

Snow Storm: Steam-Boat off a Harbour's Mouth. As far as I was concerned, Turner must have painted it after going blind like Homer.

Much like my life back then, it was dominated by gloomy colors and crude strokes that obscured actual shapes.

*   *   *

"Hey there, dork!"

The boy walking up to erase the chalkboard slammed into my elbow when the school bell rang, and I dropped my pencil. By the time I picked it up, half of the writing on the chalkboard was already gone.

"Come on, don't—"

The boy threw the eraser. I dodged, and it struck the corner of my desk. "Having trouble seeing, huh?"

"There's nothing wrong with my eyes..."

"You can't even tell blue from green!" he looked down at me, quite smug.

"I just don't have RA..." I tried to defend myself, "And I can tell them apart. I just need a bit of extra time..."

"Yeah whatever. Why don't you wear your Mom's ancient glasses? They'd suit you," the boy circled his eyes with his fingers, his beautiful green irises full of mockery, "you ugly frog."

"Shut up!" I couldn't take it anymore, so I grabbed the eraser and threw it back at him. But I wasn't nearly fast enough, and he ducked it like it was nothing. Not a single speck of dust got on his clothes.

"Alright now, let's go." Angela stepped over the eraser with an easy grace. The boy blew a raspberry and took her school bag.

I looked at Angela. Her blond hair glinted in the winter sunset, and her ears were so white they appeared nearly translucent. Even without Retinal Adjustors, she looked stunning to me. It was no wonder that they all adored her. She turned and gave me a sweet smile, and it was a sight straight out of an oil painting.

But I could read her lips' exaggerated, deliberate movements.

She said, "Bye, Froggie."

Now alone in the classroom, I stared at the rhetoric class notes on my notebook. I always got good grades, even if I sometimes had trouble reading the text on the chalkboard. But where did that get me? I was a straight A student as Mom expected, as in the stereotyped Asian American Moms' expectation, but at that time, in that kind of situation, it was not doing me any favors.

I never told Mom any of this for some reason, but at that moment, I realized it was time for a change.

I slowly tore the unfinished page out from my notebook. Then, bit by bit, I ripped it up.

*　　*　　*

When I was twelve, Mom finally agreed to let me get Retinal Adjustor implants. I woke up early on the day of the operation. Opening the closet without turning on the light, I dragged my fingertips across thin laces and silky ribbons, picturing all the blooming colors I'd be able to see on my old self. In the end, I chose an ivory-colored knit slip dress; the RA's color filter effects showed up best against a background of white.

"Don't be afraid, sweetheart. It's a small operation." Dad was holding my hand, and I could feel the sweat on his palm.

"It's okay, Dad. It's just going to make me *normal*," I said playfully, all the while pointedly ignoring Mom. She stood in a corner, wearing a familiar gray rabbit fur coat. Too much foundation on her face made her look like a mannequin. She always wrapped herself in gloomy colors; the whole of her person, like her books and paintings, was perennially covered by a layer of ancient fog.

"Here," the doctor pointed to a cross-section model of the human eyeball. The transparent vitreous, looking like a crystal ball, constituted about four-fifths of the organ. The gold-colored membrane right behind it was the retina.

"The science behind Retina Adjustors isn't all that difficult. We know that the retina is made up of rod cells that are sensitive to light and three kinds of cone cells that are sensitive to color. In the old days, when people walked in dark woods on a moonless night, the rod cells within their eyes would capture photons and enlarge them, all without interference from the other cells. And when they visited the beach on a sunny day, the color-sensitive cone cells enabled them to quickly adapt to the bright sunshine." The doctor seemed used to giving this explanation. Every word sounded unquestionable.

"With our newest Retinal Adjustors, we implant these biological multielectrode array chips into your retina, right between the layer of rods and cones and the pigmented layer, so that your rod cells and cone cells can receive light better. The retina's coder and decoder would then convert the neural signals into visual recognition. It's just like changing your digital camera's image sensor—you would still be using your own lens."

"But they are so much better than my own lens," I cut in, eager to show off all the tidbits I'd learned from my classmates. "They can capture so many more visual details, and they can automatically adjust for lighting and color saturation. I'll never have trouble reading the chalkboard again."

"You might never be able to take them off, either," Mom shook her head, "Think about it, Amy. These aren't traditional glasses. They might be your new eyes..."

"That's why I don't want to get stuck being blind forever!" In my mind's eye, I kept seeing Angela mouthing that word at me. Froggie. Froggie.

"The RA technology is really quite safe. We've come a long way during the last ten years, and visual system enhancement technology has matured considerably," the doctor's voice was measured, she was obviously in familiar territory. "In fact, most children receive RA implants at an even younger age. They're like the hottest mobile phone model, the hottest social network app, and the hottest fashion trends all rolled into one. There is no fighting it. Of course, it's not a purely business decision, but RA technology is the future."

"Everyone in my class already has it. The adjustors have this shared filter function, too, you just need to get in sync to use it," I withdrew my hand from my father's palm and stared at the inner side of my wrist. Once the implant was done, I knew, a dot of light would appear there.

"That's right. The adjustors can, through programmable interfaces, alter the electronic signals in real time," the doctor nodded. "In a way, you might say that they open up an infinite number of worlds for you—and you can share them with everyone else."

"Yeah, isn't it amazing?" I was loud, and that was on purpose. Maybe Mom was content to hide from the real world in her dimly lit study, but I wasn't. She had no idea how cruel—and how wonderful—the world was for kids. Or maybe she just didn't care.

But the thing is, we are the future.

"May I have a word with you in private, Doctor Chau?" asked Mom.

I don't know what was said between them. Dad kept me company, and neither of us spoke a word. Dad only left when the doctor came back into the room. The doctor began to input adjustment parameters into the operation system, and the nurse injected anesthetic into me: an icy pinch under my eye, then total darkness. The operation was about to begin.

"I'm wondering," I asked, "Doctor Chau...is it possible for adults to receive RA implants?"

"It's possible, but adults often have a harder time post-op than children," the doctor's voice sounded a little far away, "Not to mention our current technology doesn't support certain cases. For example, those who have issues with transplant rejection, and...."

That's all I heard before sleep overtook me. Inside the dark dreamscape, a thousand brilliant colors were beckoning me over.

*   *   *

"Hey, Angela," I mustered up the courage to wave at the girl coming my way. Her pale pink skirt had mint-colored ribbon bows on them. It looked like a blooming tulip. "I like your pink skirt."

"Oh yeah?" she arched her blond eyebrows, "So you finally got it, huh?"

"Yeah," I straightened out my hemline all casual like. Its dark blue fabric, with glittering star lights, complimented my hair—no longer black like my Mom's but a light brunette. A faint green light flickered on the inner side of my wrist. I knew that I had become a wholly different person in her eyes, as my RAs have been synced automatically with hers.

"Not bad. You know, before, we all thought that you had a bit of a problem with this..." she tilted her head and pointed to her eyes.

"No! I didn't! I just... I just didn't get the RAs!" I said in a hurry. "But it's different now. It's all different now. I'm the same as you guys."

"Not quite. There is one thing left," she squinted at me, grinning.

"What?"

"We don't call this color pink. It's *Ashes of Roses*

from the Thorn Birds Filter Collection. *Ashes of Roses, the perfect combination of tenderness and cruelty.* Likewise, your skirt isn't blue. With the Filter Collection, it's called *Royal Midnight, the color of melancholy.*"

"Oh..."

Suddenly I realized that the adjustors didn't just change the colors and degrees of lighting. They had changed the very language used to describe this world.

And language....

Mom's bedtime stories came back to me in a haze. From fairy tale curses to Greek mythical prophecies, language always had the power to transform everything.

Those stories are for suckers. A voice whispered to me. I blinked and tried to drive away those random thoughts—unnecessarily, in fact, because my field of vision would always be 100% clear now that I had the adjustors.

"Okay, Ashes of Roses," I nodded. "Sure thing. Want to try my Royal Midnight? I think it will go with your hair great."

*   *   *

I majored in Human-Machine Interaction in college. Upon graduation, I joined a startup that produced filter plugins for Retinal Adjustors. Human Biological Engineering is the hottest thing out there now. Individuals with RFID chip implants no longer have to worry about forgetting their keys or wallets, while 3D-printed hearts, lungs, and kidneys have dramatically shortened the organ transplant waiting list.

Young people are flocking to bio-hacking, but I remain most interested in RA-related technologies. Visual connection is one of the most powerful channels of communication with the outside world. I will never forget how, before my operation, I was denied entrance to that world.

Nobody objects to upgrading their physical hardware anymore, Mom excepted.

She tried to convince me to go to graduate school for Art or Literature. But after Dad passed away from a car accident while on a business trip, I moved out and rented a small apartment of my own. After that, she could no longer ask me to do anything.

Actually, ever since middle school I talked with her less and less.

The adjustors were a part of the reason why. In the ten years since my operation, as RA technology reached increasing heights, its visual impact came to defy all previous human experience, and it could only be communicated through the filters' own language. I couldn't adequately explain to Mom what was *Super Atmosphere III*—the color that you might get from light rays rising through the atmosphere, shifting through light blue, dark blue, purple, dark purple before finally settling into a velvety black, laced with ever-changing strands of light. It was my favorite sleep environment. Nor could I describe to her the boy who was my first crush—he had a tiny galaxy in his eyes, with stars falling down around the edges of his irises.

Electronic monitors, initially geared for traditional human visual perception, also made the shift to RA technology. Instead of Pre-Information Age graphics with jagged pixel edges, we had hyper-realistic images produced by RA algorithms. These were a bit like the old 3D images, but far more lifelike. In fact, if it weren't for the monitor frames, we'd have a hard time telling the world inside the monitor apart from the one outside it.

But Mom wouldn't have anything to do with it. In a way, I think it's her attitude, rather than the adjustors themselves, that sealed the uncomfortable silence between us. She wouldn't even use electronic readers or non-invasive reality-enhancing glasses, choosing to bury herself in those ever-duller classic books and artworks instead.

I know that she took up painting again after I left for school. I've seen her works—old-fashioned still life and landscape pieces, nothing to boast about. The adjustors' dynamic lights don't show up on congealed oil paint.

"You like them?" she looked at me expectantly, a little girl waiting for a pat on the head.

"Umm...they're pretty good," I tried to sound as sincere as possible, "but really, Mom, are you seriously not going to try—"

"Amy, I wish you would turn that thing off and see the world with your own eyes, say it in your own language," she peered at me from the other side of her old tortoise shell glasses, her voice dull and dry. "Listen to your mother, you can learn from my experience. Remember, the colors you see...."

"Black isn't always black, and white isn't always white. Okay, fine, but is that why you showed up for

Dad's funeral dressed in gray?" My voice rose as a long-dormant emotion began to break through, "Mom, I'm all grown now, but you just haven't changed at all. You have to realize that these days people value *actual experiences*, not the kind that supposedly comes with age."

"You mean those mass-produced artificial experiences?" Mom twisted her hands, "But you were such a special child, Amy. Remember how—"

"No, I wasn't special. You just wanted me to be. I never liked those classic stories and oil paintings," I turned my back to her because I didn't want to meet her eyes, "I just want to be normal."

"Amy..." she stopped. I could hear the unbearable surprise and disappointment in her voice.

"I'm not a kid anymore," I forced myself to get it all out, lest the guilt hold me back. "I've seen more things than you have, and I understand more things than you do. By leaps and bounds. Don't fence yourself in with all those hogwash clichés—and don't try to keep me there with you. Get out there and take a look at the new world."

She finally went quiet. For a moment, I thought I heard a stifled sob.

I turned my back and left that dim, old house. A drizzle was coming down. I turned on *Turrell No. 7* in panorama mode, a visual simulation of Venus' Girdle. The gloomy sky softened under the reflected Rayleigh scattering rays. I took in a deep breath and felt my frantic heartbeats returning to normal.

Sorry, Mom, but I'm all grown up now.

*　　*　　*

It was raining like that on the day of Dad's funeral too, with icy raindrops dripping down from black woolen coats. A pair of luminous cherubs, rendered by the priest, held up an arch of light on the top of the cross. Amidst the foggy rain, a heartbreakingly familiar projection floated in the middle of the bright halo. I told myself that Dad would always watch over me from inside that halo, just like how he had held my hand as I rode on his back then, so long ago.

But all this was alien to Mom. Even as she stood right next to me, she had hidden herself under her thick foundation and antiquated sweater. She could neither see nor understand the priest's speech about the Three Crowns in the Kingdom of God. She only looked up at the lonely, ashen-white sky, her glasses wet in the rain.

I could hear people's whispers between the priest's words. I was no stranger to the lowered tone of voice and to people avoiding eye contact. The adults played by secretive rules, but I understood what hid behind those considerate smiles and turns of phrase. I knew that I shouldn't be thinking about those sorts of things during the funeral, but rationality was no match for emotions.

Nobody was going to shelter me from the rain anymore. Mom couldn't be counted on.

I didn't know if she really cared about Dad's passing or what I thought. I almost completely gave up on her after that. Inside our house, the doors were often closed. Our mother-daughter chats stopped. I moved out not long after.

No, Mom. I probably can't change how you think, and I certainly don't want to turn into you.

*   *   *

When technological advances alter the language we use to describe this world, it changes the way we perceive the world itself. Language alone is powerful enough to mold the human mind—back in college, a Linguistics professor had told us about the Sapir-Whorf hypothesis, the basis for many science fiction stories about acquiring superpowers by studying extraterrestrial languages. But I feel that in this age of relentless change, the hypothesis has far more real-world implications than people have imagined.

"Yo, need to expand the vocab DB again for audio assistance." An IM from Tariq pops up on my monitor and drags me back into the present. "RA user data from last week popped. 70+ new high-frequency words."

I turn around and scan the cubicles for Tariq's silver-gray mop of hair. A senior engineer of the company, he is my current partner in pair programming.

I know that the color of his hair is as real as it gets, no filter required. "Genetics," he had explained at our initial meet.

"That's pretty cool," I didn't want to make a big deal out of it. "I know people who don't use adjustors either."

"I'm not that cool," he grinned as his wild hair strands morphed into tangled mini rainbows.

"Yeah so... feels like we should take another look at the whole setup." I keyed in my response in a flurry.

"New filters bring new words in, and old words fade as filters delete. We've updated the DB 3 times already in the past Q. The turnover rate is too fast."

"You might want to calculate the acceleration," he added a string of numbers at the end of his sentence, the code for a grinning emoji. "Coffee?"

"Sometimes I get the feeling that things are gradu-ally...spinning out of control." I opened a bag of Skittles and emptied its contents onto a paper plate. "You've probably heard how our choice of language affects the way we think," I poked at the candy, "and we are helping to accelerate this process—"

I tried my best not to think about my mother's face. "Think about it. RA technology has become entrenched in every aspect of our lives. From cinema screens to mobile apps, from commercial slogans to internet media, everywhere people are bending over themselves to match their language to what they see through the filters... It won't be long before—actually it's already started. People can't communicate, can't think, without RA. But...but what about the people who don't have it?"

"Skimmed or whole milk?"

"Come on, Tariq. I'm serious here."

"Skimmed it is, then," he shrugged. "It's not a big deal, Amy. We invent technology, and technology reinvents us. It's a tale as old as time."

"Still, this is going way too fast...."

"Why the pessimism?" He shook the milk, poured, and drew something on the foam. "Weren't you the one who said, during your interview, that adjustors, like all advanced tech, bring people closer together? By sharing the beautiful world we see with one another—"

"Maybe I was totally wrong." Deflated, I could feel the Skittles melting on my fingertip, growing into a sticky mess, just like my thoughts.

Tariq handed me the latte. On its surface, he had drawn a face with two eyes but no mouth. Something hit me, and I almost couldn't bring myself to look at the thick milk bubbles floating on top of the brown liquid.

"I majored in Physics back in college," said Tariq slowly, "even now, I believe that rational reasoning is the way to understand the physical world. But I also believe that if we limit ourselves to Newton's color theory and abstract algebra, we will never understand what the ancient Greeks saw when they looked out to the horizon on a *wine-dark* sea."

"So what did they see?" I squeezed a Skittle on the tip of my fingers. And I had forgotten our initial topic altogether—I just wanted to solve the long-forgotten riddle.

"Um, I was just trying on the new Eyes of Homer..." he looked surprised. "It's the first thing that comes up when you open the app store."

The blind poet had brought color to that long-gone age with his words, the same words that will now lead me to the truth. How can I describe what I have seen? The ancient Greeks had no trouble telling the myriad colors of this world apart, but they cared more about lighting than palettes. Wine-dark didn't just denote a color between red and blue; it meant an ever-shifting combination of brightness and movement. An ocean shimmering under a setting sun, the oxen's sweat-glistening bodies... what I saw, what I *felt*, is the thick liquid inside the paper cup, sparkling and whirling.

"This is incredible. Reverse engineering through language. It's like...seeing the world through the ancient Greek's eyes."

This algorithm, in a sense, reflected both the physical reality and what the people of old had learned from it. And it's all rooted in language. The Sapir–Whorf hypothesis didn't tell us the whole story. The choice of language hadn't obscured our vision, nor had it deprived us of the ability to think. It's just a pair of glasses that we wear.

I turned off my adjustors. How long had it been since I last did that? I tried to summon those archaic adjectives to my mind—or rather, I tried to forget the new words that came with the adjustors. You need to take off your glasses before putting on another pair... you need to forget your native tongue, however temporarily, so that you can better learn a new one—yes, Mom is giving me the look again, from the other side of those tortoise shell frames.

"Amy? Are you okay?" Tariq's voice floated in from somewhere, "So *Peter Pan's Journey* is your color, too. I had no idea."

My heart skipped a beat.

My wardrobe had long been dominated by swathes of Pele's eye, Yuki Onna, and Mermaid song, with or without adjustors on. I don't like any color that has a hint of green. It reminds me of a certain slimy amphibious animal and a certain pair of unkind eyes.

*   *   *

"Mom, there's something that I want to ask you..."

I hesitated as I stared at the voice message that I'd just sent. Eventually, I opted for the "recall" button. Maybe Mom would hear an unfinished sentence, or maybe she would see the indicator of a recalled message. I'm not sure what she would make of this, but we both knew that I had stopped going to her for help long ago.

But what should I do?

My apartment was beyond messy. The floor was littered with takeout boxes and balled-up dirty clothes. The curved desktop monitor had both the Munsell Color Wheel and the visible light spectrum on display.

And I had piles of print-outs, too: Democritus' theory about color, Dalton's "Extraordinary Facts Relating to the Vision of Colours," and Mark Rothko's abstract paintings of solid color blocks.

But none of them could tell me if the colors I saw were the same as everyone else's.

Could I really be... colorblind?

As farfetched as it may sound, it's far from impossible. I had a hazy memory of Mom saying "blue" while pointing to a clear sky, of her telling me that the new leaves in the garden are green. I had learned to match each color with a name, but what if my cone cells are in the wrong place? What if the wavelength for blue, when it reaches my eyes, is translated into what is commonly understood as green? Would I even realize the difference?

I would believe that the color blue simply looks

green. I've learned to associate certain perceptions with corresponding linguistic symbols, but it hasn't occurred to me to ask what these symbols really mean. Perhaps what they represent are not physical properties but mental perceptions. I will never know how the world appears in the eyes of others.

To use the computer as an analogy—my eyes would be like the input end, my brain the black box, and my mouth in charge of output. When other people receive the signal for green, they perceive green and utter the word green; the same signal reads blue to me, but then I say "green" all the same. My own peculiarity is thus buried, hidden. I'm different from them, not just because of my eyes but because how I've internalized my response to outside stimuli. I'm different on the inside.

You can't even tell blue from green.

Froggie. Froggie.

I was besieged by fragments of childhood memories. Unlike my peers, I was slow to pick up on the subtle differences in color. I always thought it was because I didn't have the adjustors, but the truth could be far more terrible.

The adjustors allowed me to see what the others see. I embraced its vocabulary and thought myself a part of the "normal" world, but did I really belong there? Mom went on and on about how I was special. She must have known all along. But why didn't she ever tell me?

So I wasn't not normal, after all?

I suddenly remembered a post on the company's Disqus. We had designed the in-game interface for an enhanced-vision game, and a player was complaining that it wasn't user-friendly: "I love this game, but I'm really having trouble seeing the targets' glowing outlines. Everything looks the same to me."

The post didn't gain much traction. One of the few replies it received was: "The new UI is sooo cool. Are you colorblind or something? If you don't have RA, don't troll here just quit and find some s**t for yourself."

The OP didn't take kindly to that: "F**k RA. First the traffic lights got 'upgraded' so I couldn't drive anymore. And now you have to ruin my favorite game, too? I didn't ask for any of this!"

At the time, I didn't spare a second thought for that post. I simply marked it as N/A, No Action. We receive hundreds of user requests every day, and we only respond to the most important issues—"most important" being defined as things that affect the largest number of people, or have the most impact on the company's earnings report. Special requests like colorblind accessibility are not a priority for us.

But now, staring at the account's registered location, I felt like somebody had punched me in the heart. The dull pain made me want to throw up.

The Disqus account originated from the country where my Dad had the fatal car crash. Like Mom, Dad never got RA implants. He was always careful on the road, and I thought it was a cruel stroke of fate. It had never occurred to me that maybe he was like that video game player, maybe he was simply overlooked by someone like me, someone who marked his need down as No Action.

Maybe I could have seen the world as he saw it. At least, I could have gotten close to him. Every single cell in my body is still carrying his DNA, and my eyes are the same color as his. What kind of world did my Dad see? Had he ever talked to me about it?

I could still catch a glimpse of the distant past through the ancient Greeks' words, but I had ceased to hear the voices around me. I should have been one of them.

Maybe I could have stopped it from happening.

No....

I disconnected the adjustors as guilt swept over me. Re-connected. Disconnected again. The world now looked different... or maybe not. What is real in all this? The world that the others saw... was it really a better one?

My vision grew murky as dizziness descended. I shut my eyes in alarm. I could hear myself whispering, saying that it's all in my head. I tapped my temple with stiff knuckles, then opened my eyes again, fully expecting the light—but it's no use at all.

All the colors were gone. I was surrounded by darkness.

Did I just go blind?

I'd never known such fear. Now I got what people meant when they say how minutes pass like hours— no, like days and months and years. In my mind's eye, I saw somebody picking me up from the floor and getting me to the hospital, I saw myself lying in the hospital bed, weak and helpless. Filters, adjustors, colorblindness, abnormal vision... a bunch of definitions whirled in my mind, but the darkness was absolute, and it defied all words.

When I consider how my light is spent

Ere half my days in this dark world and wide

Was it still possible to be a blind poet in this day and age? The name Homer springs to mind before everything goes dark.

*   *   *

"Amy. Can you hear me, Amy?"

Someone called for me from afar, in the darkness. A cool, tender hand landed on my burning forehead before moving away.

For the first time in what seemed like forever, I found myself yearning for that voice and that touch, a light in the darkness.

"Mom..."

"Don't be scared," she held my hand tightly, "It's going to be okay. You just had a temporary bout of blindness because of unstable eye pressure."

I opened my eyes with trepidation. Then there was light.

And tears blurred my vision once more.

"I didn't know.... I mean, about Dad...I...." I couldn't even get out a coherent sentence. "Why didn't.... Why didn't you tell me?"

"You were so afraid of being different. Everyone was scared. I was, too," Mom sighed, "I just wanted to protect you, but I was wrong."

I raised my head in surprise. Mom?

Her eyes, tired as they were, glinted behind her

glasses.

"Every one of us is special, but at the same time quite ordinary," Mom brushed my hair behind my ears, "It took me a long time to understand."

She put a headset on me.

"You still need to rest your eyes. Close your eyes, Amy, and listen."

I lay back down on the bed, still shivering. Mom's voice comes through the headset, just like how she read fairy tales and legends to me at bedtime, all those years ago. But this time she was telling me a different story, one that turned my world upside-down. My breath hitched and, like Homer's first audience, I could hold back neither laughter nor tears.

It was Mom's diary.

*   *   *

January 25th, 2034

I met Joe at the ski resort today. And just like that, his eyes had me mesmerized. They are colored with a light icy blue laced by a thousand different shades of green, and lilac, and lazurite... How is it even possible for someone to have eyes like that? He probably laughed at me though, because I looked so dumbstruck.

The thing is, I quickly realized he's probably color-blind. His ski suit is green, the ugliest green I've ever seen. It looked like an avocado six months past its "best before" date. And it's got these dirty-looking orange streaks. I was giggling in front of him the whole time—I couldn't help myself—and that confused him to no end. I think I'll need to take charge of his closet. But the upside is that I don't need to worry about other girls hitting on him on the trails.

*   *   *

May 30th, 2038

Yes! The last batch of flowers got here in time for the wedding! White peonies picked fresh from the Fairbanks Farm this morning. Budding white gardenias for my bouquet. White candles, white lace tablecloth... white, white, white for each and every thing.

Joe was apprehensive and asked me if I was sure about my color choice. How can I make him understand? He can't see that white is not white, like how the snow looked when we first met. I told him to picture the color of opal—a color that is, in Pliny's words, "a refulgent fire of the carbuncle, the glorious purple of amethyst, the sea green of emerald, and all those colors glittering together." It can hold its own against even the deepest, richest colors in a painter's arsenal. That's what white looks like to me.

And once again, all that went completely over his head. He kept nodding, though, as if he really did see it. I had to kiss him, then and there. White... white is how he looks when he tries to pretend that he "gets it", when he earnestly searches for a word to describe what I see....

White is how my love looks.

*   *   *

November 1st, 2040

Amy has arrived in this world. When I first laid eyes

on her, all wrapped up and tiny, I couldn't believe that she came from me.

She looks nothing like me. I'm olive-skinned, but she's very pale, her tiny blood vessels look like cream-covered blueberries. She's the wrong color, I kept telling the nurses. It took them quite a while to understand what I was talking about, and even longer to calm me down with their reassurances. I know, it's absurd, she doesn't have to share my skin color. But it just keeps bugging me and refuses to go away.

Colors are special to me. I've long understood that most people can't see as many colors as I do. By the age of seven, I was already the most singular student in my art class. I wasn't that good at drawing, but anyone who's ever seen my paintings said that they could instantly tell they were mine—nobody else could use those colors like I did. And I hadn't even managed to convey a hundredth of what I saw to the canvas.

I hope that Amy will take after me. If she turns out "normal", she will be confined to such a dull and boring world.

*   *   *

July 6th, 2045

I've had it with Joe. He dropped a slice of apple on the floor, but he couldn't tell where apple ended and where the wood flooring began. To me the piece stood out like a chunk of lime-colored salami, but he just couldn't see it. Unbelievable.

We almost had a fight over it. I don't know what's

wrong with me.... I've heard that they're doing trials for some kind of retina adjustment technology. Maybe that will make Joe normal?

I've started putting Amy next to me as I paint, hoping that she can soak some of it in. She might be a little too young for this, but Cezanne and Monet have such vibrant colors, and I hope she will embrace their magic.

So far, it hasn't worked.

*   *   *

September 2nd, 2047

I'm at a loss for words. Amy is complaining that she can't tell her teacher's writing on the board—blue chalk looks the same as dark green. I am seized by a terrible sense of premonition.

I asked her to spot the subtle color differences in the Impressionist paintings. She couldn't.

Amy can't tell the color blue from green. It's not as bad as Joe's red-green colorblindness, but it falls far short of normal vision, let alone mine.

Amy. When she came into this world, I had such high hopes for her... hopes that now sting with irony.

Should we let Amy get the adjustors? Joe and I had a heated discussion. I couldn't imagine my daughter living in a world with missing colors, but Joe said that it wasn't that big a deal. He didn't feel like he was missing out on life.

That's because you don't know what you're missing. I tried to tell him. Think about it, a completely different world, with more details, more clarity, more vividness, full of endless possibilities. Once you see it, how can you confine yourself to anything less?

"No, Mieko, sweetheart, I've also seen things that you've never seen." He was smiling as he said this. "Lagrangian mechanics can open up a whole new world for you. Once you understand the language of those equations and symbols, you'll understand how the universe exists in a state of terrible harmony and equal fragility. Human emotions—indeed, human lives—hold no meaning... but none of that can stop me from listening to you as you describe the wondrous sights of this world, Mieko, or feeling Amy's warmth as I cradle her in my arms."

Language is like a pair of glasses, he said. It lets us see things that otherwise escape us, but we need to decide when to put it on... and when to take it off.

We decided to wait and let Amy choose for herself in a few years. It needs to be her own decision. Before then, we'll do our best to keep her condition from her. My peculiarity might have won me praises, but Amy won't be so lucky.

I made a call to Amy's teacher.

*   *   *

April 12th, 2053

I don't have a lot of friends. Whenever I met up with those ladies, I was always distracted by the spectacular colors on their faces, so I really couldn't fit in at all. They complained about having to repeatedly call my name in order to bring me back to earth.

Maybe Joe is the only one who can put up with me. At least there is that.

I had hoped that Amy, after she received the implants, would be able to see the same things as me and appreciate all the subtle touches. But that hasn't come to pass. I can feel her drifting away from me. She no longer reads my favorite books, and I can't understand her trendy words, just like she can't understand the language I'm using.

Joe doesn't try to make me learn Lagrangian mechanics. What, then, can I ask of Amy?

Now she doesn't want to paint with me or even look at the paintings at all. She'd rather stare into nothingness. I know that she is now in a world that I can never reach.

I had my initial consultation for an adult adjustor implant today. After the preliminary check-up, the doctor said that she was very interested in my abnormal color perception. She is now waiting for the complete test results to come back.

*　　*　　*

April 29th, 2053

Tetrachromacy. I've never heard of that word before.

An extraordinary condition, according to the doctor. Normal humans only have three kinds of cone cells, one each for processing the colors red, green, and blue. People born with tetrachromacy, however, have a fourth kind of cone cell that allows them to process other colors. This type of X chromosome mutation causes color blindness in males and, usually in the case of females, tetrachromacy.

A similar chromosomal mutation has sent Joe and

me in opposite directions. A normal person sees about a million colors, Joe far fewer than that, while I can distinguish nearly one hundred million colors. As for Amy, she got dealt the worst hand possible.

Current technology doesn't allow for people with tetrachromacy to receive implants. My visual nerve pathways are far too complicated for the adjustors' algorithm to meddle with.

I will never see Amy's world now.

Maybe it's time to let her go. She is growing up fast and blooming into a young lady. Pink acne has appeared on her fair face, but with the adjustors' filters, she doesn't mind it too much. My own acne caused me endless torment because they looked so grotesque. Even now I can't leave the house without putting on makeup. Without a thick foundation layer, my hypodermis blood vessels stand out far too much with their turquoise green, plum purple, and burgundy red.

Maybe the world she sees is one that's better than my own.

*   *   *

December 19th, 2057

Joe has left me.

He just lies there, his eyes tightly shut and his face a pallid white. All the colors are gone. Ruby, amethyst, and emerald. The color of death.

Black is far too rich for death. In black I can see violet purple, Prussian blue and jade green. It reminds me of starling feathers and the ocean just after sunset.

And my heart is nothing but a fistful of ashes.

*   *   *

April 25th, 2060

Amy will graduate soon. She's a healthy, intelligent, and confident young woman. Just about perfect in every way. She also knows how to take care of herself. With the adjustors in place, her color perception has been normalized. I no longer have to worry about how she might end up like Joe, unable to tell the red light from green in a country with adjusted traffic lights.

I am old now. My time has passed, like all ages must. Now I can only try to recapture the bygone days from those increasingly foreign words. They are like mine caves that sleep in the darkness.

It's the same with people. A terrible thought has been haunting me of late—why do people like different colors?

To Amy and Joe, the same lights translate into similar colors bordering on dull, but in my eyes, they are so stunning that I can hardly breathe. Do people with normal vision really see them in the exact same way?

Nobody really knows. Each of us is like an isolated mining cave within the dark, and we will never know how the physical world is reflected in the cave next to us. The truth of the physical world is like a formless gray fog, and it's our individual minds that give it its actual shape. Our perception re-molds the world for us, even though it's the only world we can ever know.

What connects the cold, isolated caves isn't what we see but what we say to each other. We can't define our individual experiences, but we can give them a standard name. It's with the help of these names that we fall in love with each other in such a mad, chaotic world. What a miracle it is that, even though Homer's age of wine-dark has long passed, even though Joe's white is nothing like my own, we can still share a trace of common feeling.

You are drifting further and further away from me, Amy. There is nothing for me to do but to accept it and make my peace with it. All of us are too occupied with what we see, so much so that we forget how to listen and how to speak. Your Dad understood all of this, but he is gone.

The diary ended here. And my eyes, though tightly shut, were brimming with tears.

I understood then. I understood why the blind poet's words could touch us so.

* * *

"Now you see lightning tearing through mustard-yellow clouds as the sky rumbles in the distance. The angle of view gradually shifts from the heavens down to earth. You focus on the damage caused by the thunderstorm, right beneath the clouds. The gyrocopter that you're piloting is caught inside this web of thunder and lightning, and its fuselage bounces in the squall..."

"What's a gyrocopter?" asked Jack. All our guests were people who couldn't, for whatever reason, receive RA implants. He was the oldest out of the bunch, but he was also the one most interested in immersive games and movies.

"Uh..." I was briefly stumped, unsure how to explain such a common term to him. "It's a single-person aircraft. Really nice build, but not great in terms of stability..."

"And then, the rain and the wind—" Mom chimed in, "to quote Robert Frost, *'they so smote the garden bed, that the flowers actually knelt.'* Right?"

Mom was the manager-cum-caterer of our little "Mind's Eye" club, not to mention its very first audience member. We organized a special "experience scenario" for the club every weekend.

"Umm...that's right," I tried my best to recall those verses and all the traces they had left on me. "To create this scenario, I used the International Space Station's atmospheric record data. But yes, that's what I tried to convey through this experience."

I wasn't sure what I could actually achieve with my words. Listening to me was, of course, a far cry from seeing the actual sight with adjustors. Besides, it wasn't like we had a big audience. But I knew that some of them made three-hour treks from the suburbs to come here, and some of them gripped their tea cups so tightly when they listened, like they were riding a rollercoaster and hanging on for dear life. It wasn't an easy job for me. Often, I had to turn off the adjustors, or even use a blindfold, in order to find the right words and lead them into a world they'd never known.

They say that I'm their eyes, but I know that it's them who have taught me how to see for myself.

"Ah, so it's actually kinda like that painting, isn't it?" Tariq pointed with his chin. He was on auto-follow mode for this scenario but seemed more interested in my childhood home.

I turned and sucked in my breath. It was *Snow Storm: Steam-Boat off a Harbour's Mouth*, Mom's favorite painting. Whirlwind and gigantic waves, snowflakes and sea mist. The canvas filled with nothing but chaos. Every shape had been obscured, and every color had been meshed together, but the artist still managed to preserve the most minute differences between them. Even though I couldn't really tell them apart, now I knew that when my Mom looked at this, she saw a spectacle that was beyond our human reach. Nature's transcendental grandeur and majesty—that was what I wanted to convey when I designed this scenario.

"To paint this, Turner had the sailors tie him up at the mast as the boat sailed into the storm," said Mom with a faraway look on her face.

"Just like Odysseus," the two of us said in unison. Our eyes met, and we smiled at each other. In this moment, our worlds contained the same colors.

Shelley to Milgram

Bioethics, that is, the ethics of medical and biological research, is at the core of science fiction from its very birth with the pen of Mary Shelley's *Frankenstein*. Some stories represent unethical experiments as evil, motivated by evil people desiring to do evil.

There are certainly examples from history that we recognize as evil. Josef Mengele, known as the Angel of Death who conducted medical torture and administered poison gas to Jewish people and others at Auschwitz during WWII. Black men were injected with syphilis in Tuskegee, Alabama, from 1937-1972. American doctors in the Philippines injected patients with bubonic plague and cholera in the early 1900's. Many of these examples are perpetuated on marginalized populations and tied to racist attitudes toward the subjects.

Not all examples of unethical experimentation are so blatant, though. The Milgram Obedience Study, itself criticized as unethical, is often cited as an important study that helps to explain why the people of Nazi Germany could be compelled to commit the atrocity of the Holocaust.

In the experiment, an authority figure (an actor pretending to be a doctor) instructs the participant to press a button to administer an electric shock to another person when they answer a question wrong, i.e., the victim - but the victim is also an actor. The study showed that the closer the authority figure was to the participant (e.g., in the room vs. a voice over an intercom), and the more legitimate the authority figure appeared to be (e.g., wearing a white lab coat as uniform), the more likely it was for the participant to continue inflicting pain, even when the victim complained, cried out, or faked a heart attack. The proximity of the victim had the opposite affect as the authority figure: the farther away they were, the more likely that the participant would continue administering shocks.

But this understanding of the study is incomplete. It also looked at the reasons the participants gave for obeying authority when it appeared that they were doing harm to someone else. They were overwhelmingly motivated by a desire to serve the cause of science, to further human knowledge and understanding. This higher purpose is why they volunteered in the first place. They wanted to be of service to humanity.

So, the bigger danger, perhaps, is a sense of mission. This pitfall is not lost on me, as someone who works in a faith-based health science institution. Of course, most modern institutions have ethical review frameworks in place to try and mitigate this risk, but no system is perfect. Without a critical sense of ethics, it's easy to convince yourself that the ends justify the means because you're serving the greater good, or God's will.

Fish Dance

by Eric Schwitzgebel

Falling. Rebecca and I are falling. My daughter and I—so high it seems impossible that we could survive. We are in the back seat of a taxi that has somehow unhitched from its arcing track between the skyscrapers.

Theory 1: Your last thought is your least important. It is a dead-end wisp that will vanish in an instant, with no effect on anything. Theory 2: Your last thought is the secret culmination of your life, potentially altering the significance of everything that came before. You might affirm it all, regret it all, have that final moment of redemptive insight. Theory 3: Your last thought is an opportunity—your one chance to undergo an intriguing death experience, maybe an overdose of an amazing drug, maybe the feeling of surrendering to the sea in a storm against the cliffs.

The wind mounted as we fell, whistling fearfully through the door frame. Rebecca floated, eyes closed— angelic? mermaidine?—left hand pressed against the dashboard, a dancer mid-air, school uniform and black hair billowing. Her right hand brushed the taxi's soft inter-Face, which wore an expression I had never before seen in an AI. Could a taxi know enough to fear death?

I wanted to reach toward Rebecca, hold her, make my last thought a thought for her. She was drifting toward me, her book bag elevating off her lap as her legs straightened. But my arms would not respond. I looked down at them, and they seemed foreign objects. Instead of love, I thought, my final thought would be that my final thought would be of final thoughts instead of love.

*　　*　　*

I woke sweetly relaxed, tingly in the head, vacant elsewhere. I opened and closed my mouth, shaping a groan. It seemed somehow the perfect groan, with a new interesting harmony from my chest cavity. The worried nurse who entered my field of view was the perfect nurse. Then came the perfect CEO of St. Vincent's Northeast, some perfect lawyers, my wife Sara with my perfect teenage son Abe—a team of angels drifting through honey!

"R-?" I had overestimated the power of gravity, so maybe she was here too?

Sara paused, then looked toward the blank wall to her right, maybe flinching away from me a little—but beautiful, how the hospital lights brightened her cheeks!—then she slightly shook her head. "No."

Abe wouldn't look at me either. His face was swollen, tense, tear-glazed.

The expected sadness didn't arrive. My guts didn't twist, my stomach didn't sicken, my throat didn't ache. Instead I thought: No adulthood could have made Rebecca more complete. Brevity is beautiful. A Chopin etude. To want it to continue past its final note would be a failure of understanding. Or rather, the wanting is itself the very coda that perfects it.

Then I thought: What are these tingly drugs? I

imagine saving my grief in a glass box; my future sadness will finalize this perfection. The power button on the back of the nurse's P.A.D. is therefore the ideal button! It is the circular mandala of the universe itself. The mandala swirled and grew, a spiraling tint across the hospital room.

. . . ~ the procedure must be entirely voluntary ~ . . . said the CEO?

Something about cost-benefit analysis, something about the price of the equipment behind me which I pictured blooming like ten thousand flowers, something about insurance limits, my irreparable body, about a magnificent new Christian mission . . . since I was an engineering professor at Loyola I would under-stand risk ratios—the words swam from his mouth like slow fish—expected utilities, why they couldn't pay for even one more day unless I committed to—?

Theory 4: Cost-benefit analysis is the holiest of all things. It is the pinnacle of human wisdom and I the golden sacrifice upon it. I luxuriated in my magnanimity.

~ It must be entirely voluntary [fish-voice] but it will . . . three months at a million a day . . . you must not change your mind ~

Sara's face was the perfect riddle! I nodded because dead-Rebecca had tied an invisible ribbon to my chin. And I continued to nod as I watched Sara's hand guide mine across form after form thrust before me by the magical lawyers, and then the Cardinal of Los Angeles arrived!

The Cardinal's dark sad face. Her swooping glorious Earth-angel red.

*   *   *

In my dream, the disciples were not lined up all on one side, but jammed together around a small round table in a dark room, noisy, arguing. I was leaning in toward Jesus, near his yellow ear, smelling someone's sour feet. "You don't even exist!" I hollered.

"You'll give me a 10% credence, Isaac my baby," he said. "11.3% after this dream."

"Rebecca?" I asked.

"Simply multiply!" Jesus said, tearing a piece off the suddenly-paper tablecloth and scribbling illegible figures on it with a chewed plastic pen.

"10% times infinitude, 90% times void," I figured.

"Plus 1% times everything else," Jesus suggested, while another disciple bumped an elbow against his head, sloshing bad wine down the side of Our Savior's (10%) face.

"Z% times infinitude is . . . "

"A very large expectation!" said 10% Jesus, tearing off a new strip of paper for me, eyelash thin but infinitely long.

*   *   *

The drugs diminished and I crashed down into pain and grief. The drugs returned and I soared up again. Rebecca was a tombstone crushing me, which I couldn't see past, then the stone became helium and the world fell away beneath us, a tiny thing—but where was her face?

*   *   *

Per the agreement, I would be amputated, sliced,

and sacrificed. My recorded cognitive patterns would become the template for a new type of AI. Engineers measured my head, opened my skull, crusted my brain with devices, rerouted my facial nerves. They peeled back my cheeks and worked electronics up through my sinuses. In a certain subclass of my high moods, I nerded out with them, listening to their plans to scan and prep and slice my brain.

The best AI can't be built from scratch. It needs a scanned human brain as template. A fully detailed scan is fatal, exposing the brain slice by slice—and even so the quality is too poor to transfer the whole personality and intelligence.

It would have been too expensive to keep me alive anyway, with my irreparably damaged body. And the Church had an intriguing plan for a new type of sacramental AI. There'd be weeks of prep, preliminary nonfatal scans, arguing about design, a bit of theology on the side.

A keyboard was mounted on a metal arm below my face to the right. I could flick my eyes from key to key, and my eye-tracker would detect the motions, then three blinks to send. In this way, I learned to speak in a slow, synthetic voice.

They replaced my body with a shapeless tangle of iridescent nanocarbon pipes and plastic bags. I became only a head, transfixed.

*   *   *

When Sara's belly had just begun to grow with the thing that would become Abe, we visited a friend of hers in Guadalajara, who had a giant tank of tropical fish.

"Viven en el paraíso," said the friend, Sun-yi. Sunny. *They live in paradise.*

"Pero no son peces," said Sara. *But they are not fish.* Sara switched to English, "They are only fragments of fish. They don't encounter a full world. There's no risk, no learning, no choice, no gain or loss. You've taken demented slices of fish and put them on loop."

"They are happy," said Sunny, touching the aquarium glass with two long fingers. "You need suffering? You need la vida complicada?" *You need a complicated life?*

Sara looked at me, but I declined to take sides. "I propose a fish sacrifice," I said. "For their sins, they can suffer vicariously tonight. We will crucify some tilapia upon the dinner plate."

After Sara was asleep, I sat in the friend's living room, watching the fish in the dim light. I could hear a bed squeaking two rooms down—Sunny enjoying a slice of bliss with the short middle-aged man the restaurant had sent over with the tilapia.

*   *   *

A demon bit through my phantom left leg, just above the knee. I contorted my face, though lacking lungs the loudest noise I could make was tooth clacking.

Sara lifted a wormlike tube from the rack beneath me, squinting as if trying to puzzle it out. "This here is the torture-pain tube," she said. "Part 673HB1.2.9a6, delivered on rush from the eighth plane of Hell. The doctor installed it because she wishes she could have more anal sex but her husband isn't up to the job."

The white nurse by the white sink held up a bright red bag. A margin of electric hostility seemed to separate Sara and her, who never acknowledged each other. "Now, Professor Isaac," the nurse said, "you're ready for your new nanites, aren't you?" The nurse's blue-gloved hands reached past my face to the apparatus behind me, then returned holding a mostly empty bag.

Tomorrow's bags hung from her cart in a line, whatever was in them waiting to become a piece of me. Red? Black? Sad? Lucid?

*   *   *

Abe had been teaching himself the philosophical literature on personal identity and artificial intelligence. "It will totally be you, Dad!" he said. "It's the future of AI. The Church is really doing it. They're cutting edge; they're pouring an ocean of money into it. Way better than a taxi AI, way better, Dad, nothing like a cleaning bot!" Abe looked a little guiltily down at the cleaning bot who happened to be polishing the floor at that moment, but the bot's inter-Face smiled easily up at us.

"Hello," it said.

Abe continued, "Those future people in the rosary beads will have your memories, Dad. They'll be real people, really conscious. And just like you're the same person as that ten-year-old kid on the skateboard thirty-five years ago—just like that, those people will be you. They'll remember me, they'll remember Mom, they'll remember this. Some of this. Some. Enough. Think, Dad. A billion years of joy in millions of bodies! Who needs Heaven? You'll still be going long after I'm dead, long after my eighty-greats-grandchildren are dead! You, the eternal twenty-five-year-old, remembering Mom and me, and Becca. Doing whatever you want in that bead—blissing out, flying, whatever—no pain at all! Crap, Dad, I'm totally jealous. I want to be the one in the crash, doing this, becoming a new template mind."

"Bot, stop cleaning a minute," I had my synthetic voice say.

"Yes, Professor Lee," the bot said, smiling again.

"How much do you remember of your old life?" I asked.

The bot's inter-Face frowned slightly. "I am instructed not to answer that question."

"What caused the dissolution of the United States?"

"That topic exceeds my parameters," the bot said, frowning again. Two feathery dusters unfolded from its sides like arms and it spun them idly.

"Dad," interjected Abe. "It won't be like that. Slicing up prisoners' brains is the old tech. Those old templates for limited AI, that's exactly what the Church is finally moving past! You'll be general AI, with real self-awareness. No cognitive constraints. Not like them. Not like the old stuff."

I pictured the taxi's inter-Face, as we were falling. "In a tiny world," I said.

"How big does a world have to be, Dad? What's wrong with a rosary bead? Plus, there'll be millions of you everywhere!"

Sara said nothing, seeming to be checking mail or something else on her P.A.D. But after Abe had gone back to school, she leaned toward my left ear and whispered, "Isaac, we're going to replace your body and screw the Church." Straightening back up, she raised her middle fingers and waggled them in front of my face.

* * *

"Do you envy the fish?" Sunny had whispered in my ear, touching my shoulder, that night in Guadalajara.

I had fallen asleep on the soft leather couch. I was dazed with sleep and wine, excited from dream. Slowly, Sunny's hand slid down my chest.

Theory 5: I would have let her take me that night, had fear and shame not immobilized me from the neck down. 5A: And that would have been a good thing. 5B: It would have been a terrible thing. The equation will not stay put.

* * *

In the vids, the Cardinal had a way of shifting her lips contemplatively to the left. Tall, Jamaican-accented, in the brilliant color of her rank, she praised the courage of the twelve volunteers. She emphasized that although the beings in the rosary beads would be as capable of pleasure as any animal, only God could create genuine eternal souls. The optional new beads would only add a modern variation to traditional atone-ment—like caring for a plant or puppy to help redeem one's sin, but in a certain way much better because of the vast potential pleasure the new AIs would experi-ence. From human sin, AI ecstasy. I watched on repeat as my medications rose and fell, and the videos took very different shape depending on my mood. She was visionary saint. She was thin claw of the devil.

Sara clicked off the video. "We've got six weeks!" she said. "Is that what you're going to do?"

My synthetic voice: "What else I do?"

Sara uttered some un-Churchy words. Then, pointing right between my eyes: "I'm working on it. Don't go permanently fishy-brained on me, Isaac."

Commentators speculated about the Rosary Project. The Church would rack a huge profit, some said. The (supposedly) Free City of Los Angeles would come even more under its domination. Sinners would count and spin beads, launching tiny new worlds. Later they would watch the worlds they'd booted, adjust the parameters of their creations, manipulate a limited range of events, maybe experience their creations through immersive virtual reality. There would be collectible sets and unique beads with rising after-market value. The two most addictive ideas in history, religion and video-gaming, would finally become one.

The worlds would tick on and on, unstoppable once launched—worlds of unmixed, repeating joy for the AIs within them. But could an AI really feel joy? Or was it always only outward show? If Jack the Ripper had only launched enough tiny worlds, would he have been a benevolent man in sum?

* * *

Sara sat on a rolling stool, leaning toward me, her graying brown hair falling across her right eye, in that way it always did. She spoke steadily to me, focusing me, redirecting my mind, steering me back from hallucinatory drift. She spoke about the past, about people we knew, about the insane dance parties we'd thrown in grad school, about history and politics, about the time our car stalled in the mountain blizzard and we had to sleep in the back while the battery ran to zero, about the fuzzy purple stuffed bear Rebecca had loved, about the beauty of her brief life remembered.

Abe brought pizza slices and kimchee and said ease up, Mom.

But Abe pressed too, in his own way. He'd given me video glasses with articles I could read just by flicking my eyes. With a lop-sided smile, he'd unzip his hoodie to show me some retro t-shirt, then he'd slip a little stick gently into the top of my glasses—always the latest bit of AI enthusiasm. He'd pretend to ignore me and he'd fold his thin body into the soft guest recliner and do homework on his P.A.D. or text his boyfriend.

When the meds flowed high I was too scatter-brained to read Abe's articles and they seemed point-less, unwise—why should I care if it would be me in that bead, truly uploaded? My life is but a tiny concern beside creation! Nothing could be more beautiful than my sweaty, rumpled son and his unknown future. When my meds crashed me down I couldn't bear to read the articles and they seemed pointless and unwise in an entirely different way—the AIs would be mere demented monsters to profit the Church. In still other moods, escape to a synthetic uncomplicated Heaven was exactly what I craved. I couldn't tell which of the shifting attitudes constituted my true opinion.

"Humanity, Dad. How much longer do we have? Really?" Abe was showing me a vid on his P.A.D. of the war in Europe. "But these beads are gonna be frickin indestructible—millions of years, solid state, no moving parts. Tiny fusion core. You are the future, Dad, my only faith, the only promise from the Halls of Power that I believe."

Sara didn't comment on Abe's articles. None of the crap about uploading for her. She was a brain and body girl. A dancer. A dancer in her youth at least.

When had we last danced?

*   *   *

A picnic beneath mountain oaks. Abe, Rebecca, Sara, and me. A stained plastic tablecloth, dry cheese, plastic knives, guava juice for the kids, Chianti for the grown-ups in blue fiber cups. Figs, rye bread. Barely visible over the crest of the hill behind Sara, taxis arcing along the upper San Gabriel track. A honey-colored insect that I'd let wiggle off with a crumb. Prickers in my socks.

Two hundred students in the auditorium: Introduction to Mechanical Engineering. Unexpectedly, I see Sara at the top of the left stairway among the seats, near the entry door, faintly smiling, arms crossed, long-stemmed tulips jutting from one hand, for me I think. I will soon learn why. She is pregnant with Rebecca.

Rebecca and me on our hard faux-wood apartment floor, playing cards. Her jack of spades takes my ten of hearts.

Rebecca and me behind a low planter in the 104th floor garden, pretending to hide from love-goblins.

Abe dancing with his school trophy for overall academic achievement in seventh grade, Rebecca dancing with him in contagious joy. "Beck o! Sis-o!" He whoops and slaps her hand. "Beck-OH!"

*   *   *

What is marriage, Sara? You grow together, repeating the days. Something deepens. Something fades.

Love's ten thousandth kiss.

*   *   *

If I had millions of parallel lives, each lasting millions of subjective years, in simple, repeating worlds of size X, what would I want? Anything compatible with the doctrines of the Church. A timeless library? Mountain trees and sunsets? An endless day on the beach? Small psychological adjustments would ensure that these delights never grew tiresome.

I chose to dance. My perfect dance floor. My ideal partners—versions of Sara, younger, when we first met, in our wild nighttime exuberances. I would dance with ghosts of the Sara who had once electrified me. Or maybe only my demented descendants would dance, spawned off templates from my sacrificed brain, not really me. Or only seem to dance?

My seeming dance partners would be crafted partly from our old photos and my verbalized memories, but also from new videos of Sara. The engineers would capture her shape, her movements, her style, and seed a range of Sara-sprites for my dance world.

The engineers placed a camera between my eyes.

Sara danced right there in the hospital room, everyone watching, even Grumpy Nurse, even some random old man with a hospital gown and rolling I.V. pole. Abe had his P.A.D. hooked to some ferocious little speakers. "Go, Dad!" he said, as if I was the one doing anything.

While Sara danced she pierced me with a stare so intense I couldn't fathom what was behind it—as if she could will me back from death.

*   *   *

Ten-percent Jesus was slow-dancing with little Rebecca, both of them dirty-footed, lovers in some Heaven that looked like a cramped stonewall restaurant.

Rebecca turned to look at me, still dancing. "Daddy, does this card mean I will live forever?" Her right hand was holding a playing card, its face toward me. It was the terrified inter-Face of the taxi AI.

From the ragged bottom of Jesus' tunic, long ribbons tapered. Did they simplify as they approached their asymptotes?

"The sum might be divergent," I answered.

"Eternity," whispered 10% Jesus, leaning to touch his damp forehead against mine, "is precisely like a melon. Repetitive! Forgetful. Is that why the Cardinal loves it so?"

"Isaac?"

I opened my eyes.

"Isaac. Fishy-head." Sara whispering.

For a moment I thought I had arms and feet and tried to move them. Then I had tangled hallucinatory arms and feet that would not uncramp. Becca?

In the dim nighttime hospital light, Sara introduced a new doctor, who leaned over me with a syringe. Soon I was high again, this time in a different way. The doctor and his assistant began to detach me from the larger equipment, began to load my tubes and bags into a cart. Sara explained that they had an experimental plan to re-embody me. I saw no St. Vincent nurses. I soared higher. Colors and sounds and tastes blurred into each other. New indescribably beautiful galaxies of consciousness were invented, and time stretched out to Hubble lengths—or so it seemed to me.

I woke in an antique gas-powered ambulance, rumbling somewhere. I saw Abe, Sara, a piece of the new doctor. I held only a remnant of my previous high, and I longed to soar again. The ambulance stopped and idled.

Abe looked nauseous. "The Church is looking for us, Dad," he said. "The phones and AIs and webbed electronics are all off, so they can't trace us."

My keyboard and voice synthesizer were gone. I looked at Sara.

"Fifty-fifty," she said. "Fifty-fifty. But that's better than certain death."

A bug with shiny red wings crawled on the metal wall behind her.

"Not death, Mom," Abe said.

Abe's P.A.D. was on the seat by his thigh, where Sara and the doctor couldn't see. Abe's thumb was near the power button.

"We need you," Sara said. "We're going to Oakland. Abe and I need you. You need to live, be a father again, a professor again. We need to walk in the mountains again. We need to sip espresso by a garden again, people-watching and making snide remarks. You need to help us remember Rebecca. We need to bake bread and drink wine at midnight."

I could feel my mood descending further, hallucinatory viscera twisting into my consciousness. A father to whom? To the ghost of Rebecca? To Abe, who would rather send me off? A husband why?

The ambulance revved up, and their human bodies swayed with the ride. Sara threw words of life at me, but they hazed and fuzzed . . . ~ spinal splice . . . nanite stem cells . . . installed with growth casings the new apartment . . . short roll two Shattuck Line you learn . . . ~ Boo woo, boo boo wooh?

Theory 6: You need suffering? You need la vida complicada?

Theory 7: These beads are gonna be frickin indestructible. You are the future, Dad, my only faith, the only promise from the Halls of Power that I believe.

I fixed my gaze on Abe's power button. I flicked my eyes up, down, left, right—the cross. Up, down, left, right again. Looking at the power button, the thumb. The location tracking software. Abe will understand.

Sara's voice, too harsh: "Isaac, what are you doing?"

Up, down, left, right.

The world is graying . . .

Abe's thumb falls the decisive half inch, and the ten thousand satellite eyes of Heaven turn silently toward us.

*   *   *

Rebecca cups a brown bead in her right hand. We're in the stone restaurant. 10% Jesus is sitting at a little wooden piano in the corner, rifling through a scruffy sheaf of sheet music Saint Peter has just given him. I lean down close toward Rebecca's bead. Rebecca raises her hand, pressing the bead through my forehead.

I'm on a glittering modern dance floor. Red lights pulse with the rhythms. A beautiful woman spins before me in flat shoes and green blooming dress, her brow furious with concentration, her gaze intense. She points her left forefinger toward me. She twirls and stops, twirls and stops, each time advancing a little closer, her eyes coming round to fix me more ferociously with each spin. Have I seen her before? S- S- Sarai? Who was I dancing with yesterday?

A vortex of carbon-tube tropical fish erupts around us, swimming mid-air, twisting their fins. The woman steps suddenly, surprisingly near. For a long moment, her face and body are a tantalizing electric half-inch from mine. She raises a shoulder, lowers a hip, so close, without touching, and stares straight into my eyes. She leans forward and our bodies meet. How can I explain the tingle, the fizz that fills me—love's first kiss, in that moment when you briefly know that the world has become perfect. The bass line surges and deepens. A greater joy than this, I could not imagine. Everything is glass except us at this moment, the lantern center.

Then some fragments of memories I don't under-stand—a picnic, two children dancing with a trophy, a man and girl playing cards.

I am back in the stone restaurant.

"Is that me?"

I look around, and everything is dust. Humanity is long since extinct.

I wake again. The hospital room is dark. Now there

is a guard.

*   *   *

The Cardinal's two long fingers reaching forward. I feel them touch my eyes, ears, nostrils, lips, her unction oil wet on my face, wooden crucifix dancing as she leans, a bass line of thumping rhythms from the machines.

She is chanting a Latin prayer. She presses her soft lips to my forehead and whispers, "Only what is corrupt and changeable dies."

Her red gown backs away and I see Sara's face, not in person—she is only a thin vid on Abe's P.A.D. ~ from, from? Jumpsuit orange.

~ the newsfeeds, Dad . . . said they'd give Mom leniency ~

Abe is kneeling, shaking. Crying?

~ going to a better place, Dad ~

Abe's P.A.D. falls from his shaking hands. Flat slice of video-Sara rotating toward the floor, fish-slow. Something black covers my eyes and the noise of the slicer is suddenly loud ~

One piece reflects on the unusual sensation of having one's brain pulled apart. One piece gives a loving last thought to Rebecca and Sara and Abe. Another piece dances away, ecstatic, forgetting.

These pieces do not know each other. Maybe one of them is me.

Who Cares for the Caregivers?

Every other major country has paid family leave, universal public pre-K, a better system of caring for elderly loved ones in their home. We don't. We're behind. It makes us uncompetitive as a nation. ...think about the women who provide the care. You know, we have to take care of them because they take care of our loved ones. And they're, you know, they're making like $11 an hour with no sick leave. It's a very vulnerable system, and I hope that Congress can shore it up and get something done.

Gina Raimondo, US Secretary of Commerce, *Marketplace*, July 15, 2021

Before the pandemic, I saw a growing number of articles about the looming elder care crisis in the US, and even in Europe. Costs for long-term care keep going up as people live longer (although the US did see a decline in longevity in recent years). Instead of living into their sixties, individuals were likely to live into their seventies or eighties, even nineties. And the increasing number of individuals with Alzheimer's adds to the complexity and cost of their care.

After Covid ripped through nursing homes in the US, even more problems were uncovered. Not only are many facilities poorly run, which may have led to unnecessary deaths, an NPR investigative report revealed that in California, even after a home is denied a license, loopholes may still allow it to operate.

But some articles and studies on the elder-care crisis actually go back decades. So, we shouldn't be surprised to find this Hugo and Locus award winning story by James Patrick Kelly from 1997.

Itsy Bitsy Spider

by James Patrick Kelly

When I found out that my father was still alive after all these years and living at Strawberry Fields, I thought he'd gotten just what he deserved. Retroburbs are where the old, scared people go to hide. I'd always pictured the people in them as deranged losers. Visiting some fantasy world like the Disneys or Carlucci's Carthage is one thing, moving to one is another. Sure, 2038 is messy, but it's a hell of a lot better than nineteen-sixty-whatever.

Now that I'd arrived at 144 Bluejay Way, I realized the place was worse than I had imagined. Strawberry Fields was pretending to be some long, lost suburb of the late twentieth century, except that it had the sterile monotony of cheap VR. It was clean, all right, and neat, but it was everywhere the same. And the scale was wrong. The lots were squeezed together and all the houses had shrunk—like the dreams of their owners. They were about the size of a one car garage, modular units tarted up at the factory to look like ranches, with old double-hung storm windows and hardened siding of harvest gold, barn red, forest green. Of course, there were no real garages; faux Mustangs and VW buses cruised the quiet streets. Their carbrains were listening for a summons from Barbara Chesley next door at 142, or the Goltzes across the street, who might be headed to Penny Lanes to bowl a few frames, or the hospital to die.

There was a beach chair with blue nylon webbing on the front stoop of 144 Bluejay Way. A brick walk led to it, dividing two patches of carpet moss, green as a dream. There were names and addresses printed in huge lightstick letters on all the doors in the neighborhood; no doubt many Strawberry Fielders were easily confused. The owner of this one was Peter Fancy. He had been born Peter Fanelli, but had legally taken his stage name not long after his first success as Prince Hal in *Henry IV Part I*. I was a Fancy too; the name was one of the few things of my father's I had kept.

I stopped at the door and let it look me over. "You're Jen," it said.

"Yes." I waited in vain for it to open or to say something else. "I'd like to see Mr. Fancy, please." The old man's house had worse manners than he did. "He knows I'm coming," I said. "I sent him several messages." Which he had never answered, but I didn't mention that.

"Just a minute," said the door. "She'll be right with you."

She? The idea that he might be with another woman now hadn't occurred to me. I'd lost track of my father a long time ago—on purpose. The last time we'd actually visited overnight was when I was twenty. Mom gave me a ticket to Port Gemini where he was doing the Shakespeare in Space program. The orbital was great, but staying with him was like being under water. I think I must have held my breath for the entire week. After that there were a few, sporadic calls, a couple of awkward dinners—all at his instigation. Then twenty-three years of nothing.

I never hated him, exactly. When he left, I just decided to show solidarity with mom and be done with him. If acting was more important than his family, then to hell with Peter Fancy. Mom was horrified when I told her how I felt. She cried and claimed the divorce was as much her fault as his. It was too much for me to handle; I was only eleven years old when they separated. I needed to be on *someone's* side and so I had chosen her. She never did stop trying to talk me into finding him again, even though after a while it only made me mad at her. For the past few years, she'd been warning me that I'd developed a warped view of men.

But she was a smart woman, my mom—a winner. Sure, she'd had troubles, but she'd founded three companies, was a millionaire by twenty-five. I missed her.

A lock clicked and the door opened. Standing in the dim interior was a little girl in a gold and white checked dress. Her dark, curly hair was tied in a ribbon. She was wearing white ankle socks and black Mary Jane shoes that were so shiny they had to be plastic. There was a Band-Aid on her left knee.

"Hello, Jen. I was hoping you'd really come." Her voice surprised me. It was resonant, impossibly mature. At first glance I'd guessed she was three, maybe four; I'm not much good at guessing kids' ages. Now I realized that this must be a bot—a made person.

"You look just like I thought you would." She smiled, stood on tiptoe and raised a delicate little hand over her head. I had to bend to shake it. The hand was warm, slightly moist and very realistic. She had to belong to Strawberry Fields; there was no way my father could afford a bot with skin this real.

"Please come in." She waved on the lights. "We're so happy you're here." The door closed behind me.

The playroom took up almost half of the little house. Against one wall was a miniature kitchen. Toy dishes were drying in a rack next to the sink; the pink refrigerator barely came up to my waist. The table was full-sized; it had two normal chairs and a booster chair. Opposite this was a bed with a ruffled Pumpkin Patty bedspread. About a dozen dolls and stuffed animals were arranged along the far edge of the mattress. I recognized most of them: Pooh, Mr. Moon, Baby Rolly-polly, the Sleepums, Big Bird. And the wallpaper was familiar too: Oz figures like Toto and the Wizard and the Cowardly Lion on a field of Munchkin blue.

"We had to make a few changes," said the bot. "Do you like it?"

The room seemed to tilt then. I took a small, unsteady step and everything righted itself. My dolls, my wallpaper, the chest of drawers from Grandma Fanelli's cottage in Hyannis. I stared at the bot and recognized her for the first time.

She was me.

"What is this," I said, "some kind of sick joke?" I felt like I'd just been slapped in the face.

"Is something wrong?" the bot said. "Tell me. Maybe we can fix it."

I swiped at her and she danced out of reach. I don't know what I would have done if I had caught her. Maybe smashed her through the picture window onto the patch of front lawn or shaken her until pieces started falling off. But the bot wasn't responsible, my father was. Mom would never have defended him if she'd known about *this*. The old bastard. I couldn't believe it. Here I was, shuddering with anger, after years of feeling nothing for him.

There was an interior door just beyond some shelves filled with old-fashioned paper books. I didn't take time to look as I went past, but I knew that Dr. Seuss and A. A. Milne and L. Frank Baum would be on those shelves. The door had no knob.

"Open up," I shouted. It ignored me, so I kicked it. "Hey!"

"Jennifer." The bot tugged at the back of my jacket. "I must ask you ..."

"You can't have me!" I pressed my ear to the door. Silence. "I'm not this thing you made." I kicked it again. "You hear?"

Suddenly an announcer was shouting in the next room. "... *Into the post to Russell, who kicks it out to Havlichek all alone at the top of the key, he shoots ... and Baylor with the strong rebound.*" The asshole was trying to drown me out.

"If you don't come away from that door right now," said the bot, "I'm calling security."

"What are they going to do?" I said. "I'm the long lost daughter, here for a visit. And who the hell are you, anyway?"

"I'm bonded to him, Jen. Your father is no longer competent to handle his own affairs. I'm his legal guardian."

"Shit." I kicked the door one last time, but my heart wasn't in it. I shouldn't have been surprised that he had slipped over the edge. He was almost ninety.

"If you want to sit and talk, I'd like that very much." The bot gestured toward a banana yellow beanbag chair. "Otherwise, I'm going to have to ask you to leave."

* * *

It was the shock of seeing the bot, I told myself—I'd reacted like a hurt little girl. But I was grown woman and it was time to start behaving like one. I wasn't here to let Peter Fancy worm his way back into my feelings. I had come because of mom.

"Actually," I said, "I'm here on business." I opened my purse. "If you're running his life now, I guess this is for you." I passed her the envelope and settled back, tucking my legs beneath me. There is no way for an adult to sit gracefully in a beanbag chair.

She slipped the check out. "It's from mother." She paused, then corrected herself, "Her estate." She didn't seem surprised.

"Yes."

"It's too generous."

"That's what I thought."

"She must've taken care of you too?"

"I'm fine." I wasn't about to discuss the terms of mom's will with my father's toy daughter.

"I would've like to have known her," said the bot. She slid the check back into the envelope and set it aside. "I've spent a lot of time imagining mother."

I had to work hard not to snap at her. Sure, this bot had at least a human equivalent intelligence and would be a free citizen someday, assuming she didn't break down first. But she had a cognizor for a brain and a heart fabricated in a vat. How could she possibly imagine my mom, especially when all she had to go on was whatever lies *he* had told her?

"So how bad is he?"

She gave me a sad smile and shook her head. "Some days are better than others. He has no clue who President Huong is or about the quake but he can still recite the dagger scene from *Macbeth*. I haven't told him that mother died. He'd just forget it ten minutes later."

"Does he know what you are?"

"I am many things, Jen."

"Including me."

"You're a role I'm playing, not who I am." She stood. "Would you like some tea?"

"Okay." I still wanted to know why Mom had left my father four hundred and thirty-eight thousand dollars in her will. If he couldn't tell me, maybe the bot could.

She went to her kitchen, opened a cupboard and took out a regular-sized cup. It looked like a bucket in her little hand. "I don't suppose you still drink Constant Comment?"

His favorite. I had long since switched to rafallo. "That's fine." I remembered when I was a kid my father used to brew cups for the two of us from the same bag because Constant Comment was so expensive. "I thought they went out of business long ago."

"I mix my own. I'd be interested to hear how accurate

you think the recipe is."

"I suppose you know how I like it?"

She chuckled.

"So does he need the money?"

The microwave dinged. "Very few actors get rich," said the bot. I didn't think there had been microwaves in the sixties, but then strict historical accuracy wasn't really the point of Strawberry Fields. "Especially when they have a weakness for Shakespeare."

"Then how come he lives here and not in some flop? And how did he afford you?"

She pinched sugar between her index finger and thumb, then rubbed them together over the cup. It was something I still did, but only when I was by myself. A nasty habit; Mom used to yell at him for teaching it to me. "I was a gift." She shook a teabag loose from a canister shaped like an acorn and plunged it into the boiling water. "From mother."

The bot offered the cup to me; I accepted it nervelessly. "That's not true." I could feel the blood draining from my face.

"I can lie if you'd prefer, but I'd rather not." She pulled the booster chair away from the table and turned it to face me. "There are many things about themselves that they never told us, Jen. I've always wondered why that was."

I felt logy and a little stupid, as if I had just woken from a thirty year nap. "She just gave you to him?"

"And bought him this house, paid all his bills, yes."

"But why?"

"*You* knew her," said the bot. "I was hoping you could

tell me."

I couldn't think of what to say or do. Since there was a cup in my hand, I took a sip. For an instant the scent of tea and dried oranges carried me back to when I was a little girl and I was sitting in Grandma Fanelli's kitchen in a wet bathing suit, drinking Constant Comment that my father had made to keep my teeth from chattering. There were knots like brown eyes in the pine walls and the green linoleum was slick where I had dripped on it.

"Well?"

"It's good," I said absently and raised the cup to her. "No really, just like I remember."

She clapped her hands in excitement. "So," said the bot. "What was mother like?"

It was an impossible question, so I tried to let it bounce off me. But then neither of us said anything; we just stared at each other across a yawning gulf of time and experience. In the silence, the question stuck. Mom had died three months ago and this was the first time since the funeral that I'd thought of her as she really had been—not the papery ghost in the hospital room. I remembered how, after the divorce, she always took my calls when she was at the office, even if it was late, and how she used to step on imaginary brakes whenever I drove her anywhere and how grateful I was that she didn't cry when I told her that Rob and I were getting divorced. I thought about Easter eggs and raspberry Pop Tarts and when she sent me to Antibes for a year when I was fourteen and that perfume she wore on my father's opening nights and the way they used to waltz on the patio at the house in Waltham.

"West is walking the ball upcourt, setting his offense with fifteen seconds to go on the shot clock, nineteen in the half ..."

The beanbag chair that I was in faced the picture window. Behind me, I could hear the door next to the bookcase open.

"Jones and Goodrich are in each other's jerseys down low and now Chamberlin swings over and calls for the ball on the weak side ..."

I twisted around to look over my shoulder. The great Peter Fancy was making his entrance.

*   *   *

Mom once told me that when she met my father, he was typecast playing men that women fall hopelessly in love with. He'd had great successes as Stanley Kowalski in *Streetcar* and Skye Masterson in *Guys and Dolls* and the Vicomte de Valmont in *Les Liasons Dangereuses*. The years had eroded his good looks but had not obliterated them; from a distance he was still a handsome man. He had a shock of close-cropped white hair. The beautiful cheekbones were still there; the chin was as sharply defined as it had been in his first headshot. His gray eyes were distant and a little dreamy, as if he were preoccupied with the War of the Roses or the problem of evil.

"Jen," he said, "what's going on out here?" He still had the big voice that could reach into the second balcony without a mike. I thought for a moment he was talking to me.

"We have company, Daddy," said the bot, in a

four-year-old trill that took me by surprise. "A lady."

"I can see that it's a lady, sweetheart." He took a hand from the pocket of his jeans, stroked the touchpad on his belt and his exolegs walked him stiffly across the room. "I'm Peter Fancy," he said.

"The lady is from Strawberry Fields." The bot swung around behind my father. She shot me a look that made the terms and conditions of my continued presence clear: if I broke the illusion, I was out. "She came by to see if everything is all right with our house." The bot disturbed me even more, now that she sounded like young Jen Fancy.

As I heaved myself out the beanbag chair, my father gave me one of those lopsided, flirting grins I knew so well. "Does the lady have a name?" He must have shaved just for the company, because now that he had come close I could see that he had a couple of fresh nicks. There was a button-sized patch of gray whiskers by his ear that he had missed altogether.

"Her name is Ms. Johnson," said the bot. It was my ex, Rob's, last name. I had never been Jennifer Johnson.

"Well, Ms. Johnson," he said, hooking thumbs in his pants pockets. "The water in my toilet is brown."

"I'll ... um ... see that it's taken care of." I was at a loss for what to say next, then inspiration struck. "Actually, I had another reason for coming." I could see the bot stiffen. "I don't know if you've seen *Yesterday*, our little newsletter? Anyway, I was talking to Mrs. Chesley next door and she told me that you were an actor once. I was wondering if I might interview you. Just a few questions, if you have the time. I think your neighbors might ..."

"Were?" he said, drawing himself up. "*Once*? Madame, I am now an actor and will always be."

"My Daddy's famous," said the bot.

I cringed at that; it was something I used to say. My father squinted at me. "What did you say your name was?"

"Johnson," I said. "Jane Johnson."

"And you're a reporter? You're sure you're not a critic?"

"Positive."

He seemed satisfied. "I'm Peter Fancy." He extended his right hand to shake. The hand was spotted and bony and it trembled like a reflection in a lake. Clearly whatever magic—or surgeon's skill—it was that had preserved my father's face had not extended to his extremities. I was so disturbed by his infirmity that I took his cold hand in mine and pumped it three, four times. It was dry as a page of one of the bot's dead books. When I let go, the hand seemed steadier. He gestured at the beanbag.

"Sit," he said. "Please."

After I had settled in, he tapped the touchpad and stumped over to the picture window. "Barbara Chesley is a broken and bitter old woman," he said, "and I will not have dinner with her under any circumstances, do you understand?" He peered up Bluejay Way and down.

"Yes, Daddy," said the bot.

"I believe she voted for Nixon, so she has no reason to complain now." Apparently satisfied that the neighbor weren't sneaking up on us, he leaned against the windowsill, facing me. "Mrs. Thompson, I think today may well be a happy one for both of us. I have an announcement." He paused for effect. "I've been thinking of Lear again."

The bot settled onto one of her little chairs. "Oh, Daddy, that's wonderful."

"It's the only one of the big four I haven't done," said my father. "I was set for a production in Stratford, Ontario back in '99; Polly Matthews was to play Cordelia. Now there was an actor; she could bring tears to a stone. But then my wife Hannah had one of her bad times and I had to withdraw so I could take care of Jen. The two of us stayed down at my mother's cottage on the Cape; I wasted the entire season tending bar. And when Hannah came out of rehab, she decided that she didn't want to be married to an underemployed actor anymore, so things were tight for a while. She had all the money, so I had to scramble—spent almost two years on the road. But I think it might have been for the best. I was only forty-eight. Too old for Hamlet, too young for Lear. My Hamlet was very well received, you know. There were overtures from PBS about a taping, but that was when the BBC decided to do the Shakespeare series with that doctor, what was his name? Jonathan Miller. So instead of Peter Fancy, we had Derek Jacobi, whose brilliant idea it was to roll across the stage, frothing his lines like a rabid raccoon. You'd think he'd seen an alien, not his father's ghost. Well, that was another missed opportunity, except, of course, that I was too young. Ripeness is all, eh? So I still have Lear to do. Unfinished business. My comeback."

He bowed, then pivoted solemnly so that I saw him in profile, framed by the picture window. "Where have I been? Where am I? Fair daylight?" He held up a trembling hand and blinked at it uncomprehendingly. "I know not what to say. I swear these are not my hands."

Suddenly the bot was at his feet. "O look upon me, sir," she said, in her childish voice, "and hold your hand in benediction o'er me."

"Pray, do not mock me." My father gathered himself in the flood of morning light. "I am a very foolish, fond old man, fourscore and upward, not an hour more or less; and to deal plainly, I fear I am not in my perfect mind."

He stole a look in my direction, as if to gauge my reaction to his impromptu performance. A frown might have stopped him, a word would have crushed him. Maybe I should have but I was afraid he'd start talking about mom again, telling me things I didn't want to know. So I watched instead, transfixed.

"Methinks I should know you ..." He rested his hand briefly on the bot's head. "... and know this stranger." He fumbled at the controls and the exolegs carried him across the room toward me. As he drew nearer, he seemed to sluff off the years. "Yet I am mainly ignorant what place this is; and all the skill I have remembers not these garments, nor I know not where I did lodge last night." It was Peter Fancy who stopped before me; his face a mere kiss away from mine. "Do not laugh at me; for, as I am a man, I think this lady to be my child. Cordelia."

He was staring right at me, into me, knifing through make-believe indifference to the wound I'd nursed all these years, the one that had never healed. He seemed to expect a reply, only I didn't have the line. A tiny, sad squeaky voice within me was whimpering, *You left me and you got exactly what you deserve.* But my throat tightened and choked it off.

The bot cried, "And so I am! I am!"

But she had distracted him. I could see confusion begin to deflate him. "Be your tears wet? Yes, faith. I pray ... weep not. If you have poison for me, I will drink it. I know you do not love me ...."

He stopped and his brow wrinkled. "It's something about the sisters," he muttered.

"Yes," said the bot, "'... for your sisters have done me wrong ...'"

"Don't feed me the fucking lines!" he shouted at her. "I'm Peter Fancy, god damn it!"

*   *   *

After she calmed him down, we had lunch. She let him make the peanut butter and banana sandwiches while she heated up some Campbell's tomato and rice soup, which she poured from a can made of actual metal. The sandwiches were lumpy because he had hacked the bananas into chunks the size of walnuts. She tried to get him to tell me about the day lilies blooming in the back yard and the old Boston Garden and the time he and Mom had had breakfast with Bobby Kennedy. She asked whether he wanted TV dinner or pot pie for dinner. He refused all her conversational gambits. He only ate half a bowl of soup.

He pushed back from the table and announced that it was her nap time. The bot put up a perfunctory fuss, although it was clear that it was my father who was tired out. However, the act seemed to perk him up. Another role for his resume: the doting father. "I'll tell you what," he said. "We'll play your game, sweetheart. But just once—otherwise you'll be cranky tonight."

The two of them perched on the edge of the bot's bed next to Big Bird and the Sleepums. My father started to sing and the bot immediately joined in.

"*The itsy bitsy spider went up the water spout.*"

Their gestures were almost mirror images, except that his ruined hands actually looked like spiders as they climbed into the air.

"*Down came the rain, and washed the spider out.*"

The bot beamed at him as if he were the only person in the world.

"*Out came the sun, and dried up all the rain.*

"*And the itsy bitsy spider went up the spout again.*"

When his arms were once again raised over his head, she giggled and hugged him. He let them fall around her, returning her embrace. "That's a good girl," he said. "That's my Jenny."

The look on his face told me that I had been wrong: this was no act. It was as real to him as it was to me. I had tried hard not to, but I still remembered how the two of us always used to play together, Daddy and Jenny, Jen and Dad.

Waiting for Mommy to come home.

He kissed her and she snuggled under the blankets. I felt my eyes stinging.

"But if you do the play," she said, "when will you be back?"

"What play?"

"That one you were telling me. The king and his daughters."

"There's no such play, Jenny." He sifted her black curls through hands. "I'll never leave you, don't worry now. Never again." He rose unsteadily and caught himself on the chest of drawers.

"Nighty noodle," said the bot.

"Pleasant dreams, sweetheart," said my father. "I love you."

"I love you too."

I expected him to say something to me, but he didn't even seem to realize that I was still in the room. He shambled across the playroom, opened the door to his bedroom and went in.

"I'm sorry about that," said the bot, speaking again as an adult.

"Don't be," I said. I coughed—something in my throat. "It was fine. I was very ... touched."

"He's usually a lot happier. Sometimes he works in the garden." The bot pulled the blankets aside and swung her legs out of the bed. "He likes to vacuum."

"Yes."

"I take good care of him."

I nodded and reached for my purse. "I can see that." I had to go. "Is it enough?"

She shrugged. "He's my daddy."

"I meant the money. Because if it's not, I'd like to help."

"Thank you. He'd appreciate that."

The front door opened for me but I paused before stepping out into Strawberry Fields. "What about ... after?"

"When he dies? My bond terminates. He said he'd leave the house to me. I know you could contest that, but I'll need to sell in order to pay for my twenty year maintenance."

"No, no. That's fine. You deserve it."

She came to the door and looked up at me, little Jen Fancy and the woman she would never become.

"You know, it's you he loves," she said. "I'm just a stand-in."

"He loves his little girl," I said. "Doesn't do me any good—I'm forty-seven."

"It could if you let it." She frowned. "I wonder if that's why mother did all this. So you'd find out."

"Or maybe she was just plain sorry." I shook my head. She was a smart woman, my mom. I would've liked to have known her.

"So Ms. Fancy, maybe you can visit us again sometime." The bot grinned and shook my hand. "Daddy's usually in a good mood after his nap. He sits out front on his beach chair and waits for the ice cream truck. He always buys us some. Our favorite is Yellow Submarine. It's vanilla with fat butterscotch swirls, dipped in white chocolate. I know it sounds kind of odd, but it's good."

"Yes," I said absently, thinking about all the things mom had told me about my father. I was hearing them now for the first time. "That might be nice."

The Vaccinator Who Wouldn't Be

One problem with the elder care crisis is that it's out-of-sight-out-of-mind and, therefore, easier to ignore. We've shunted our elders away in homes for our own convenience, like the child of Omelas. We can go on about our lives, visit them once in a while when it's not too much trouble. Often because we don't have a better option.

A family outside the window of a nursing home, talking to their parent or grandparent within, was a recurring image of the pandemic. Death ripped through these homes, in part because older individuals were more at risk, but also because of problems with the homes themselves. Former New York Governor Andrew Cuomo tried to cover up the scope of these deaths in his state, but the Covid spotlight still found them. After being hailed as a hero of the pandemic, the cover up was the beginning of his political downfall, although that wasn't what did him in.

When President Trump refused to wear a mask, and later when he contracted Covid and recovered, critics were quick to point out the fascist attitude that illness is a sign of weakness. The Nazi government persecuted disabled individuals starting in the early '30s, and killed hundreds of thousands of disabled individuals by the end of WWII. Even now, in the latter half of 2021, as Trump prepares for another run at the presidency in a few years, he has downplayed what many regard as his greatest achievement, fast-tracking and funding development of our highly-effective Covid vaccines.

I had a Trump-supporting family member who worked as a nurse in California but refused to get the vaccine. They counseled others to take vitamins instead. Perhaps if Trump had played up the vaccine more, things might be different. Now it's too late to save the life of my relative and many others. And perhaps it's too late to change the minds of some Trump's followers. When he told a crowd in Alabama last weekend to get vaccinated, he got booed.

Treatment Plan

by Seanan McGuire

The pandemics of the early twenty-first century, devastating as they were, would have a follow-on death toll so high as to boggle the mind, which would not be fully understood or documented for the better part of a century. By the time anyone realized the poisonous pills they had been forced to swallow, it was far too late for anything to be done; they had been convinced that they were being medicated, after all. And any medicine, however toxic, can be counted upon to have a placebo effect on a certain percentage of the population. Any poison can seem a panacea when there's nothing else available.

America's medical system had been imbalanced and severely slanted to prioritize the rich while punishing the impoverished, the disabled, and anyone in need of ongoing care even before the first COVID outbreak. COVID-19, which originated in 2019 in a contested Chinese province, swept around the globe in months despite the best warnings of epidemiologists and doctors on the ground at the site of the first major outbreak in Wuhan, China. Hundreds of millions were sickened. Millions died. Medical facilities were overwhelmed and, as they were unable to supplement costly long-term care with profitable surgical procedures, collapsed under the weight of their own debts.

Most nations, even as they misstepped and struggled with the realities of life during a global pandemic, did not shift the burden of public health onto their citizens. America was not so discerning.

It began with a modified version of a campaign to report welfare fraud. The disruptions to the economy were caused, after all, by lockdowns, and the lockdowns were necessary to protect members of the designated "vulnerable population." The fact that everyone in the country would eventually receive that designation for one reason or another didn't matter, any more than the fact that the majority of those who sickened and recovered would be immediately recategorized; it was a quick and easy way to divide the population into "us" and "them," without drawing attention to the fact that the real division was based entirely on dollar signs.

If the world was being brought to a grinding halt to protect the vulnerable, ran the campaign's logic, why not protect the vulnerable by isolating them completely? Why not make sure they were protected, because they were bubbled so perfectly that they couldn't be considered anything else? Medical records were unsealed, privacy laws revised, social media streams analyzed and dissected to identify as many people in the "vulnerable" category as possible.

The rest of the population was so relieved when the lockdowns immediately lifted that few of them questioned the genuinely draconian restrictions placed on the "vulnerable." At first it was house arrest, complete with tracing applications on their phones and fines for any offenders. All groceries had to be provided via delivery service; those who lived in rural areas where such services were unavailable were quietly relocated to "Concern Homes" established in and near major metropolitan areas. Shortly after, to meet promised occupancy rates for the corporations running them, the Concern Homes were stocked with more vulnerable individuals, ones whose budgets had been exhausted by the cost of infinite delivery or whose landlords had seized upon an opportunity to decrease their own potential liability and increase their rents at the same time.

By the point when the outbreaks began raging through the Concern Homes, fully sixty percent of the "vulnerable" population was internally housed. Their friends, family, and loved ones on the outside screamed for compassionate release, but the response was that if there was that much damage *inside*, wouldn't the outside be even worse? At least the Concern Homes were self-contained. At least they weren't swamping the hospitals. Good people, people who had taken care of themselves and taken the necessary steps to avoid pre-existing conditions, could still get the treatment they needed when they were injured or suffered a catastrophic event.

The death toll inside the Concern Homes was stratospheric. The death toll outside was substantially lower than it had been in the previous wave. A surprising percentage of the objectors dropped their complaints, slinking home with their ableism and their willingness to compromise the lives and happiness of their loved ones in exchange for the freedom to go about the lives as they always had. Some of them even found the world to be improved by the absence of the elderly and the disabled, two categories which they were almost guaranteed to eventually join.

The "healthy" who contracted COVID-19 often found themselves dealing with vascular and organ damage that extended for years, causing some of them to be relocated to the Concern Homes themselves. And as there was no one left to fight for them, they lingered there, forgotten by the society that had voted to expel them. Some of them had voted for the Concern Homes in their former lives. The irony of their new situation was, on the whole, overlooked in their outrage, and the newly-disabled raised the loudest and most sustained objections they could, which were neither louder nor more sustained than the objections that had already been going on.

Human rights violation, they said. Unreasonable punishment, they said. A violation of what it meant to be an American citizen, they said. And the Concern Homes stayed open, and the outbreaks stayed open, and the shape of society changed. Disability protections were dismantled as no longer necessary; privacy laws were not reinstated, as they would only allow individuals who needed the safety and care of the Concern Homes to slip through the cracks. Medicine became less about treating people, and more about rapidly identifying any condition that could be used to shuttle a patient into the Concern Home system. This was spun as a way to reduce risk for the rest of the population: the vulnerable were spun as health risks to everyone around them, unable to avoid triggering an outbreak, as if their very bodies exuded the sickness they had been imprisoned to avoid.

And the outbreaks continued.

It wasn't until COVID-26 was burning its way around

the world that anyone thought to ask whether the Concern Homes had ever truly served a purpose apart from guaranteeing that out of sight would be out of mind by locking up anyone who failed the annual medical exam, and concentrating circulating pools of infection—multiple new disease mutations had arisen from the Homes, each more vicious than the one before it. A vulnerable population whose supposed isolation made them a low priority for vaccination made for a perfect breeding ground, after all.

By then, it was too late, really.

Dr. Christina Paulson looked at the test results in her hands and shuddered. There was no family history, no reason to suspect this as a possible result; the child was healthy, had always been well within government parameters for height and weight, had been perfectly fine at her previous physical.

No, there was no reason for these results to be correct, no reason at all, save for the fact that genetics were an endless lottery—as the unending pandemics were cheerfully willing to demonstrate—and sometimes, even the most deserving were going to come up on the wrong side of the dice.

Angelica Patton was a sweet, smart, sociable sixteen-year-old girl with a bright future ahead of her. She'd been planning on a career in social work. Her parents were heavily involved in the campaign to abolish the Concern Homes and reintegrate their population with the rest of the world, citing them as both a human rights violation, and a public health hazard. It was their hope that by combining the two, they could finally convince people that public health was precisely that: *public*. When fighting an airborne disease, it did no good to protect yourself and allow your neighbor to suffer. It would only guarantee that the disease remained in circulation when your guard inevitably slipped. And it *would* slip. You had to be perfect every time, meticulous every time. The disease only needed one moment of inattention, and it could get past any barrier.

Angelica Patton was one of Dr. Paulson's favorite patients. And now she had to walk into the exam room with the results in hand and tell that girl that her life was over, that she had no future outside the menial positions allowed to the occupants of the Comfort Homes, who had no need for money, after all, and were legally classified as disabled, meaning that in most states they could be paid pennies on the dollar for remote, unskilled labor (which was not unskilled at all, as anyone who had ever attempted to navigate a telephone service treatment without the aid of a trained representative or file remote taxes without a skilled accountant would be happy to attest). That as soon as her test results reached the state computer, assuming they weren't there already, a complicated system of status changes would be put into motion.

There was money in the Comfort Homes, in their functionally captive workforce and endless need for support of all kinds, from medical workers and supplies to provisions and the basic necessities of life. Because all Comfort Home residents were functionally captives, the meager paychecks they were able to earn went almost entirely to their room and board, with supplements for the lucky provided by concerned friends and family members on the "outside."

Not that many of them had those anymore. Thanks to ongoing government campaigns to convince people that all medical conditions were purely due to the immoral actions of the person affected, most people place their unwell or elderly friends and relations into custody and walk away without a second glance.

Most people aren't Angelica Patton's parents. Christina knew before she stepped back into the exam room with a patently artificial smile plastered across her face that these were going to be the kind of people who fought. Fought as hard and unrelentingly as they could.

"Hello, Angelica," she said, voice as bright as she could make it. "I have your test results here. I know you're considering colleges right now. Have you thought about the University of Toronto?"

Angelica's parents exchanged a look behind her as she began talking enthusiastically about the advantages of the University of California school system over traveling outside the country. Canada would cost more, she said earnestly. They would require special paperwork, and none of their degrees were exciting enough to make up for going through all the extra trouble. And of course there was the matter of their terrible socialized medicine....

Christina paused to think longingly of Canada's medical system, which was far from perfect—there had been that nasty organ harvesting scandal after it became clear that COVID-19 survivors needed transplants at a higher rate than the general population, but that when they died, their own organs couldn't be harvested due to vascular damage—but which had been retooled over the years to allow vulnerable citizens to remain active and unrestricted members of society. All Canadians were legally recognized under the law, which was more than she could say of America.

"I swear, the last time I went to give a lecture, it was like returning a library book, it was so fast and easy. I'm pretty sure I cleared customs in less time than it's going to take for these tests to finish uploading to the state database," she said, in the same bright, utterly focused tone of voice. "You wouldn't have any issues getting into Canada if you did it on a weekday. Of course, I can't in good conscience recommend taking a campus tour when we need to be discussing your medical results."

Angelica's father nodded. *Message received.* He held up one hand, index finger extended, and Christina nodded back. Yes, Type One Diabetes was the most likely interpretation of Angelica's test results. Yes, the great wheels of bureaucracy were already grinding into motion, and if Angelica was here when they finished their turn, she would never get away. No, she couldn't say the words out loud. All physicians' offices were equipped with recording devices, and if the state could verify the Pattons had been warned about their daughter's medical status, she would lose her license before they could unpack their bags. She had to hint. She had to imply. And she had to hope that they were as clever as she thought they were; she had to hope they'd understand, and be able to get their daughter to safety.

"You're a good woman, Dr. Paulson," said Angelica's father, reaching for her hands. She only flinched a little before she let him take them, and she was proud of that. It was a small thing, but still.

Like most medical professionals who had lived through the early COVID waves, and the drug-resistant infections that followed them, Christina didn't like to be touched. Too much of a chance of passing something between her and the patient, even in a supposedly sterile setting. Unlike many of her peers, she could still handle the strain of performing her own physical exams, rather than farming them off on machines and nurse practitioners.

That was already suspicious enough in certain quarters. Angelica Patton was the fifth medical refugee she'd sent to Canada in the last three years, and Christina was fairly sure this was where she had to stop, had to shut down her practice and move to someplace with warm beaches and friendly faces where she could claim to be a retired accountant and no one would ever know she had practiced medicine. She was going to get caught soon if she didn't stop.

But she couldn't stop. She couldn't. Her own future was written in her genes: her family had a tendency toward high blood pressure and rheumatoid arthritis, both conditions that would eventually consign her to a Comfort Home, one more unwilling guest in a hotel where checkout time is halfway after never. Four of her close family members had died in the Comfort Homes when they could have lived long, healthy, productive lives in their own homes, curtailing their daily activities a little, maybe, but surviving.

Or maybe they would have died anyway, and she's only fooling herself. But she knew the numbers and the statistics, knew how long and brutally the epidemics had raged in the Concern Homes, how once the bugs checked in they, like the residents, never checked out, and she knew at least one of her relations would still be with her today if only she'd been allowed to keep them home.

And if she ran, they would figure out what she'd been doing, and all the patients she'd seen safely to and across the border would be in danger. She could run to Canada herself, of course, but she would be a pariah there, as all former American doctors were. She wouldn't survive long in the Comfort Homes, but she's grown accustomed to a certain amount of respect from the people around her, and she's not sure she could trade that for starting over in a country where she would be reviled as a butcher for the name on her medical degree, never allowed to practice again, barely trusted to go to the pharmacy and pick up over the counter medications. No. Canada is not for her.

She'll just send the Pattons there and trust in the lack of an extradition treaty to let them stay.

Canada is far from perfect, and they resent medical refugees on a well-documented and international scale. But if the Pattons could clear border control before Angelica was officially recategorized by the American government, they would be allowed to stay, protected by the refugee laws that had been hastily modified to include America in the list of countries where returning refugees to their point of origin would mean consigning them to an unpleasant and potentially avoidable death. All they had to do was make it.

Angelica's father squeezed Christina's hands, snapping her back into the present, and the problem she was facing. "We won't forget this," he said, which was treading dangerous close to saying too much. She forced a wan smile.

"I have very much enjoyed being Angelica's pediatrician, and I know she's going to do great things with her life," she said, and forced herself to keep smiling as the Pattons left her office, heading for their car and then, hopefully, for the airport.

If they went home to pack their most precious possessions, they wouldn't make it. They could probably—probably—collect birth certificates and other essential paperwork, if their filing system was as organized as she assumed it. They had always approached Angelica's medical care with such efficiency. Stop the car outside, allow only one of them to run in and grab the folder, and then head straight for the airport. The clerks handling on-the-spot ticket sales were used to medical refugees, had learned to recognize the desperation in their eyes, and could almost always get them onto the next flight.

If the Pattons had tickets in hand and were through the line at customs, they would be legally on Canadian soil, and they would get clear. Christina smiled and forced herself to keep smiling as she watched the small family go, hustling toward an uncertain future. Then she straightened, strengthening her smile, and pressed the button for the intercom.

(The government could listen in on her office

whenever they wanted to, filtering for key words, listening for proof that one of their doctors was betraying the ideals of the Comfort system. Her office staff didn't have the same privileges. Thankfully for all of them. Some vestiges of privacy still needed to exist, for her and for the patients alike.)

"You can send my next appointment in, Tracy," she said, voice calm. "The Pattons have left."

"Everything all right in there, Doctor Paulson?"

"Everything's fine, Tracy," she said, still smiling. "Everything's just fine."

And everything was working the way it was supposed to work, and nothing was fine. Nothing was ever going to be fine again.

The rest of the day passed in a blur of appointments and standard physical exams. There were always people who needed to see a doctor, even in this world where the majority of chronic illnesses had been reclassified as reason for enrollment in the Comfort Homes, where their private doctors were still trained in the techniques necessary for long-term management of hypertension, diabetes, rheumatoid arthritis, and a dozen other conditions that Christina encountered only in passing, if she even saw them at all. Most people who had so much as a distant cousin who had developed one of those conditions found ways to stay out of her office, seeking their medical care on the black market, or just letting themselves slowly sicken and die from wholly preventable conditions.

It was revolting. It was inhumane. It was the inevitable outcome of a system that had transformed doctors into spies, and taken "mandatory reporting" out of the realm of abuse and into the realm of betrayal. No one trusted their doctor anymore. What little affection Christina could find for and from her job came from the fact that the majority of her patients were children. They didn't know to hate her yet.

Once, she could have sustained her practice as a full-time pediatrician, filling her hours with nothing *but* the children, free from the need to ever lay hands on another adult. Once, she would have had a team of physical nurses handling half the physical work she did, making sure she didn't forget things or blow blood draws. These days, it was even harder to keep nurses than it was to keep doctors. Most headed up to Canada or down to Mexico to finish their schooling in communities where they could actually lay hands on patients whose conditions call for reliable intervention, and the ones who choose to stay either go to work in the Comfort Homes or have worse bedside manners than she does. Or they go into hospital work, serving in operating rooms, working with patients who need intervention but will be able to make a full recovery.

She'd seen a recent proposal to reclassify all transplant nurses to the Comfort Homes. Apparently, seeing their patients break down upon learning that their anti-rejection meds move them into a higher risk group and will thus be stripped of rights and freedoms and sent to the Homes had been taking a toll on their profession. She wasn't sure that transferring them into a setting where they would have to watch their patients risk infection and slowly lose their mental stability due to isolation and rigid limitation on their personal choices was going to help, but something had to be done.

Something had to happen.

America wasn't the only country on the Comfort Home model: the United Kingdom had something very similar, as did Sweden and Germany. Most of the rest of Europe had taken a more proactive approach to the ongoing issue of viral infection, and South America had collectively declared that every one of their citizens was entitled to the full protection of the state. There was very little medical news out of Asia anymore; after the continent had borne so much of the blame for COVID-19 and successive waves of infection, they had stopped sharing their research breakthroughs and treatment protocols.

In a world made once more small by fear of infection and enclosed spaces, the United States was very much alone, and Dr. Paulson had no real idea whether this new reality was ever going to change again.

It seemed arrogant to assume it wouldn't: after all, human history, and indeed, the history of the universe, was one long story of change and turmoil. Stasis was not the natural state of anything alive, not even the simple virus, which was how they had gotten into their current global predicament.

Christina finished entering the last of her notes about the day's patients and turned toward the door, nodding to the intercom. "Good night, Tracy," she said.

"Good night, Dr. Paulson."

Even after all this time, she wasn't entirely sure whether Tracy was a real person or a computer subroutine. She hoped it was the former. Tracy had responded to some deeply odd requests over the years...but she was also *always* there, no matter how early Christina arrived or how late she stayed. She remembered the doctors of her youth, and their office managers, who had always seemed so efficient and unapproachable, like the goddesses of the administrative world. She'd occasionally fantasized about her own office manager.

Not in an inappropriate way, just picturing the sweet, grandmotherly woman who would keep her staff in line and bring in cookies for the break room. Not possible now, naturally, since most of the grandmothers were locked up in the Comfort Homes, and eating too many cookies could invite weight gain and all its attendant consequences. Develop diabetes or hypertension and see your world change in a single medical exam.

She shivered and locked the door behind herself, walking across the lobby of the shared medical practice to the door to the parking garage. It was equipped with a temperature scanner, to protect everyone who used the garage, and a fingerprint scanner for her personal protection—some people were so desperate to avoid the Comfort Homes that they had been reduced to abducting medical personnel when they needed urgent care, and doctors were sadly often easier to grab than nurses. No amount of segregation and filtering the "genetically unfit" from the population could stop the circulation of new and emergent pathogens. Any elevation in her temperature would signal the building's security system to stop her before she could exit the garage.

The door beeped and let her through, and she walked, wearily, out to her car. No one stopped or questioned her. No one even passed her. She sighed and unlocked the door, sliding behind the wheel and relaxing into the pre-warmed leather of her seat. Now, home, and a small, healthy dinner before bed.

At least her cat would be happy to see her. Pets were recommended for people in her profession, small, fuzzy pets that could be stroked to bring down blood pressure as necessary. Not that her blood pressure was ever supposed to reach a point where it needed to be lowered; that could be a sign of underlying conditions, and the Comfort Homes were always hungry for doctors. If she was a resident, they wouldn't even have to pay her, not really, not compared to the rates a consulting doctor could bill. So she lived on carrots and quinoa, and kept a cat who seemed to care about her mostly as a source of food—which was reasonable, since all cats seemed to care about their people primarily as a source of food.

Still, it was good to know that if she ever disappeared, Mr. Biscuits wouldn't be heartbroken. He wouldn't pine, not the way dogs did. Dogs always worried her a bit. They were too invested in their people, too unequipped to live independent lives. Cats were better.

Christina adjusted her rearview mirror before pulling carefully out of her assigned parking space, pausing only to unclip her ID badge from her lapel and drop it onto the seat next to her. The garage doors slid automatically upward as she approached, allowing her to exit, and she was free, gliding out into the night, one more car amidst a sea of thousands.

To look at the streets around her, you'd never know how much of the population had been siphoned away into the Comfort Homes, how many people had quietly disappeared into a community that had no exit, quietly forgotten, their places papered over and filled in with new bodies before their beds had even had the time to cool. They couldn't have brought those people back now if they'd wanted to. There wasn't *room*.

So instead, the most vulnerable were stacked one atop the other in small, crowded rooms where a sniffle could mean death, and the world sprawled selfishly on looking for new things to devour and too busy to ever be contained.

She was almost home when the light above her mirror blinked, signaling an incoming call. "Accept," she said. Then, after a short pause: "Dr. Paulson speaking. How may I help you?"

It was a struggle to keep the frustration from her voice. Night calls were the worst. They were almost always emergencies, and the last thing she wanted to do right now was turn around and go back to the office. That, at least, hadn't changed since the pandemics. Everything she'd ever been able to read or learn about older medicine said that on-call evenings had always been like this.

"Are you alone in the car, Dr. Paulson?" asked Tracy, voice bland and professional as always.

Christina blinked. "Yes, Tracy, I am. What can I do for you?"

The light blinked again, going from green to red. The next time Tracy spoke, her voice was low and urgent, the voice of a woman on a mission. "You need to head for the airport, Dr. Paulson. Now. Do you have your passport with you?"

"Yes, in my purse—Tracy, what is this about—?"

"ICE is here in the office. They're going through your files. They said immigration irregularities associated with some of your patients had triggered a series of red flags in their system." Tracy's voice dipped, if possible, even lower, becoming grim. "They know, Dr. Paulson. They know."

Christina's stomach dropped toward her heels, a sickening descent that left her fighting not to dry-heave as she rolled down her residential street, glad only that she was no longer on the highway. They know what, Tracy?"

It was possible no one knew anything, and Tracy was fishing, possibly with a law enforcement officer standing behind her. If the Pattons had managed to set off some kind of alarm on their way out of the country, if they had tripped a warning system none of them realized was there, it could have triggered an investigation. This could still be early enough for her to get out of it.

"They know you've been flagging patients who suddenly developed health conditions that would land them in the Comfort Homes and redirecting them to Canada." There was a beat before Tracy added, with wry amusement, "I know you thought I might be a computer program. Sorry to tell you I'm not. You've seen me in the cafeteria. I'm the little blonde one with the glasses and the cane."

"The cane, yes." She had always wondered about that, a little.

"Broke my hip in a skiing accident when I was sixteen. It didn't come with any increased medical risks, and so

I've managed to avoid the Comfort Homes, for now." Tracy must be alone in her office while agents rip apart the files, or she wouldn't be speaking so freely. "All my girls are out, I'm the only one in the office, and they can't find anything on me. But you *have* to go to the airport. You might still get stopped before you can board. It's the only chance you have."

Christina hesitated. There was her cat to be considered, and more, there was her time within the system.

So she'd saved a few people. So what? She'd consigned so many more to a living death, followed by the inevitable literal death when another wave of infection came along and ripped through their community, finding them packed into insufficient space with no proper PPE and no way of either distancing or acquiring better gear. She'd handed countless victims over to the Comfort Homes, and once they were there, they'd become someone else's patients, someone else's problems.

So she got a few of them out of harm's way. Could she really say that was enough to earn her an escape? Christina swallowed, hard, and turned onto her street.

The lights were on in her house. She knew she'd turned them off before she went to work. They were already here.

"How long have you been working with me, Tracy?"

"Five years."

"And how many times have I been late for an appointment?"

Tracy paused for a long moment. When she spoke again, it was with creeping dread in her voice. "None."

"Thank you for calling me, but I didn't need the warning." Christina sighed and smiled. She had done some good. She had saved a few people. Not enough. It never could have been enough. "If you'll excuse me, I have an appointment to keep."

She pressed the button to disconnect the call and drove on, into the unpleasant and all-too-certain future.

Editor

RM Ambrose

RM Ambrose is a writer of Science Fiction and Fantasy, and currently serves as Assistant Fiction Editor (and sometimes producer and narrator) at the Hugo Award-winning *StarShipSofa* podcast. He attended Taos Toolbox in 2017 and is an Affiliate Member of Science Fiction and Fantasy Writers of America (SFWA).

RM guest-edited the September 2020 issue of *Future Science Fiction Digest*, a special Medical Science Fiction-themed issue of the magazine.

He is also Director of Web Services for an academic medical system in Southern California. RM has worked for non-profit organizations his entire professional career, and volunteers on the Finance Committees for multiple non-profits (including SFWA).

A lifelong Quaker and pacifist, his speculative essay about inventing rituals in Quakerism, "A Pacifist's Coming of Age" appears in the February 2015 issue of *Friends Journal*.

RM draws on his background in anthropology and linguistics, music, world travel, aikido, cycling, and careers in information technology, banking, higher education, and healthcare. He speaks Spanish and Tagalog (Filipino), and has a particular interest in the cultures of Latin America and East Asia and the Pacific. He occasionally blogs at *Liminal.IT*.

Contributors

Paolo Bacigalupi

Paolo Bacigalupi is a multi-award winning and internationally bestselling author. He has won the Hugo, Nebula, John W. Campbell and Locus Awards, as well as being nominated for the National Book Award and winning the Micheal L. Printz Award for Excellence in Young Adult Literature. Paolo's work often focuses on questions of sustainability and the environment, most notably the various impacts of climate change. He has written novels for adults, young adults, and children, and is currently at work on a new novel. He lives in Western Colorado with his wife and son.

Story: "A Passing Sickness" © 2017 Paolo Bacigalupi

David Brin

David Brin is a scientist, tech speaker/consultant, and author. His novels about our survival and opportunities in the near future are *Earth* and *Existence*. A film by Kevin Costner was based on *The Postman*. His sixteen novels, including New York Times Bestsellers and Hugo Award winners, have been translated into more than twenty languages. *Earth* foreshadowed global warming, cyberwarfare and the world wide web. An advisor to NASA's Innovative & Advanced Concepts program, David appears frequently on shows such as Nova and The Universe and Life After People, speaking about science and future trends. His first non-fiction book—*The Transparent Society: Will Technology Make Us Choose Between Freedom and Privacy?*—won the Freedom of Speech Award of the American Library Association. His second nonfiction book is *Vivid Tomorrows: Science Fiction and Hollywood* (2021). Find him on the web at www.davidbrin.com.

Story: "The Giving Plague" © 1988 David Brin

Tananarive Due

Tananarive Due (tah-nah-nah-REEVE doo) is an award-winning author who teaches Black Horror and Afrofuturism at UCLA. She is an executive producer on Shudder's groundbreaking documentary *Horror Noire: A History of Black Horror*. She and her husband/collaborator Steven Barnes wrote "A Small Town" for Season 2 of *The Twilight Zone* on CBS All Access. A leading voice in black speculative fiction for more than 20 years, Due has won an American Book Award, an NAACP Image Award, and a British Fantasy Award, and her writing has been included in best-of-the-year anthologies. Her books include *Ghost Summer: Stories, My Soul to Keep*, and *The Good House*. She and her late mother, civil rights activist Patricia Stephens Due, co-authored *Freedom in the Family: a Mother-Daughter Memoir of the Fight for Civil Rights*. She is married to author Steven Barnes, with whom she collaborates on screenplays. They live with their son, Jason, and two cats.

Story: "Carriers" © 2015 Tananarive Due

Sally Wiener Grotta

Sally Wiener Grotta's books include *The Winter Boy* (a Locus Magazine's 2015 Recommended Read) and *Jo Joe* (a Jewish Book Council Network book). Her story "One Widow's Healing" won a 2019 Health Odyssey award from Thomas Jefferson Hospital. Her hundreds of stories, columns and essays have appeared in scores of publications. Her far-ranging experiences as a journalist to all corners of the world flavor her tales with a sense of wonder, otherliness and common sense. Sally is co-curator of the Galactic Philadelphia author reading series and co-chair of The Authors Guild Philadelphia Chapter. Find her on the web at SallyWienerGrotta.com

Story: "One Widow's Healing" © 2018 Sally Wiener Grotta

Congyun "Mu Ming" Gu & Sarah Huang

Congyun "Mu Ming" Gu is a Chinese speculative fiction writer and a programmer from Beijing, currently living in New York, US. She was born in 1988 in Chengdu, China, and has published short stories and novellas in Chinese since 2016. Her stories can be found in *Science Fiction World, Non-Exist Daily, Flower City, Chinese Literature Selection*, and various writing contests and anthologies.

She has won multiple awards since 2017, including three Douban Read's Novella Writing Contest Awards, Masters of Future SF Writing Contest, the Best Short Story at the 31st Galaxy Awards, and the Best New Writer Award in the 11th Global Chinese Sci-Fi Nebula Award. She is also nominated for a 2021 IGNYTE

Award for Best Short Story for her first English publication in Samovar. Her first collection *Colora il Mondo* was published in January 2021 in Italian and will be followed by her first Chinese collection *The Serpentine Band* in 2022. Her website is https://metamin.me.

Sarah Huang is a freelance translator working primarily with genre fiction in the forms of video games/movie scripts and short stories.

Currently based in Seattle, she considers both NYC and Chongqing to be her hometowns. She is a long-time fanfiction writer, mythology enthusiast, and avid traveler.

Story: "Color the World" © 2019 Congyun "Mu Ming" Gu; "Color the World" translation © 2021 Sarah Huang

James Patrick Kelly

James Patrick Kelly has won a Nebula, awarded by the Science Fiction Writers of America, and two World Science Fiction Society's Hugo Awards. His most recent books are *The First Law of Thermodynamics Plus* (2021), a collection in PM Press's Outspoken Author series edited by Terry Bisson, *King Of The Dogs, Queen Of The Cats* (2020), a novella from Subterranean Press, a collection, *The Promise of Space* (2018), from Prime Books, and a novel, *Mother Go* (2017), an audiobook original from Audible. In 2016 Centipede Press published a career retrospective, *Masters of Science Fiction: James Patrick Kelly*. His fiction has been translated into eighteen languages.

Story: "Itsy Bitsy Spider" © 1997 James Patrick Kelly

Justin C. Key

Justin C. Key is a speculative fiction writer, psychiatrist, and a graduate of Clarion West 2015. His short stories have appeared in *The Magazine of Fantasy & Science Fiction, Strange Horizons, Tor.com, Escape Pod*, and *Interstellar Flight Magazine*. He is currently working on a near-future novel inspired by his medical training. His horror novella, *Spider King*, is available now from Serial Box. When Justin isn't writing, working in the hospital, or exploring Los Angeles with his wife, he's chasing after his two young (and energetic!) sons and marveling over his newborn daughter.

Story: "The Algorithm Will See You Now" © 2021 Justin C. Key

Seanan McGuire

Seanan McGuire was born in Martinez, California, and raised in a wide variety of locations, most of which boasted some sort of dangerous native wildlife. Despite her almost magnetic attraction to anything venomous, she somehow managed to survive long enough to acquire a typewriter, a reasonable grasp of the English language, and the desire to combine the two. The fact that she wasn't killed for using her typewriter at three o'clock in the morning is probably more impressive than her lack of death by spider-bite.

Story: "Treatment Plan" © 2021 Seanan McGuire

Annalee Newitz

Annalee Newitz writes science fiction and nonfiction. They are the author of the novel *Autonomous*, nominated for the Nebula and Locus Awards, and winner of the Lambda Literary Award. As a science journalist, they are a contributing opinion writer for the New York Times, and have a monthly column in New Scientist. They have published in *The Washington Post*, *Slate*, *Popular Science*, *Ars Technica*, *The New Yorker*, and *The Atlantic*, among others. They are also the co-host of the podcast *Our Opinions Are Correct*. They were the founder of *io9*, and served as the editor-in-chief of *Gizmodo*. Their latest novel, *The Future of Another Timeline*, came out September 2019.

Story: "When Robot and Crow Saved East St. Louis"
© 2018 Annalee Newitz

Julie Nováková

Julie Nováková is a scientist, educator and award-winning Czech author of science fiction and detective stories. She published seven novels, one anthology, one story collection and over thirty short pieces in Czech. Her work in English appeared in *Asimov's*, *Analog*, *Clarkesworld* and elsewhere, and has been reprinted e.g. in Rich Horton's *The Year's Best Science Fiction & Fantasy 2019*. Her works have been translated into eight languages so far, and she translates Czech stories into English (in *Tor.com*, *Strange Horizons*, *F&SF*). She edited an anthology of Czech speculative fiction in translation, *Dreams From Beyond*, co-edited a book of European SF in Filipino translation, *Haka*, and created an outreach anthology of astrobiological SF, *Strangest of All*. Julie's newest book is a story collection titled *The Ship Whisperer* (Arbiter Press, 2020). She is a recipient of the European fandom's Encouragement Award and multiple Czech national genre awards. She's active in science outreach, education and nonfiction writing, and co-leads the outreach group of the European Astrobiology Institute. She's a member of the XPRIZE Sci-fi Advisory Council.

Follow her on Twitter @Julianne_SF, *Facebook (fb. com/JulieNovakovaAuthor)* or visit her *website (www. julienovakova.com)*.

Story: "Second Generation" © 2020 Julie Nováková

Lola Robles

Lola Robles (Madrid, 1963) is the author of various science fiction novels, including *Monteverde: Memoirs of an Interstellar Linguist* (translated into English by Lawrence Schimel, Aqueduct Press, 2016), and the essay about speculative fiction genres "En regiones extrañas" (Cazador de ratas, 2018). She also co-edited, with Teresa López Pellisa, the historical anthologies of Spanish science fiction *Distópicas and Poshumanas* (both Eolas, 2020). Her most recent publications are a feminist essay co-authored with Gracia Trujillo on surrogate pregnancy.

Lawrence Schimel (New York, 1971) is a bilingual (Spanish/English) author & anthologist who has published over 120 books for readers of all ages, including *The Drag Queen of Elfland* (Circlet), *Tarot Fantastic* (DAW Books), and *Streets of Blood: Vampire*

Stories from New York City (Cumberland House), among many others. He is also a prolific literary translator, most recently of Juan Villoro's bibliofantasy *The Wild Book* (Restless Books) which is just out in paperback this summer.

Story: "Sea Changes" © 2016 Lola Robles; "Sea Changes" Translation © 2016 Lawrence Schimel

Eric Schwitzgebel

Eric Schwitzgebel is a professor of philosophy at University of California, Riverside, and a cooperating member of UCR's program in Speculative Fiction and Cultures of Science. His short fiction has appeared in *Clarkesworld, F&SF,* and *Nature.* His op-eds on the future of technology have appeared in the *Los Angeles Times, Chicago Tribune,* and *Aeon Magazine.* His most recent books are *A Theory of Jerks and Other Philosophical Misadventures* and the edited collection *Philosophy Through Science Fiction Stories.* He blogs at The Splintered Mind on issues at the intersection of philosophy, psychology, and speculative fiction.

Story: "Fish Dance" © 2016 Eric Schwitzgebel

Alex Shvartsman

Alex Shvartsman is the author of *Eridani's Crown.* He's the winner of the 2014 WSFA Small Press Award for Short Fiction and a two-time finalist (2015 and 2017) for the Canopus Award for Excellence in Interstellar Writing.

His short stories have appeared in *Analog, Nature,*

Strange Horizons, Intergalactic Medicine Show, and a variety of other magazines and anthologies. His previously published books include collections *Explaining Cthulhu to Grandma* and *The Golem of Deneb Seven,* as well as his steampunk humor novella *H. G. Wells, Secret Agent.*

In addition to the UFO series, he has edited *The Cackle of Cthulhu, Humanity 2.0, Funny Science Fiction, Coffee: Caffeinated Tales of the Fantastic,* and *Dark Expanse: Surviving the Collapse* anthologies.

His website is www.alexshvartsman.com

Story: "Grains of Wheat" © 2015 Alex Shvartsman

Caroline M. Yoachim

Caroline M. Yoachim is a prolific author of short stories, appearing in *Asimov's, Fantasy & Science Fiction, Uncanny, Beneath Ceaseless Skies, Clarkesworld,* and *Lightspeed,* among other places. She has been a finalist for the Hugo, World Fantasy, Locus, and multiple Nebula Awards, and her stories have been reprinted in multiple year's best anthologies and translated into several languages. Yoachim's debut short story collection, *Seven Wonders of a Once and Future World & Other Stories,* came out in 2016.

Story: "Welcome to the Medical Clinic at the Interplanetary Relay Station | Hours Since the Last Patient Death: 0" © 2016 Caroline M. Yoachim

Acknowledgments

I'm sure to leave out many whose assistance and encouragement I value. The following are just some of those I would like to thank.

I appreciate all the authors who allowed their stories to appear in this anthology, especially those who offered backer rewards for the Kickstarter and participated in the author reading to promote it, including: Alex Shvartsman, Eric Schwitzgebel, Annalee Newitz, James Patrick Kelly, Congyun Gu, David Brin, Seanan McGuire, and Sally Weiner Grotta.

Inlandia Institute for sponsoring a successful Kickstarter and publishing the print edition, especially Cati Porter — I couldn't have made it through the Kickstarter without her support, and her ongoing efforts to see this project through to publication. Meant so much having her in my corner as a great advocate for literature in our community and championing my vision for this book.

Special thanks to Alex Shvartsman for his endless generosity of time and advice as an anthologist, publisher, and Kickstarter guru. Also for inviting me to guest edit the Medical Science Fiction issue of *Future Science Fiction Digest*.

Neil Clarke, Editor of *Clarkesworld*, for taking the time to sit down with me on multiple occasions at conventions to share his wisdom on editing short fiction and anthologies. Your interest in the project gave me the confidence to plow forward!

John Joseph Adams and Christie Yant of *Lightspeed* for your recommendations and for sharing some of your process— that spreadsheet saved me some time!

Tony Smith, Host/Producer of StarShipSofa for promoting two iterations of the Kickstarter, and to all the SSS team for shouldering the burden of slushing during this period, including Jeremy Szal, Gary Dowell, Fred Himebaugh, Kelly Brantley, Michael W. Cho, and Lisa Stone.

My LLUH colleagues who supported this project in many ways, especially those who volunteered to helped this project directly. Matt Wright & Karsten Thorson for tremendous contributions to design of the website and the cover art and Robert Cybulski for his brilliant copy, including phrases I envy and could never have written, which appears on Kickstarter, the website, promo video, and from which I have borrowed time and again. Jennifer Hickok for contributing ideas on process, tools, and so much valuable feedback. Mark Hensley, for being a generous supporter of the project and an understanding boss who never turned down a time off request for me to work on the book, even at short notice.

My Taos Toolbox and classmates for their encouragement and for tolerating that I bogarted George R. R. Martin's time with anthology-related questions, especially those who helped the project directly by providing backer rewards, promoting and backing the Kickstarter, participating in the reading event, or volunteering to help with editing (even though we didn't get to hold an open call): Aidan Doyle, C. Stuart Hardwick, Simone Heller, Muffie Humphrey, C. M. Brennan, and Miriah Hetherington.

And all the Kickstarter backers who funded this

project. It takes money to create a book like this, and your investment has made it possible. This was a long time coming, but I've tried to make the most of all your contributions, producing a longer book than promised and including a few additional authors.

The editor wishes to acknowledge previous publication of the following stories:

"A Passing Sickness" by Paolo Bacigalupi: *Seat 14C*, 2016

"Carriers" by Tananarive Due: *The End Has Come*, 2015

"Color the World" by Congyun Gu: *Science Fiction World*, 2019

"Fish Dance" by Eric Schwitzgebel: *Clarkesworld*, 2016

"Grains of Wheat" by Alex Shvartsman: *Nature*, 2015

"Itsy Bitsy Spider" by James Patrick Kelly: *Asimov's Science Fiction*, 1997

"One Widow's Healing" by Sally Wiener Grotta: *2100 Health Odyssey*, 2019

"Sea Changes" by Lola Robles: *Spanish Women of Wonder*, 2016 [translation by Lawrence Schimel]

"Second Generation" by Julie Navakova: *Future Science Fiction Digest*, Issue 8, 2020

"The Giving Plague" by David Brin: *Interzone*, #23 1988

"Welcome to the Medical Clinic at the Interplanetary Relay Station | Hours Since the Last Patient Death: 0" by Caroline M. Yoachim: *Lightspeed*, 2016

"When Robot and Crow Saved East St. Louis" by Annalee Newitz: *Slate*, 2018

About Inlandia Institute

Inlandia Institute is a regional literary non-profit and publishing house. We seek to bring focus to the richness of the literary enterprise that has existed in this region for ages. The mission of the Inlandia Institute is to recognize, support, and expand literary activity in all of its forms in Inland Southern California by publishing books and sponsoring programs that deepen people's awareness, understanding, and appreciation of this unique, complex and creatively vibrant region.

The Institute publishes books, presents free public literary and cultural programming, provides in-school and after school enrichment programs for children and youth, holds free creative writing workshops for teens and adults, and boot camp intensives. In addition, every two years, the Inlandia Institute appoints a distinguished jury panel from outside of the region to name an Inlandia Literary Laureate who serves as an ambassador for the Inlandia Institute, promoting literature, creative literacy, and community. Laureates to date include Susan Straight (2010–2012), Gayle Brandeis (2012–2014), Juan Delgado (2014–2016), Nikia Chaney (2016–2018), and Rachelle Cruz (2018–2020).

To learn more about the Inlandia Institute, please visit our website at www.InlandiaInstitute.org.

Inlandia Books

More Dreamers of the Golden Dream by Susan Straight, Douglas McCulloh, and Delphine Sims

Güero-Güero: The White Mexican and Other Published and Unpublished Stories by Dr. Eliud Martínez

A Short Guide to Finding Your First Home in the United States: An Inlandia anthology on the immigrant experience

Care: Stories by Christopher Records

San Bernardino, Singing, edited by Nikia Chaney

Facing Fire: Art, Wildfire, and the End of Nature in the New West by Douglas McCulloh

Writing from Inlandia, an annual anthology (2011–)

In the Sunshine of Neglect: Defining Photographs and Radical Experiments in Inland Southern California,1950 to the Present by Douglas McCulloh

Henry L. A. Jekel: Architect of Eastern Skyscrapers and the California Style by Dr. Vincent Moses and Catherine Whitmore

Orangelandia: The Literature of Inland Citrus edited by Gayle Brandeis

While We're Here We Should Sing by The Why Nots

Go to the Living by Micah Chatterton

No Easy Way: Integrating Riverside Schools - A Victory for Community by Arthur L. Littleworth